Paper Trail

Paper Trail

Written by
Lyndon Haynes

Copyright © 2023 by Lyndon Haynes

All rights reserved. No part of this book may be reproduced or used in any manner without written permission of the copyright owner except for the use of quotations in a book review.

FIRST EDITION

978-1-80541-449-0 (paperback)

978-1-80541-450-6 (eBook)

https://authorlyndonhaynes.com

Contents

Introduction: Who's that girl? 1
Chapter One: Welcome back 9
Chapter Two: Don't believe the hype 17
Chapter Three: Bloodstream 33
Chapter Four: Dancing Queen 49
Chapter Five: Work mode 55
Chapter Six: Missing words 69
Chapter Seven: Riding through the desert 77
Chapter Eight: Farewell summer 91
Chapter Nine: Never is a promise 99
Chapter Ten: Affirmative action 109
Chapter Eleven: Can I live? 113
Chapter Twelve: Rain on me 123
Chapter Thirteen: Don't cry for me 133
Chapter Fourteen: Sweet serenade 141
Chapter Fifteen: Only if you knew 153
Chapter Sixteen: Who will save your soul? 161
Chapter Seventeen: The man with the child in his eyes 169
Chapter Eighteen: Wandering romance 185
Chapter Nineteen: Numbers on the board 197
Chapter Twenty: This can't be life 211
Chapter Twenty-One: Sleep to dream 213

Chapter Twenty-Two: I'm working 221
Chapter Twenty-Three: A Childrens Story 229
Chapter Twenty-Four: Pray for me 235
Chapter Twenty-Five : Run, run 249
Chapter Twenty-Six: Moment of clarity 259
Chapter Twenty-Seven: Do you know? 269
Chapter Twenty-Eight: Sober thoughts 273
Chapter Twenty-Nine: Same problems? 287
Chapter Thirty: Tomorrow 293
Next Installment 321

Introduction

Who's that girl?

Friday night in The Griffin pub was always a good night, packed out with locals enjoying the start to the weekend. This was an old-school pub—sticky carpet, wooden tables, fruit machines, a jukebox and an old dartboard hanging on a white wall that had been pinpricked by stray arrows more times than the actual board.

It was situated on the corner of Radley Street, a few yards from the notorious Kingfisher Estate. Ask anyone around here about that estate and they'll offer a raised eyebrow or a scratch of the chin. Most of the punters were either from the estate or had friends or family who lived there.

Barry Evans, still in his post office uniform, sat stuffing the last bits of a bag of peanuts into his mouth. He was with his usual mates, Stumpy Jones and Pete Grainer; they laughed hard above the din of other exaggerated conversations around them.

An hour later, a merry Barry sank the remains of another pint. 'That's it—I'm done. I'll see you clowns tomorrow,' he slurred, getting up and shaking hands with Stumpy, who was gently stewing that he couldn't finish his story about his dream car restoration, and Pete, who winked at him. 'Be lucky, Baz.'

Barry stumbled his way through the crowded pub and out into the street.

Barry bumped into a group of girls having a cigarette outside. He recognised one of them from the estate. 'Oops, so sorry. Night, ladies,' he mumbled, staggering past them, and throwing up a wave as he made his way home. It was a cold evening in the midst of winter. The streets were quiet apart from the buzz coming from The Griffin behind him.

Barry zipped up his jacket, swaying as the icy air hit him. Luckily, his flat on the Kingfisher was only a short walk through the arches. Barry looked down, noticing his bootlaces were undone. He stopped and bent down to tie the loose strings. As he did so, a fifty-pound note fluttered across the pavement in front of him. He looked around but could see nobody. He chuckled to himself and picked up the stray currency.

'Blimey.' He stood up, shrugging, before scrunching the note in his fist. After a few more steps, he saw another few notes dancing across the pavement. 'Bloody hell, what's going on?' He managed to bend and scoop up the other stray notes, again looking around, wary of any watching eyes.

As Barry approached the arches, he saw a steady swirl of fifty-pound notes loosely circling on the ground. He rubbed his eyes. 'Jesus.' He again looked over his shoulder, ensuring he was alone. This was the entrance to Kingfisher Estate, after all, and he knew full well that there could be eyes on him. Unsteadily, he managed to scrape some of the notes up, stuffing them into his pocket gleefully. Then he heard the soft whimper of someone weeping.

Barry steadied himself and walked towards where the money was coming from, the large dustbins stacked against the dark bricks of the arch walls. 'Hello?' He cleared his throat as he tentatively stepped towards a pile of black bin liners. He trapped a few more notes under his foot, bending to pick them up. He peered ahead and saw what he thought was the slender leg of a woman. 'Who's there?' he asked, stuffing the money into his pockets and moving slowly to the source of the floating notes.

The snivelling cries became clearer as he edged closer. The leg moved slightly, causing Barry to jump back. 'Oi, who the fuck…?' At first he thought it was a homeless person, but why would they be the source of a stream of fifty-pound notes? He peered down at the bundled body lying amongst the trash.

'Help… me,' came a faint, breathy voice. Barry froze.

'Are you hurt?' he asked, his voice quivering, as he inched forward. He could see a young black woman dressed in a sparkly black cocktail dress, one foot bare, the other with a black stiletto dangling by the strap, her thighs covered in blood.

Barry covered his mouth, choking back the fizzy liquid which frothed in his throat. He began to back away. 'Don't leave. Please help me,' the woman pleaded, her breath shallow.

Barry hesitated, spooked by the wail of a fire engine's siren as it sped past on the main road. 'Shit,' he whispered, circling and wiping his mouth, then walked back towards her. He could see a leather bag clasped in her hand. It was open and stuffed with money.

'Fuckin' 'ell, Cindy? Is that you?' Barry knelt beside her. It was Cindy Harper, his neighbour on the estate. He knew her well and her brother, Dwayne. 'Where does it hurt?' His mind scrambled as he tried his best to sober up.

'Just… get… me… home,' Cindy whimpered, barely able to breathe.

Barry raked his fingers through his thinning hair before trying to drag her to her feet. 'Oww, slowly.' Cindy grimaced as he rolled her onto her side. She stared at him, her eyes sleepy, almost comatose.

Barry noticed the gaping wound on her upper thigh, revealed by her dress snagged up on her hip. 'Oh Jesus Christ,' he muttered, instinctively placing his hand over the wound as the blood seeped out. 'Ok, take it easy now. I'll call for an ambulance.' He shook his head violently, trying to clear the alcohol out of his brain, and dug in his pocket for his phone.

'No!' Cindy gasped. 'No ambulance, no police.'

'But you're hurt, bleeding, you need help!'

'Just take me home.'

Barry kept his phone in his pocket. 'Ok, I'm gonna count to three, then I'll lift ya,' he said. 'One… two and three…' Barry struggled to get her into any kind of upright position, stumbling briefly before using all his might to stand Cindy up. 'Got you—just hang on.' He swung her arm around his neck and steadied himself.

Cindy was a dead weight and awkward to hold up. She was barely conscious, mumbling under her breath in obvious pain. 'Zip the bag.' She gritted her teeth, wheezing huskily. Her head hung limply.

The two staggered their way through the back arches which led to Kingfisher Estate. Being a Friday night, it was busy, with a few youths hanging out and couples making their way out for the night.

Barry sweated profusely, struggling to drag Cindy along while holding onto the bag. Up ahead he could see a few youths; his heart thudded in his chest. 'Cindy, stay with me. Try to walk now.' He was panicking as they drew closer to the young men.

'Get her waved, then drag her home to bed.' One of the youths—tall, white, shaved head—shot a cheeky remark. He laughed, seeking validation from his gang as they watched on and cackled. Barry nodded his head. A wry, strained smile broke across his face as he bundled his way past them. Cindy's head was down, so the gang didn't recognise her. 'Get lucky, fam. Fuck her brains out!' Another crude comment echoed behind them as Barry inched Cindy closer to the stairwell and lift.

'Wait! Gimme a sec. Fuck, I'm out of breath.' Barry, not the most fit or physical specimen, leant against the wall as he pressed the silver metal button to call the lift. He panted as he waited. Cindy groaned, the pain from the wound to her leg biting in. 'Come on, Cindy, lift's here.' Barry spoke in almost a whisper, his breaths shallow.

The lift doors slid open and an African woman dressed in her nurse's uniform stepped out. 'Hi, Barry.' She was a familiar neighbour. 'Everything alright?' She looked down at a bent-over Cindy, inspecting the state of her bloodstained leg and noticing she had one bare foot. 'Hi, Agnes. Yeah, fine thanks.' Barry gave her an uncomfortable smile, then bundled himself and Cindy into the tight lift. 'She fell over—been celebrating all day.' He tried his best to shrug her off, laughing unconvincingly.

Agnes watched on uneasily, not buying his story. 'You want me to check that wound?' She held the lift doors open as she looked at the two of them.

'Nope! We're ok. Just wanna get her home… Cheers.' Barry tried to offer a sincere response, but his sweaty, flustered face showed his real feeling of panic. Agnes observed Cindy for a few seconds, unable to see her face, before removing her arm and allowing the metal door to scrape shut.

Inside the confined space of the lift, Barry breathed a massive sigh. He couldn't muster the energy to hold Cindy up any longer. He let go, crouching over to catch his breath. Cindy crumbled in a heap onto the disinfected, piss-stained floor. 'Oh Jesus, what am I doing?' He banged his head against the metal panelling.

Once again he summoned his strength to pick her up. They had reached his floor, the doors scraping open on arrival. 'Cindy, stay with me. Please, come on, one last bit.' Barry did his best to keep her awake, gently slapping her face. She was drifting in and out of consciousness. Her body was like a sack of potatoes as he dragged her out of the lift. 'Fuck me,' Barry huffed. 'Nearly home. Cindy, stay with me.' He was shaking and almost in tears, but he pulled her the last few yards to his door.

Barry dug in his pockets frantically and found his keys, the crumpled fifty-pound notes spilling out onto Cindy's slumped body. His bloodied hand shook and he tried to compose himself. 'Bloody hell,' he mumbled, fiddling until he pushed the key into the Yale lock, turned it and pushed open the door.

Barry wheezed, drained from his exertions, coughing up saliva, wiping his hand across his mouth and sniffing loudly. He looked down at the floor. Cindy had passed out in a heap. The sparkly dress barely preserved her modesty, her bloodied thigh a stark reminder of her recent journey.

Barry dragged her up and pulled her inside brusquely, staggering back inside the narrow passage of his home. He lost his balance and fell onto his back. 'Arrgh, flipping heck!' he screamed in pain. For a few seconds, he stared up at the ceiling, his intoxication replaced by the rush of fear. 'Shit,' he gasped before getting up clumsily.

Cindy's feet were lying across the threshold. Barry folded her legs, bringing them in, and slammed the door shut. Her body was posed inelegantly. He sank down onto his haunches, back to the door, and placed his head in his hands. At that point, the loud ring of his mobile made him jump.

'Fuck's sake.' Barry dug into his pocket and pulled out the vibrating phone. On the screen flashed Pete Grainer's name. 'Shit.' He rubbed his face vigorously, then answered. 'Alright, Pete.' Barry's voice quivered as he spoke. He could hear busy background noise and loud music.

'Oi, Baz, it's proper lively down here now, mate,' Pete bellowed through the phone speaker.

'Yeah… sounds it,' Barry answered feebly, staring at the blood glistening on Cindy's brown skin and the large leather bag stuffed with money. He felt dizzy and lightheaded. He choked back tears, the stark realisation of his situation kicking in.

'Baz, get back down here! There's a cold pint waiting. Stump's up dancing!' Pete gave a wheezy laugh. Barry sat in silence, unable to reply. 'Baz!' Pete's voice shook him back into the present.

'Nah, mate… have a good un,' he replied dryly, clicking on the phone and dropping it onto the floor. He leant his head back against the door, closing his eyes as he and Cindy remained motionless.

Chapter One

Welcome back

One year earlier.

Cindy Harper stood happily in her kitchen putting the finishing touches to a large cake. She threw some sprinkles onto the white icing. She was wearing a tight pair of jeans and a tight white T-shirt with a printed photograph of her brother Dwayne. The words 'Welcome back' were written in rainbow-coloured glitter. She was vibrant as other adults came in and out carrying bottles of wine, champagne and a variety of snacks and food.

Cindy was a thirty-six-year-old single mother with a glowing smile, short bobbed black hair and cheekbones which enhanced the clear, brown skin of her youthful and attractive face. She was excited that her brother was due in a few minutes, unaware of the surprise party she had organised for his release after serving three-and-a-half years at Her Majesty's pleasure. Her daughter, eight-year-old Cece, a cute, bright-eyed mini-me, was dressed in the same T-shirt and jeans, with sparkly trainers which lit up each step. She skipped in to watch her mother place the last decorations on the cake.

Reggae music played in the background, mixing with the aroma of Jamaican cuisine. Friends and family members mingled in the living room. 'Mummy, what time will Uncle Dwayne get here?' She tiptoed up to the counter to view the cake.

'He'll be here soon.' Cindy looked down proudly at her, offering her the last few coloured sprinkles. 'Go and check everyone is ready while I finish this.' She smiled, watching Cece hoover the sweet sprinkles into her mouth before skipping off into the living room.

'Right, done.' She wiped her hands on a tea cloth, admiring her work. She picked her phone up from the counter and took a picture of the cake. 'Not bad at all, Cindy.' She gave herself a verbal pat on the back before lifting it carefully and walking into the living room. 'Coming through!' she announced to a response of ooh's and ahh's when she entered.

The room was decorated with balloons, banners and fairy lights. A large table was covered with a clean white cloth on which bowls of sweets, snacks and the centrepiece cake were placed.

Cindy still fussed, ensuring everything was as it should be. The sound of a text alert came through on her phone; she read the message. 'He's here! Come on, get ready,' she announced. Cindy turned the music down and closed the door to the living room. 'Sssh, quiet everybody,' she instructed, putting her hand to her lips.

'Mummy, is Uncle Dwayne coming now?' Cece asked.

'Yes, darling. Quiet, get ready.' She placed her hands on Cece's shoulders and gave them a rub.

The sound of the front door being unlocked could be heard, along with voices as people entered the house. Unsuspecting,

Dwayne walked in. He was stouter than before, his hair and beard overgrown, masking his twenty-eight-year-old features. He carried a large brown paper bag containing his belongings. His old school friend, Ricky, who had collected him from prison, walked in behind him—average build, low fade haircut, dressed in a tight Trapstar T-shirt and black jogging bottoms.

'Bro, it's good to be home.' Dwayne smiled at Ricky. 'I can smell that home cooking.' He dumped the bag in the hallway and proceeded towards the front room.

Ricky smiled, nodding and checking his phone. 'Yeah, smells decent.' He put his phone into camera mode and began filming behind Dwayne's back, watching him as he pushed open the living room door.

'Surprise!' everyone in the room shouted in unison, pulling party poppers. Dwayne stepped back in shock, staring at the faces that welcomed him as the paper streamers descended in front of him.

Cece was the first to rush and hug him. 'Uncle Dwayne!' Her little trainers lit up more than her wide smile.

'Cece!' He scooped her up into his large arms. 'Wow, look at you! Big girl now.' Finally, a smile burst across his face.

Cindy also came forward, embracing him, planting a kiss on his cheek and ruffling his hair. 'Welcome home, bro.' She turned to everyone, proud to show off her wayward brother.

Dwayne, overwhelmed, turned to Ricky, who smiled and shrugged, still filming his mate. Dwayne puffed out his cheeks, Cece still clinging to him like a koala bear. 'Jeez, you knew about this, innit?' Dwayne pointed at his friend, who was capturing it all on his phone. 'Kinda.' Ricky shrugged, thrusting the phone camera in his direction. Dwayne stepped forward, greeting the friends and family, who all gathered around him.

A champagne bottle popped, followed by cheers. 'Come, you must be hungry. Put the music on!' Cindy, still hyped up and in command, did not allow Dwayne to settle; she pulled him into the kitchen.

The background music started again and everyone in the room began to dance, mingle and indulge in the food and beverage. 'Let's just have a minute.' Cindy smiled, looking at Dwayne, who, in turn, looked a bit embarrassed by all the fuss.

'They've proper fed you up in there, innit,' she joked, squeezing his biceps. Dwayne laughed, tensing up his arm. 'Gym time. Helped with the boredom,' he replied, stepping over to the pots of food on the cooker and lifting the lids. 'Now that's proper tings.' He sniffed in the aroma of stewed chicken and curried goat.

'Bro, listen.' Cindy grabbed his hand; her almond-shaped eyes gazed up at him, glassed over with emotion. She blinked, forcing a tear to roll down her cheek. 'Let this be the last time, Dwayne. No more fuckery.' Her voice was stern yet had a quiver of tenderness.

'Nah, sis, I'm done, trust me. Straight and narrow from now on,' Dwayne replied, his tone hushed, sensitive to his sister's plea.

'I mean it, Dwayne! I'm in a good place with work, and Cece don't need...' Cindy stopped in her tracks, taking a breath as one of her aunts came into the kitchen.

'You ready to serve?' her aunt asked. Cindy turned to her.

'Yes, Auntie, give me a minute,' she replied. Her aunt, sensing her interruption, left the room.

'Sis, swear down, I'm done with that life,' Dwayne reassured her, with an element of sincerity in his voice. He held out his fist.

Cindy stared back at him. She wanted to believe him, deep down she did, but with Dwayne and his past, there would always be a nagging doubt in the back of her mind. Regardless, she held out her fist and touched his.

'Serve up, nah! The smell of this homecooked food is killing me,' Dwayne joked, engulfing Cindy with a big bear hug.

'Alright, get off me!' she laughed, playfully pushing him away and wiping her eyes.

Dwayne and Ricky stood on the balcony eating their food from paper plates. 'Hmm, this is what I missed, man.' He munched down on a piece of chicken.

'Proper tings, man. Cindy cheffed up, bro,' Ricky agreed, stuffing a forkful of coleslaw into his mouth. They stood in silence, chowing down, staring out to the adjoining Tetris tower blocks that made up Kingfisher Estate.

The dark evening skies blanketed the dull landscape. 'Bro, things round 'ere have changed. The youngers running shit now,' Ricky mused, turning to Dwayne, his cheeks still bulging with food.

'Can imagine,' Dwayne said, wiping his mouth with a white tissue napkin. 'Let dem. I'm not on it; just wanna stay on the low.' He picked up a red plastic cup from the ledge and took a sip. 'Heard dat Mad Man K Fire got smoked last year,' he mentioned casually.

'Yeah, a younger smoked him—imagine that' Ricky replied, picking his teeth with the fork. 'He was always moving mad anyway.'

Dwayne downed the rest of his drink. 'Come, let's go back inside.' He opened the door and went back in, followed by Ricky.

Later in the evening, Dwayne placed a sleepy Cece onto her bed. He eased off her flashing trainers and placed them neatly on the floor. He softly rubbed her forehead. 'Can't believe how much you've grown,' he whispered, his voice hushed. He covered her with her favourite *Frozen* blanket, then kissed her cheek gently. He sat for a few seconds just watching over her as she slept peacefully. He patted her, shaking his head. 'Missed you, my little niece,' he muttered under his breath, taking a moment to himself.

Dwayne rubbed his face, tired from the day's events. He looked worried, scratching his bearded chin roughly. He stood up to leave, but before he left the room, he dug into his jean pocket and pulled out a white piece of paper. He leant his ear towards the door, making sure Cindy was not near, and looked at the paper. In handwritten scrawl, the note read 'Willy Notch 07922143280'. Dwayne stared at it intently for a few seconds, then stuffed it back into his pocket before tiptoeing out of the room.

Cindy was alone in the living room, clearing up the remains from the party, when Dwayne joined her. He began to help, picking up paper plates and half-empty cups. 'That was a nice welcome, sis; respect for that.' He playfully nudged her as they threw the trash into a black bin liner.

'It's all good, bro. I think I was more excited than you!' she quipped, putting the last of the party popper streamers into the bag.

'Chill, I'll do the rest.' Dwayne took the bag while a grateful Cindy, wearing a pair of fluffy rabbit-eared slippers, flopped onto the huge sofa. She watched in silence as Dwayne scraped the last bits of debris into the bag.

'Did I tell you I got that PA job at Shuster and Klein's?' She yawned, pulling her knees up to her chest.

'Only a million times, sis.' Dwayne yawned mockingly. 'Nah, blessed for you; sounds good.' He flopped beside her.

Cindy smiled. She was tired now but wanted to spend every waking moment with her brother. 'Yeah, I love it,' she continued. 'Never thought I'd work for a blue-chip company doing medical research.' She still spoke with enthusiasm, although her yawns were telling a different story.

'Go on, sis, go to bed. I'll chill here for a bit,' Dwayne ordered. Cindy slowly raised herself and stood.

'Ok, the blankets in the airing…' She yawned again.

'Cupboard. Don't worry, I'll find them.' He finished her sentence with a smile.

Cindy waved and left the room. 'Night, then,' she said, trudging up the stairs.

'Night,' he replied, kicking off his trainers and resting back on the sofa. Letting out a big sigh, he looked up at the banner stretched across the wall. 'Welcome back' the colourful, shiny letters read. 'Welcome back,' he sighed, scratching his head.

Chapter Two

Don't believe the hype

The sun peeked out from behind the grey clouds which framed the city landscape. The piercing glow beamed into the large, glass-walled offices of the Schuster and Klein building. Cindy sat alone in a large meeting room, going through her lunchtime briefing. She stared up at a large projector screen at her presentation, scribbling notes on a notepad. Well dressed and smart in a crisp, white, fitted blouse, she clicked through to the next slide and read for a few seconds. Other employees walked around busily outside in the vast, open plan office.

Cindy stood, pushing her chair backwards, and walked over towards the screen. She was focused and in the zone, business mode, black pencil skirt and high heels to match. She had just started reading when a gentle tap on the frosted glass door distracted her.

She turned around and saw Lena Schmit smiling through the pane of glass. Tall, blonde hair brushed perfectly; her neat fringe framed her pale face, hovering just above her thick, black-framed glasses; late twenties with the figure of an Olympic high jumper. She entered holding a laptop under her arm and a cardboard drinks carrier holding two burgundy Costa coffee cups.

'Hiya, ready then?' Lena placed the drinks holder on the desk before putting the laptop beside it. Cindy puffed out her cheeks as she acknowledged Lena. 'Ready as I'll ever be,' she responded while walking back towards her seat. Both sat in silence. Lena sipped her coffee while tapping on the keyboard of her silver laptop.

'Deep breath, they'll be here in a minute.' Lena's perky voice echoed in the large room, her German accent subtle. Cindy nodded, clicking the mouse to queue up the presentation before grabbing her coffee. 'Thanks, Lena, I needed this.' She took a quick sip before an entourage of sharply suited men converged in the room, 'Showtime,' Lena quipped, winking at Cindy as the men all took their places around the table. Cindy smiled at them, taking a deep breath.

Andersen De Breuk came in last. Light blue suit, open-necked white shirt and white trainers, looking every bit the modern-day boss; his highlighted blonde hair was slicked to the left with a sharp parting. Cindy looked up and smiled at him.

'Afternoon,' he said confidently. 'Cindy, let's kick off.' Andersen took his seat and set up a large tablet, focused on his screen. Lena nodded towards Cindy, who stood up.

'Good afternoon, everyone. I've compiled a report of our monthly performance in our Middle East and African territories.' She clicked the mouse and confidently began her presentation.

* * *

Old-school hip-hop music blasted throughout the flat as Dwayne, in a white vest and shorts, performed a rapid set of sit ups in the middle of the living room floor, lifting his knees as he pulled up his stout frame.

'Forty-eight... forty-nine... fifty, jeez.' He collapsed on his back, staring up as the din of the heavy bass beats descended into silence. 'Fuck me...' Gassed out, he barely managed to lift his torso into an upright position, then sprang to his feet. He walked towards the balcony and stepped through the doorway onto the ledge.

He stared out across the blocks of Kingfisher Estate, the grey clouds stubbornly blocking out the sun. He took a few moments catching his breath while stretching out his back. The sound of the doorbell stopped him in his tracks. *Who's that?* he wondered, walking back into the house to answer the door.

Dwayne opened the door to see Ricky standing there in a white Nike hoodie, phone to his ear. 'Yeah, gotta go.' He took the phone away from his ear. 'You up then?' He smiled at seeing a sweaty, half-dressed Dwayne.

'Up from time, bro. Had to take Cece to school.' He fist-pumped Ricky and let him in. Ricky sat back on the sofa, scrolling through his phone. 'No work today?'

'Nah, it's long,' Ricky mumbled, barely dragging his eyes away from the phone screen.

'What you on?' Dwayne walked into the kitchen for a few seconds then returned gulping down a bottle of water.

'Not much,' Ricky responded, scratching a tuft of hair on his chin. 'Got a little suttin later, tho, if you're on it.' He showed

Dwayne a picture of a sexy young female on his phone. 'That's Paige; she runs an event in the city. Some boujee shit, top-tier links,' he enthused, winking at Dwayne.

Dwayne studied the photo. 'Rah, if they all look like her, I'm there.' He nodded his approval, handing the phone back to Ricky. 'Need some garms, tho.' He sucked on the water bottle.

'Bro, I got you,' Ricky responded. 'Let's take a drive.' He stood up, signalling to Dwayne to leave.

Dwayne closed the balcony door. 'Let's go.' He picked up some keys from the dining table and led the way out of the flat.

The lift doors opened. Dwayne and Ricky stepped out into the fresh air and walked towards the car park. Ahead of them stood a group of youths, no older than eighteen. They looked menacing, all dressed in black tracksuits with hoodies.

The smell of weed wafted through the air. One of the youths, short and light-skinned, with braided hair, stared at the approaching Dwayne. 'What's this prick preeing me for?' Dwayne kissed his teeth, his prison bravado still apparent as he trained his eyes on the youth.

'Fresh out the can, yeah.' The youth, known locally as L Boi, smirked at Dwayne, who puffed out his chest as he walked slowly up to them. He stopped staring directly at L Boi, who kept his glare in Dwayne's direction.

'Do I know you?' Dwayne stood boldly in front of them, a few inches away from L Boi.

Ricky rolled his eyes and pulled on Dwayne's arm. 'Allow dem, bro,' he said calmly, trying to persuade Dwayne to keep walking, but Dwayne stood firm, his pride stubbornly not allowing him to move on.

'L Boi, innit?'

'That's me.' The youngster held his gaze. A slim reddened scar was embedded in his right cheek. A thin, wispy moustache barely formed across his top lip.

'Well, L Boi, I'm not fruity, so tek your eyes off me, innit,' Dwayne rasped.

L Boi turned to his friends and started to laugh. 'Funny guy. Nah, bro, I'm calm,' he retorted, tucking his hand into his jogging pants as if to indicate he had a weapon of some sort.

Ricky huffed and tugged Dwayne's arm again, 'Come, bro, forget them.' He ushered Dwayne away.

Dwayne nodded and smiled back at L Boi. 'See you about, innit.' He pointed at him before walking away. 'Little prick.' He shot his comment in earshot of L Boi and his gang.

Driving to the stores, Ricky shook his head while keeping his eyes on the road. Dwayne, still fuming, stared out of the window. 'Bro, fuck dem youths,' Dwayne seethed.

'Yo, that L Boi is the new king of the block. He buss up K Fire.'

Dwayne turned to Ricky. 'What, him?' he responded, shocked.

Ricky sighed. 'Yeah, he's a little shit.' Dwayne went back to staring out of the window, the cogs in his mind turning, digesting the information.

* * *

'Size ten.' Dwayne handed a fresh pair of white Nike Airs to the young student-like assistant, who took the shoes and talked into a handheld radio, placing the order. Dwayne looked around the trendy store, which was filled with brand name sportswear, drill and rap music pumping loudly through the speakers. 'In just three years, so much has changed.' He watched a couple of young girls grabbing a bunch of T-shirts and jogging pants. 'I feel old man,' he mused, turning back to the large wall displaying a variety of trainers.

Ricky's phone rang, not for the first time; it seemed to ring or receive a text every other minute. 'Need one of them, too.' Dwayne nodded to Ricky, watching him answer another call before the young assistant came back with the bright orange Nike trainer box.

Walking through the shopping mall, which was busy with throngs of people, Dwayne trained his eyes on a flock of girls coming towards them. He eyeballed all of them as they passed him.

'They're pickney, bro,' Ricky chimed in between his phone conversations.

'I've been away too long, man.' Dwayne craned his neck, continuing to check them out.

A couple of hours later, Ricky had parked up outside a primary school. 'Let me go get her.' Dwayne opened the door, exited and slammed it shut. Ricky watched him through the windscreen as he made his way to the school gates to wait with the other adults. Dwayne stood patiently, feeling slightly awkward as the parents chatted amongst themselves.

'Dwayne Harper?' An inquisitive female voice forced him to turn around. A pretty woman stood smiling at him, her brown skin clear with little make-up, her striking red-dyed hair tied in a ponytail, and large gold earrings hanging from her ears.

'Don't remember me?' she quizzed.

'Lisa… Walker!' Dwayne's brain clicked into memory mode on recognition.

'Yeah, you alright? What you doing here?' She came forward, her ample figure visible through her baby blue velour tracksuit.

'Jeez, how long's it been?' Dwayne gave her a loose embrace, a smile breaking across his face.

'I dunno, five or six years,' she responded, happy to see him.

'I'm not a nonce or anything. My niece Cece, I'm picking her up.' He gestured towards the school gates. Lisa laughed, revealing a diamond gleam from her tooth. It suited her. She was attractive in a ghetto fabulous way.

'Never thought you was… Still a joker, I see.'

Dwayne acted bashful. 'So…'

'Yeah, my son Kai. He goes here too.' She chuckled. Within seconds, a horde of young kids dressed in little green blazers came running out towards the gate, chased by a couple of flustered teachers. 'No running!' one of them shouted as the parents formed a queue to collect their children.

Cece ran excitedly towards Dwayne. 'Uncle Dwayne!' She loved the fact her uncle was there; her face beamed with happiness as she hugged him.

'Alright, Cece.' He consumed her with a big hug.

'Here he comes.' Lisa smiled as Kai trudged towards her, looking tired and bedraggled.

'Mummy, I couldn't finish my painting,' he huffed, handing the half-coloured sheet of paper to her.

Lisa sighed. 'It's ok, Kai; we can finish at home.' She ruffled Kai's hair. 'See what I have to deal with?' She smiled at Dwayne. 'So I'll see you in the morning then?' She gave Dwayne a cute smile, putting her arm around Kai, about to walk away.

'Yeah, you will,' Dwayne replied, smirking, checking her out before turning his attention back to Cece. 'Come on, Ricky's waiting.' He stroked her head and walked towards the car.

* * *

Cindy walked through the spacious office with Lena alongside her. A large screen showing Sky News hung above the fresh, clean room where other young professionals sat in front of large Apple Mac screens. A buzz of mutterings could be heard from the busy workforce.

'That was brilliant. Andersen was impressed.' Lena turned to Cindy. Both clutched their laptops to their chests.

'You think so?' she replied, unsure.

'Of course. It was perfect.' They continued to walk until they reached a small glass-cube-like room.

Cindy pushed the door open and turned to Lena. 'Thanks. Sometimes I doubt if I'm good enough to be here.'

Lena fixed her glasses, smiling back. 'Let's do drinks after, my treat.' She trotted away quickly.

'I can't… Lena!' Cindy tried to protest but in vain; she was left with no chance to answer.

Cindy sat alone in her office, applying a new coat of lipstick and speaking on the speaker phone. 'Is Uncle Dwayne looking after you?' she asked, checking her lips in a small pocket mirror.

The sound of Cece's voice came through. 'Yes, Mummy. He's got lots of new clothes.'

Cindy's expression changed to one of surprise. 'Oh really?' she asked, knowing Dwayne was listening.

'Ricky sorted me,' he shouted in the background.

'Listen, gonna be a bit late this evening. Going for a drink with Lena.' She put it out there.

'Ahh, sis! I'm going out with Ricky.' Dwayne's voice raised a decibel in frustration. Andersen De Breuk hovered outside her office, waving playfully at Cindy. 'Listen, have to go.' She hung up the call, beckoning her boss into the room.

Andersen entered and pulled up a chair opposite Cindy, crossing his legs casually. 'Great work today.' Smiling, he brushed his hand through his golden blonde hair, the large-faced Breitling watch on his wrist reflecting the ceiling spotlight.

Cindy sat up straight, acknowledging his praise. 'Thank you. Hope it was sufficient?'

'Was perfect; our clients thought so too.' His calm Dutch accent reassured Cindy of his satisfaction.

He glanced at her Mac screen, which displayed the housing website Zoopla. 'Looking for a house?' he asked, staring at the screen.

Cindy smiled. 'Just window shopping. Can't afford any of them, but one can dream…'

Andersen nodded approvingly, resting back in the chair. He looked directly at Cindy, his sea-blue eyes transfixed. 'I have another small task for you,' he continued.

'Of course,' Cindy responded, eagerly picking up her pen, ready to scribble some notes

'No need to write anything down. I'll be in Germany for a week; we'll FaceTime.'

Andersen checked his watch and stood up. 'Any plans for the weekend?' He looked back at Cindy, who was still digesting the minimal details of his latest request.

'No… nothing much,' she responded, intrigued, tossing the pen onto her pad.

'Cindy… a fine woman like you should be going on dates.' He smiled, fixing his blazer, before leaving the room. Cindy watched him walk out and past the glass panel. She chuckled to herself, shaking her head.

* * *

Savannahs was a bar around the corner from the Schuster and Klein building—a flashy place full of trendy young office workers sipping cocktails and taking tequila shots to celebrate the end of another working week. Cheesy pop music added to the vibrancy of the room, mixed with the excited natter of the crowd.

Cindy sat at a table near the entrance with Lena, who sipped on a fancy-looking cocktail with a slice of passion fruit floating on a foamy orange liquid. 'I love London!' she exclaimed, observing the vibrant atmosphere.

'Yeah, this part is cool,' Cindy mused as she sipped on a glass of white wine. 'It's not all like this.' She observed the room. 'Anyway, what a week!' She raised her glass to Lena who responded, clinking her glass.

'Yes, crazy busy, but we made it!' She laughed, taking off her glasses and revealing her apple-green eyes. 'Any plans?' she asked Cindy, who shook her head in response.

'Nope, apart from Madam Cece,' she giggled.

'Well, I've got Pilates, then hit the markets,' Lena informed her.

'Markets?' Cindy quizzed.

'Yes, I love the little markets—Covent Garden, Portobello—really quaint.'

'I forget you're a tourist,' Cindy laughed, shaking her head at Lena's city innocence.

* * *

Dwayne carried a sleepy Cece slowly up the stairs. He was dressed smartly in his new black designer T-shirt and black jeans. 'Gonna put you to bed. Mummy will be back soon,' he whispered as they reached the top of the landing which led to Cece's room. He stepped in gently, trying his best not to disturb her.

He placed her down on her bed and covered her. 'Night, Cece.' He kissed her softly on the forehead. 'Night.' Cece barely forced out the word before dozing off. Dwayne stood over her, watching for a few seconds before creeping out of the room.

He paced up and down the front room, impatiently checking his new phone every few seconds until he heard the key in the lock of the front door. He rushed towards it as Cindy finally arrived.

'Sir, man!' He pulled the door open, causing Cindy to stumble through.

'Alright, Dwayne, gosh, gimme a chance!' She looked up at him, her eyes glazed over from one glass too many.

'Ricky's been waiting for time.' Dwayne, eager to get out, pushed past her.

'I know. I just saw him downstairs,' she answered, flustered, as Dwayne raced out.

'Don't wait up.'

'Bye then… enjoy…' She flapped a wave before slamming the front door.

Ricky and Dwayne walked hastily through the heart of the city to a trendy tower building lit up by red neon lights. A small crowd had congregated outside—mainly women all dressed expensively. Dwayne fixed himself up as he approached.

'Bro, these chicks are saucy.' He turned to Ricky, who strolled casually, popping a mint into his mouth.

'You ain't seen nothing yet.' He smiled as they neared the entrance.

Inside, the venue was swanky, the theme of red neon lights reflected against dark onyx marble floors which led to a transparent glass lift. Dwayne stood silently, admiring the bright city lights as the lift gave them levitation up to the thirtieth floor.

'How you know these kinda people?' he asked Ricky, who took a picture of Dwayne as he peered through the window at the thousands of lights which twinkled around the building like tiny snowflakes. 'Just links, innit.' Ricky looked full of himself as the lift doors slid open, revealing an almost gallery-like space with a futuristic silver bar adorned with different-coloured liquor bottles artistically placed around it.

'Bloodclart, this is suttin else.' Dwayne couldn't hold his awe stepping out of the lift into the shiny space. The place was filled by an array of girls from a variety of backgrounds dressed in high fashion, designer-fitted clothes, mingling with men who all seemed to be immaculately dressed, resembling models from expensive fragrance commercials.

Dwayne rubbed his chin, slightly uncomfortable, while Ricky walked confidently ahead, scoping out the crowd. An albino DJ with short-cropped yellow hair, dressed as if he'd come straight from the set of a Mad Max film, did his thing, spinning funky tunes as the people continued to talk and mingle.

Dwayne stood alone, observing everything. This was not what he was expecting, but he didn't mind as the view of attractive, classy women held his interest. A couple of minutes had passed when Ricky returned with two girls in tow, one of them being Paige, the girl in the picture on his phone. She looked better in the flesh, beautiful golden skin, plump lips and eyes that could capture any man's attention.

Along with her was an interesting-looking girl, almost androgynous in features, like Amber Rose. She had dark hair cut short, tanned skin and coloured sequins lining her deep brown eyes.

Ricky could see Dwayne's jaw drop with surprise to see his friend strolling comfortably flanked by these two fine specimens.

'So, this is my bro, Dwayne. Dwayne, meet Paige and Sasha.' Ricky introduced them, winking at Dwayne, who cleared his throat before speaking. 'Hi, ladies.' He sounded corny but didn't know what else to say. Both women politely smiled as Dwayne tried his best to look cool.

'Nice to meet you, Dwayne.' Sasha, the interesting-looking one, stuck out her jewelled, manicured hand towards Dwayne, who gently reciprocated, shaking her hand. 'You look like you need a drink,' she boldly stated in a European accent, taking him by the hand and leading him away. He turned back, looking helplessly at Ricky, who simply shrugged, smiling as he was left with the voluptuous Paige.

* * *

Dwayne awoke to the smell of strong coffee and toast. He stretched out his body, feeling snug yet unfamiliar. He blearily scanned the room. It was bright, and he rubbed his eyes. The brilliant, clean, white room looked like something from the space age—clinical yet comfortable. He knew instantly he was naked, lifting the blanket slightly to check his body beneath the cover.

'Morning.' Sasha's sultry voice laden with her Eastern European accent caused him to sit up. He watched her enter the room wearing just a white silk dressing gown. It was open, revealing her fit body in all its glory. She was holding a large tray with two cups and a plate with slices of toast.

'Jeez, my head's banging.' Dwayne sat up, still baffled and groggy. 'Where am I?' he croaked and cleared his throat. Sasha smiled. She looked fresh, still stunning even without her funky make-up.

'Too many vodka jellies?' she quipped, sitting on the large bed and placing the tray beside her carefully. 'Here, I made you some coffee and toast. I don't do this for everyone.' Sasha leant over, kissing him on the cheek then handing him one of the cups.

'Nice, thanks.' Dwayne took it, still trying to process her and his surroundings. 'Shit, did we?' he asked, embarrassed, taking a sip of the hot liquid.

Sasha plumped up a pillow and rested back, bursting into laughter. 'Yes we did; it was fun.' She crunched into her slice of toast. Dwayne shook his head. 'Don't worry, the fact you stayed for breakfast should tell you something.' She was cheeky, sexy and confident.

Jet sprays from the large chrome rainfall shower head splashed against Dwayne and Sasha. He held her tightly, her legs wrapped around his chunky frame. Sasha moaned with satisfaction as Dwayne gripped her tightly, her back sliding up and down the white marbled wall. He held her head while kissing her passionately, continuing to thrust as hard as he could, gripping her buttocks. The water washed over them and steam rose onto the glass panels.

Each time he penetrated, he caught a flashback of the night before—downing drinks, dancing closely, laughing, more drinks, kissing her in the back of a taxi, stumbling into her apartment building. He opened his eyes at the same time as she did; they gazed at one another. Sasha smiled, sticking her tongue out, digging her nails into his neck, clasping hard as they climaxed at the same time; their energy subsided gradually, both jerking to an inevitable halt.

'So I'll call you, innit.' Dwayne, now dressed in the same black T-shirt and jeans, held Sasha in the sleek hallway near the front door. 'I hope you'll do more than that,' she whispered shyly, for the first time showing a vulnerable side, and looking up at him, her eyes wanting.

'Call me tonight… please.' She stroked her finger against his lips. Dwayne smiled and sucked her finger for a few seconds. Both seemed mesmerised by the other. 'Deffo I will, swear down,' he confirmed, going in for another deep kiss, which made her groan then giggle.

'Go now while my pussy is asleep,' her sultry voice ordered as she allowed her gown to fall open again. Dwayne looked at her, ogling her breasts. 'I'm gone.' He held his hands up, breaking into a laugh, before opening the door and exiting, leaving Sasha watching him curiously as he left.

Chapter Three

Bloodstream

Cindy sat studiously in her office focused on the large Apple Mac screen. Rain pelted against the window, the slate-coloured clouds looming ominously over the city landscape. She clicked the mouse rapidly, only stopping to type furiously on the keyboard. The sound of her ringtone came through loudly, with the video symbol flashing on the screen.

Cindy clicked on the icon. Andersen's face appeared. 'Morning, Cindy, how are things?' He was seated in what looked like a café with baristas in the background busily working at a chrome espresso machine. His normal smooth appearance had been replaced by a stubble beard. 'All good here—just tackling this month's reports.' She took a deep breath. Andersen lifted a tiny porcelain espresso cup to his mouth and downed the shot.

'I'm going to send over some information. I need you to follow the instructions.' He spoke with authority, which was different to his usual relaxed disposition. 'Ok,' Cindy replied, intrigued by his serious tone. 'Call me if you have any issues,' he demanded. He seemed a little off, but Cindy nodded anyway without question before his image disappeared from the screen.

Cindy pondered for a few seconds until she was interrupted by a knock on the door. It was Lena, who was making a drinking gesture with her hand, indicating to come for a coffee break. Cindy acknowledged her, locked her PC screen and got up to join her.

They sat in the swanky, open plan cafeteria: pine-panelled walls, bright soft furnishings, and round chrome tables. 'So after you left Savannah's, I got talking to Cristian from the tech department.' Lena chattered enthusiastically between little sips of her beverage.

Cindy partially listened, distracted and rankled by the Face-Time call with Andersen. Her mind drifted from Lena's constant babble about a young tech buying her cocktails then pouncing on her in the back of her Uber ride home.

'Cindy? Are you listening?' Lena plonked down her cup, grabbing Cindy's arm and shaking her out of her distraction. 'Huh?' Cindy looked at Lena. 'Sorry, was miles away.' She took a breath. 'So, Cristian…' She smiled, waiting for Lena to continue.

* * *

Cece splashed her pink wellies down into a puddle on the pavement, enjoying the results of the earlier downfall and hopscotching her way home in front of Dwayne, who was too busy spilling his night with Sasha to Ricky on the phone.

'Bro, that was madness!' He chuckled loudly, swinging a pink *Frozen*-emblazoned mini rucksack as he walked slowly, keeping a careful eye on Cece. 'Fam, I'll call you back in a bit, and you got to share that side hustle with me,' he demanded, noticing Lisa Walker and her son Kai in the playground just up ahead.

'Uncle Dwayne, can we go to the park?' Cece pointed excitedly, her little caramel-skinned face a picture of cuteness looking up at him. 'Ok, just for a little bit,' he conceded, watching her turn and run towards the rusted, green-painted gates. Lisa waved them in, watching Cece and Kai head for the brightly coloured plastic climbing frame.

'Missed you this morning at the gates,' Dwayne said to Lisa as they took a seat on the park bench within sight of the children. She, as usual, was well put together, her street swagger on point, dressed in a short, shiny, black puffer jacket, black ripped jeans and black Adidas trainers with white stripes; her red hair was slicked back, showing off her flawless skin.

'Thought you was avoiding me,' she said half-jokingly, looking back for an answer. Dwayne peered ahead, watching Cece. He began to stroke his bushy beard.

'Nah, never that. Had a mad weekend, so…'

'It's cool; I get it.' Lisa's voice trailed off. She tucked her hands into the pockets of her jacket, hunching her body.

'You've changed, man; used to have all the chat. You and what's that girl's name?' he said, turning to Lisa, who broke into a laugh, nodding her head.

'Yeah, that was me, and you mean Nicole Fraser.' Dwayne nodded, breaking into a laugh as he remembered.

'Yeah, you lot were little rug rats.'

'Oi!' Lisa nudged him with her elbow. She looked at him directly. Her brown eyes, outlined by mascara, revealed a glint of emotion.

Dwayne looked back. 'What?' He nudged her back playfully. Lisa looked away.

'Such a dick,' she muttered under her breath. Cece ran back towards them. She took her coat off.

'Uncle Dwayne, come on the see-saw with me.' She threw her jacket onto the bench and grabbed his hand. 'C'mon.' She was out of breath but exuberant.

Dwayne got up, groaning, looking back at Lisa. 'If my little boss says see saw, then…' He shrugged, shaking his head and trudging over with Cece.

'Go on, Grandad,' Lisa shouted, watching on as Dwayne picked up Kai, sitting him on one end of the see-saw, making sure Cece held on at the other end.

On the way back to Kingfisher Estate, they walked through the park, watching on as Cece and Kai ran ahead. 'So back on the ends, how does it feel?' Lisa asked, tapping a text message into her phone.

'Better than jail,' he responded. 'Things have changed, though; got some young pricks now trying to play big man.'

Lisa nodded in agreement. 'Wanted to ask you—' She took a deep breath, taking her time. Dwayne stared at her.

'The suspense is killing me! What?' he said with a laugh.

'Nah, was gonna ask if you wanted to come round for dinner.' She stared ahead, not wanting to make eye contact.

Dwayne stopped in his tracks, letting her take a few steps in front of him. He checked her out, looking at her rear. 'Hmm, depends what's on the menu.' His reply was cheeky. Lisa looked back at him, smiling.

'You'll have to come and see, innit.' She sauntered away, making sure he got a full view of her shapely figure.

Dwayne eventually walked back into the estate carrying a tired Cece, who was drained from her exertions. His large frame held her up. 'Uncle, I'm tired.' Cece was barely awake, her head leaning against his shoulder.

'I know, Cee. We're home now. You can have a nap before din dins,' he reassured her, turning into the block to see the same group of youths, including L Boi, loitering next to the lift entrance.

They turned and watched him as he approached, vacant stares similar to the ones Dwayne had seen previously on the wing in jail. It didn't bother or intimidate him. He strode forward with purpose, reaching the lift.

L Boi once again took his stance, screwing his face up at Dwayne, his young face hardened with displeasure. 'Welcome back, big homie,' he said sarcastically, sneering. His eyelids were weighed down by the buzz of the weed he toked from a large, half-burnt spliff.

Dwayne ignored him, pushing the button to call the lift. Cece sleepily looked at them over his shoulder, staring back at them all. 'Ah, she's a likkle cutie. What's your name?' L Boi gave Cece a crooked smile.

Dwayne spun around. 'Nah, fam, you don't ever speak to her, get me?' His voice was laced with venom. He switched instantly, his stance aggressive. L Boi turned to his bunch of bandit friends, shrugging his shoulders.

'Rah man's sensitive, innit,' he said croakily and took another hit of his spliff. He turned back to face Dwayne, who stood steadfastly holding onto Cece.

'Tell you what. I'm gonna put her down in my yard, then come back to finish this.' His anger bubbled to the surface just as the lift door screeched open.

'Do your ting, fam; I was just trying to be nice.' L Boi puffed his spliff as it dangled from his lips, cackling to his crew.

'Soon come. Wait for me, bro.' He pointed his finger at L Boi. Fuming, Dwayne stepped into the corrugated cube, still clutching the pink *Frozen* rucksack, with Cece clinging onto him.

Dwayne charged out of the lift and walked at pace to the front door of Cindy's flat. He was so incensed he dropped the keys on the floor. 'Shit, Cece, get down for a sec.' He lowered a scared Cece to the ground and bent down to pick up the keys.

'Uncle, what's wrong?' Cece sensed Dwayne's mood and clung to his leg.

'Come on, Cece.' He grabbed her hand and marched to the door, jutting the key into the lock. He could overhear L Boi and his boys laughing and being boisterous below. He pushed open the door. 'Get inside,' he ordered Cece, who now was clearly upset by his intense behaviour.

Once inside, he quickly took Cece's coat off and switched on the television. 'Sit down and don't move,' he ordered, causing a fragile Cece to shudder. The tone of his voice ran through her little body.

Dwayne rushed about in the kitchen, opening different drawers and slamming them. He looked around the counter and saw a rack of sharp knives. He muttered furious obscenities under his breath, then grabbed the largest kitchen knife from the rack. 'Little fucker let's see if he's a fucking badman now,' he cursed within earshot of Cece, who was now standing in the kitchen doorway watching him.

'Thought I told you to sit down!' he shouted at her, unable to control his aggression. He took her by the arm, dragging her back to the sofa. 'Ow!' Cece screamed, then broke into a wailing cry which quickly became a scream of anguish. She continued to cry loudly, trying her best to fight him off. 'I said sit down and shut up!' Dwayne could not control his volcanic temper.

Tears streamed down Cece's face. She cried herself hoarse, trying to contain her fear, but only ended up choking on her snot. Holding the knife in his hand, Dwayne paced up and down the room. 'Cece, shut up man!' He was worked up and ready to leave, which made it worse as Cece went into a hysterical, high-pitched wail.

'No, Uncle Dwayne, don't leave me!' Cece ran towards him, stamping her feet and stretching out her arms. It was as if she knew the gravity of the situation; her little face was drenched with tears, lips quivering. Dwayne turned back, and on seeing the state his niece, eventually dropped the knife to the floor.

'It's ok, Cee; it's alright; come.' He knelt on the floor, offering an embrace, but Cece continued, unable to control the sheer fright which had taken hold. 'No!' she screamed, standing alone, shaking her arms in defiance. 'I'm sorry, bubba; uncle's sorry now. Ok, come on.' Dwayne shuffled on his knees. Beads of sweat formed on his forehead as he reached out his arms towards her.

Cece stood frozen on the spot, trying to suppress her tears. Dwayne shuffled a few more times until he took her into his arms. 'It's alright. Uncle's sorry, ok?' Cece fell onto his chest, burying her face into him. She was hot and sweating, trying to control her outpouring, her body jerking incessantly.

Dwayne hugged her tightly, whispering into her ear, 'I'm sorry, darling; uncle's sorry.' He kept repeating his words and rubbing her back, trying to calm her down. His phone began to buzz, shaking Cece, who gripped him tighter. He dug the phone from his back pocket and checked the screen. The name Sasha flashed as it continued to vibrate in his hand. Dwayne tossed it to the floor next to the knife, then held Cece, who had begun to calm down.

* * *

Cindy was back in her office. She gazed at the screen, puzzled by the instructions Andersen had sent her by email. It read, 'Transfer a deposit of seventy-five thousand pounds from my Swiss account to a company called United Orphanages. The details are provided below. Create an invoice to a contractor called Lunge Ltd here in Holland. Details also below. Once done, go to my office, and in the bottom drawer of my desk you will see a mobile phone. Switch it on. There is only one number in the contacts. Send a text saying "Complete", then switch it off and place it back in the drawer. This is a private and confidential transaction not to be discussed with anyone. Delete this email once complete. Thank you, Cindy. See you next week.'

Cindy read it a few times over to be sure. 'Never heard of any of these companies,' she muttered, intrigued, clicking off the email then clicking to another screen, sitting forward and analysing a spreadsheet.

'Nope, not on our books,' she said quietly. 'Hmm,' she pondered, clicking open the email again. 'United Orphanages…' She clicked into a search engine and typed in the company name. 'Nothing,' she mused, resting back in her leather chair, her brown eyes searching and a tidal wave of thoughts flooding her mind.

Cindy had done what had been requested and made her way to Andersen's office, which was another floor up in the private suite called the Orbit. She walked on a thick, grey carp through a quiet atrium until she reached the door. She pressed her building pass onto a flat black panel which turned green once her pass had been recognised. Being his PA, she was the only one who had access to his office.

Cindy entered the room, and the halogen spotlights beamed into life. It was large, more like an apartment lounge than an office. A long, L-shaped, white fabric sofa took up a sizable space opposite his desk, which was a curved clear glass table with built-in frosted glass drawers.

Cindy sat in his chair. She looked around, feeling the comfort of the space. 'Right, let's do this,' she said to herself, taking a deep breath before pulling open the bottom drawer. There it was the phone he had talked about. She took it out and switched it on; it came to life unlocked. She found the number in the contacts. Foreign. She could tell by the code. She tapped in the word 'Complete' and sent the message, which went through. 'Received' appeared in tiny letters below the message bubble.

Cindy curiously checked through the phone to see whether there were any other messages or pictures, anything to give her a clue as to why Andersen had never mentioned this company or phone before, but nothing. Like Andersen's office, everything was clean. She put it back in the drawer as instructed, staring around the desk. She picked up a picture of Andersen and his family—his beautiful wife Frieda and their twin girls, all smiling happily in a wooden chalet in a ski resort somewhere.

Cindy's mobile rang, the ringtone carrying through the large space. She saw Dwayne's name flashing and answered. 'Alright, bro.' She stood up from the desk and walked around the room, having a nosey as he spoke, 'What? Is she alright?' she asked, a strain of concern coating her voice. 'I'm on my way.' She cut the call and left the room in haste.

* * *

Dwayne sat at the dining table, head bowed, hands clenched tightly together while Cindy stood opposite him, her manicured hands planted firmly on the table. She was still dressed in her work attire, her usually attractive face tightened as she continued to berate her brother. 'Seriously? Is there rocks in that head of yours?' she shouted, her voice strained, trying to suppress her anger. 'What was you going to do? Murder him?' She stood upright, hands now on hips.

Dwayne breathed a deep sigh, shaking his head slowly. 'I lost it. That little prick…' He stopped, realising his words were futile. 'My bad, sis.' He finally raised his head, his eyes sorrowful, consumed with guilt.

'Is that all you can say? My bad, sis…' Cindy mimicked his deep voice sarcastically, scratching her short-bobbed head of hair in frustration.

'Your niece has seen you acting like a madman with a knife in your hand.' Her eyes bulged with rage. She confronted him, prodding her finger into the side of his head, which provoked a reaction, and he grabbed her hand. 'Sis, I told you I flipped out!' His eyes widened with intensity. He pushed the chair back, getting up from his seat, his big frame looming over Cindy.

'Don't touch me!' He pushed her hand away, looking menacingly at her. 'I fucked up, alright? Sorry.' He spoke harshly. Cindy crossed her arms defiantly.

'You don't scare me, bruv. What does scare me is you ending up back inside, and Cece…' She paused, biting her lip. 'She don't deserve that.'

Dwayne ran his fingers through his curly high-top, pacing up and down the living room while Cindy faffed around picking up Cece's various toys and books which were scattered on the floor.

'I don't want you bringing trouble to my door,' she muttered under her breath.

'What?' Dwayne stopped; his tone still carried a hint of aggression. The taut atmosphere was stretched to the maximum, interrupted only by the loud ringtone of Dwayne's phone. He checked the phone, seeing Ricky's name flashing.

'Just go. I want you out.' Cindy hung her head, drained by the tension.

'Who's gonna take Cece to school?' he protested, but her patience was thin.

'I'll manage,' she retorted, exasperated.

Dwayne grabbed his hoodie from the back of the chair and stomped out without a word. Cindy crouched on her haunches, throwing one of Cece's toys at the sofa, shuddering as the door slammed shut.

* * *

'Told you not to fuck with that younger, cha.' Ricky blew smoke out of the driver's window, annoyed with Dwayne, who sat motionless, head back, resting in the black leather passenger seat, his face turned towards the window.

'Bro, there's bigger tings out here; you wanna go back to jail or end up dead?' Ricky continued his rant, gesticulating towards Dwayne.

'Alright man, I heard it all from Cindy…' He was fed up with the whole affair. Ricky glanced at him, shaking his head, continuing to manoeuvre the car through the narrow back streets.

Only the low hum of the engine interrupted the bout of silence between them.

They arrived at a late-night car wash and valet building lit by large floodlights. A few Eastern European men were energetically scrubbing down a silver Mercedes C-Class. Ricky slowed the car to a halt and parked opposite. They sat for a few seconds. Dwayne looked out of the window. 'You getting your car washed or suttin?' he asked, watching the men, who stared back towards their car.

'Wait here,' Ricky ordered, before getting out of the car and slamming the door shut.

Dwayne watched Ricky walk around the car then across the road towards the men. Ricky exchanged words with them. They seemed familiar, one of them putting his arm around Ricky and leading him into the portacabin premises.

Dwayne watched on as Ricky disappeared. 'This is long.' He sighed, then checked his phone, scrolling down until he saw Sasha's name. He pressed the green call button, putting the phone on speaker. It rang loudly for a few seconds before a sleepy-voiced Sasha answered.

'Hello.' She sounded relaxed.

'You alright?' Dwayne asked, sounding calm now.

'Where are you?'

'Just out. Can I come round yours?' he asked, sounding tired, fed up and slightly sorry for himself.

'Yes, of course,' Sasha replied, perking up.

'Cool. Be there soon,' said Dwayne, still watching the men out of the window. He watched Ricky walk back out, holding a large leather bag and chatting to a stocky, grey-haired man dressed in a tight black T-shirt and jeans. They both looked over towards Dwayne in the car.

'Don't be long,' Sasha said seductively before cutting the phone.

Ricky returned and got back into the car, tossing the bag onto Dwayne's lap. 'Hold that for me,' He slammed the door and settled back into his seat.

'What's this?' Dwayne asked, pointing to the bag.

'I'll explain later.' Ricky smiled at him as he turned on the ignition.

'Who are they?' Dwayne continued his line of questioning.

Ricky laughed. 'You ask too many questions,' he replied, pulling away and accelerating down the street.

Dwayne began to open the zip on the bag. 'Oi nah, don't look in there.' Ricky stuck his arm out, pushing Dwayne's hand away. 'It's the little side hustle, courier ting,' Ricky continued, keeping his hand hovering above Dwayne's.

'Seen. So this is what you're doing?' Dwayne took his hand away from the bag, turning towards Ricky, his eyes searching for an answer. Ricky didn't look at him; instead, he kept his eyes firmly on the road.

'Truth is… my little nine-to-five retail position ain't cutting it, so this is just a flex,' Ricky replied with a grin. Dwayne patted the bag, squeezing it, trying to feel his way to the truth. 'The less you know the better it is, but I'll bring you in if you want?' Ricky turned to him. 'If you're on it, that is…'

Dwayne took the bag off his lap, tossing it into the back seat. 'Who the fuck are you working for?' He was now fully intrigued, waiting for Ricky to respond to his question as the car entered a tunnel. Just the glare from the orange lights illuminated their faces intermittently.

Chapter Four

Dancing Queen

Dwayne lay stretched out along the long cream couch, his bare feet perched on a plump brown-patterned cushion. Sasha walked over and stood in front of the large 4K flat screen television which was mounted onto a wall above a black glassed fireplace. The artificial orange flames danced behind her long legs. She was dressed in an oversized Rolling Stones T-shirt—the one with the logo of red lips and pink tongue sticking out. Her shorn hair was wet from the shower.

'What's on your mind?' Sasha asked, hands on hips, peering down at him. Dwayne yawned, stretching out his body. 'You've been quiet since last night.' Her voice was calm but her accent gave it an edge.

'Sorry, still kinda fuming from my argument with my sis,' Dwayne grumbled. Sasha walked up to him and knelt down.

'Talk to me.' She looked deeply into his eyes, hoping he would open up to her. He shifted, sitting up.

'Nah, it's just... Like what do you do?' he asked, changing the subject and breaking into a smile. 'All this.' He gestured at the large room and kitchen area.

Sasha broke into a laugh. 'I see what you did there, cheeky boy,' she replied, winking at Dwayne. She searched in her mind, taking a deep breath before answering. 'I'm a property manager.' She shrugged. 'Work for my brother.' Dwayne nodded.

'Makes sense. Is this one of your properties?' He continued to deflect her initial line of questioning.

Sasha stared at him for a few seconds, her brown eyes squinting slightly as the cogs in her mind turned slowly. 'Are you the police?' She shot a prickly response. 'Because you are asking a lot of questions.' Her mood shifted slightly. She seemed offended, judging by the tone of her voice.

Dwayne sensed this and backtracked. 'Just asking, babe. It's like I don't really know you.' He held her hand, but Sasha pulled away and stood up.

'Why do you care?' She was now annoyed, turning away from him, about to walk away, but turned back to face him. 'We fuck, that's it, so?'

Dwayne rose from his comfortable position and grabbed her hand. 'Chill, man. Not trying to start with you.' He spun her around to face him. He tried to pull her into him, but she resisted. 'I just got out… prison. Still getting used to the world again, get me?' For once he displayed an inkling of emotion, his brawny shoulders sagging heavily from the weight of his troubled mind.

'I don't even know what I'm talking about.' He broke into an uncomfortable laugh, trying to soften his approach. 'Ask me anything, innit?' He pulled Sasha towards him. She tensed herself rigid, reluctant to concede ground.

'Prison?' The word tumbled slowly from her mouth. She seemed rocked by his revelation, her expression one of confusion. 'For what?' she asked, pulling her hand away. They stared at each other, trying to figure out how to navigate this minefield. The sound of Sasha's phone interrupted their standoff.

Sasha picked up the phone, staring at the screen. 'It's my brother,' she mouthed to Dwayne, who was standing in suspense. Sasha answered, speaking in her native Romanian tongue as she walked around the kitchen. The short conversation seemed urgent. She cut the phone, throwing it onto the marble countertop.

'I have to go out.' She looked rattled, running her hands over her scalp. 'You can stay until I get back.' She walked towards the bedroom, taking off the large T-shirt on the way, revealing her elegant feline figure and rosary tattoo which was inked down her spine.

'And you should call your sister,' she shouted from the bedroom. Dwayne slumped onto the sofa, picking up the remote control and aiming it at the television. He switched the channel over to the football before resting back.

* * *

Sasha sat parked up in an empty side street, sucking down harshly on a cigarette. Her free hand tapped nervously on the steering wheel, her silver bracelet jangling. The driver's window was cracked half down, allowing the smoke to drift out. House music played low in the background. She now wore a black leather jacket and a black baseball cap pulled low on her head. She looked up into the rearview mirror every few seconds, then checked her phone.

A few minutes later, the bright glare of headlights beamed into her eyes. A chunky black Mercedes G-Class drove at speed towards her car, stopping only a few inches from the front of her vehicle. She took a final pull on the cigarette, then threw it out of the window, switched off the engine and exited the car. Sasha walked to the rear passenger door of the SUV with its blacked-out windows. She opened it and got in. The man from the car valet sat in the seat beside her—short, grey-haired, crew cut, tight black T-shirt, tattooed arms. He turned to Sasha and greeted her with a hearty hug, kissing both cheeks, his rough stubble grazing the side of her face. 'Raz.' Sasha smiled curtly, shying away. 'My little sister, we have a problem.' He patted her leg, reclining back in his seat as the car reversed then pulled off at speed.

The car crept slowly into a deserted industrial space flanked by old, dirty haulage trucks and storage units. Only the crunch of the tyres on the loose gravel of the old tarmac created any interference in the night silence. The wheels ground to a halt. Sasha and her brother exited the car wearing black bandanas to cover their faces. Next came the driver, one of his henchmen called Ilyan. Tall, young, and muscular, wearing sunglasses above his bandana even in the night. He stood by the car while Sasha led her brother to a storage unit.

A chunky padlock bound the black metal shutter to the floor. Sasha pulled a bunch of keys from her small handbag. She fiddled with them before inserting the correct one into the padlock, releasing the shutter.

'Hurry up,' Raz ordered aggressively, watching her struggle to pull the heavy shutter up. As she did so, inch by inch, the sound of whimpering and low cries could be heard. Raz activated the bright torch light on his phone, shining it into the storage unit. The eyes of several children huddled together on three double-sized mattresses stared back. A musty smell wafted out into the night.

A few of them began to cry. They were dirty, cold and afraid. One of them, a young boy no more than ten years old, ran towards Raz. He tried to cling to him. 'Get off me,' he growled, prising the child from his leg and pushing him forcefully back into the unit. The boy stumbled back onto one of the mattresses. 'Ilyan, go.' He ordered his henchman into the unit. He too shone the light from his phone into the unit, searching around, looking at all of the children's faces.

Sasha stared unmoved until she pointed. 'There, take her,' she commanded Ilyan. His torch revealed the body of a little girl slumped in the corner in filthy clothes. She could have been mistaken for a pile of old rags.

Ilyan covered his mouth, crouching down as he entered the unit. The other kids scattered like rats, clinging onto each other for some sort of protection. He made his way over to the young girl, checking on her momentarily before turning around and looking back at Sasha and Raz. He shook his head ominously, indicating that she was gone, before turning back and picking up her limp, lifeless body and carrying it out towards the car.

A pained cry sliced into the night from one of the young boys as he watched her being carried away. Raz stopped Ilyan. He used his phone to tilt the young girl's face, turning it towards him. Black curly hair, fair brown skin, she looked as if she were sleeping silently—dreaming—but he knew by the way her small body lay heavily in Ilyan's arms that her dreams were nothing but darkness.

'Put her in the boot.' He let go of her face, shining the torch directly into a shivering Sasha's eyes. 'Arrange for the rest to be moved tomorrow,' he said, raking his hands through his cropped, greying hair. There was no hint of remorse or sympathy in his tone, just a direct order.

Sasha nodded obediently, shuddering on hearing the car boot slam shut behind her. Raz went back to the car, opened the door and got in, leaving Sasha, statuesque, staring into the unit. Her arms folded, she shivered at the vacant stares of the children who looked back at her.

Sasha pulled the shutter down slowly, the creak of the rusty metal invoking a chorus of muffled cries. She pulled off her bandana and bent over to the side, retching from her gut, spewing out a mouthful of vomit and sniffing like a police search and rescue dog until she heard Raz's coarse voice. 'Hey! Come on.' His gruff tone startled her back into action.

Chapter Five

Work mode

'Slow the fuck down, bruh,' Dwayne shouted, gripping Ricky's arm. Ricky pressed hard on the accelerator, increasing the speed and whipping the steering wheel, turning the car sharply through the tight backstreets, his eyes bulging, focused firmly ahead.

'Not stopping, bro; can't get caught with this shit.' His eyes flicked up to the rearview mirror every two seconds. 'Fuck! They're still behind us.' They heard the faint sound of sirens getting louder.

Ricky continued to drive like a maniac, ignoring the red lights at the crossing. Dwayne sat stiffly in his seat, holding onto the door handle as the car veered around a sharp corner, hitting the kerb on his side and causing it to swerve and skid. It wobbled violently and Ricky struggled to keep control of the heavy vehicle.

'Ah shit, hold on!' The panic in his voice did little to reassure Dwayne that he was in control.

'Bro, beg you, just stop.' Another impassioned plea from Dwayne fell on deaf ears as Ricky continued with his rally driving through a set of dimly lit arches. Only the blue lights of the chasing police car illuminated the blackened bricks which shrouded the cocoon-like passage.

'Do you want to go back inside?!' Ricky shot Dwayne a look, his baseball cap pulled low, concealing his eyes. 'Do you?' he shouted. 'Fuck, man.' He banged the steering wheel in frustration, causing the loud horn to honk; it echoed into the night.

Up ahead were a set of yellow and black metal bollards blocking the exit from the arch. 'Yo, slow down, look!' Dwayne pointed ahead. 'Fuck, Ricky, stop man! You can't get through!' His voice was now a high-pitched squeal as he realised there was no way out. Ricky pumped the brakes, but because of the speed he was going, the car tyres just skidded along the damp tarmac.

'Bro, watch out, shit...' Dwayne barely got his words out before the car careered out of control and smashed into the bollards. Both were flung forwards like two rag dolls. On impact, the windscreen shattered, showering fragments of glass over them. The two airbags burst from the front, cushioning the blow to their faces, but were not enough to stop the force as their bodies were flung around like clothes in a tumble drier. The horn wailed like an air raid warning, mixing with the sound of the sirens behind them.

Dwayne jerked out of his sleep, taking a deep gasp of breath and clinging to the white sheet which partially covered his body. He stared wide-eyed around the room, breathing heavily, sweat running down his forehead. He turned to see Sasha sitting on the edge of the bed watching him. He jumped with fright on seeing her. 'Shit, what the...' His body tensed and he sat bolt upright, spooked.

Sasha was dressed in black vest and white knickers. She reached out and touched his shoulder. 'It's ok.' She rubbed him gently. Dwayne flinched at her touch. 'You had a really bad nightmare.' She shuffled next to him and hugged him.

'Serious? What the fuck?'

'It's ok, I'm here,' Sasha said softly, hugging him tightly, her face resting on his shoulder. Her own demons were apparent as the whites of her eyes were inscribed with thin red veins. She looked around the dimly lit room. Tears began to stream down her face. 'We're ok,' she said, her tone hushed, breathy. Dwayne, still shaking, tried to compose himself. He put his arms around her and held her tightly, his eyes also staring wildly into space. They sat together, consoling each other in silence.

* * *

Loud screams and vociferous voices, energetic and joyful, came from the excited kids who tumbled and bounced around in the giant, colourful soft-play cage. Cindy watched on from the safety of her seat at a coffee table, smiling and taking pictures. She watched Lena's long limbs, covered in black and luminous orange gym lycra, struggle to untangle themselves from the large, netted pit. Cece was equally exuberant, tossing the brightly coloured sponged cubes at a floundering Lena, who tried her best to scramble her way out to the safety of the parents' coffee lounge.

'Wow, you were really owning that playpen,' Cindy said with a laugh, watching a flushed Lena taking a seat beside her, plonking herself down and guzzling a bottle of water.

'Jesus, that little girl of yours has energy,' she huffed, putting her glasses back on. Her cheeks were red from her exertions. 'You should go in,' she suggested, but Cindy coolly sipped her coffee.

'No thanks, I'm fine right here.' She winked at Lena then waved at Cece. 'Andersen's back tomorrow; my agenda is packed.' She leant forward, elbows on the table; her hands held up her face, which hovered just above her coffee cup.

'He likes you. Pushes you hard because he knows how good you are,' a now chilled Lena chimed in. She took a bite from a brown ciabatta sandwich.

'Guess so…' Cindy sighed heavily, her voice barely audible amongst the screams from the kids.

'Did you hear from your brother?' Lena asked, after swallowing a mouthful of avocado and lettuce.

'Nope,' she mused, looking down at her phone and swiping the screen belatedly.

'Who's that man talking to Cece?' Lena asked, staring over towards the play pen. Cindy raised her head.

'Oh hell no!' she responded, jumping up quickly and dashing towards Cece, leaving Lena at the table.

'Oi! Nah, I don't think so.' She hastily budged herself between the netted fence and the man.

'Mummy, he said he's my dad!' Cece giggled playfully. Cindy stood steadfast, arms folded, staring back at the tall, dreadlocked individual. His ebony skin glistened with a coat of perspiration. He broke into a smile revealing at least three gold teeth.

'Hello, Cindy.' He flicked his locks, clearing them from his face, and his dark eyes bored into Cindy. 'Bit hostile, ain't it, that stance?' He choked out a laugh, which clearly unhinged Cindy.

She looked him up and down with a sneer. 'You stalking us or something, Leon?'

The man stepped back, taking an admiring look at Cindy. 'Looking good, Cind.' He took a white flannel from his back pocket and wiped his face.

'Don't… call me that.' Cindy turned to check on Cece. 'Come out now, Cece,' she ordered, her abrasive tone indicating to Cece that her play time was up.

Cindy felt slightly embarrassed. She glanced back at Lena, giving her an uncomfortable smile, before turning back and screwing up her face towards Leon just as Cece scampered around from the playpen. 'Mummy, I need juice.' Cece tugged on Cindy's hand, distracting her momentarily.

'Go and sit with Lena.' Again she growled unintentionally, still riled by his presence.

Cece did as she was told and ran over to Lena. 'What you doing here?' Cindy spoke through gritted teeth, staring up at him. He was tall and athletic, with long arms protruding from his designer T-shirt sleeves.

'I'm here with my…' He paused, looking back over his shoulder. 'Family.' He turned back to face her.

Cindy's eyes looked past him and saw another woman—early thirties, brown-skinned, pretty—standing with two young children, watching on. Cindy broke into a smile, albeit forced. 'Is that right?' She shrugged, unimpressed.

'I come in peace.' He smiled again, the gold in his mouth glinting. 'Just wanted to say hi to my daughter. She's grown,' he continued, glancing over to Cece and Lena. 'Is that your girlfriend?' he asked, knowing he still had the gall to get under Cindy's skin. 'Fuck you, Leon, leave us alone. Go back to your family.' She stressed the word family, a hint of envy unintentionally creeping into her tone. She turned away, ready to walk back over to her table where Lena and Cece watched on.

'I mean it, Cind. Just wanna spend time with her, introduce her to her brothers.' He had barely finished his sentence before Cindy interjected.

'Never gonna happen.' She shot a cursory glance over to the woman and the children, then walked away.

'I'm serious. Can't we at least…' Again his words were cut short.

'Don't!' Cindy turned around to face him, holding up one finger towards her mouth, shushing him. Her body shook with fury. She turned, breathing heavily. 'Come on, we're going.' Her voice drifted towards Lena, who sensed the mood and started hastily gathering their belongings.

Cindy took Cece's hand. Her phone began to vibrate on the table, so Lena picked it up and handed it to her. She looked at the screen and saw Dwayne's name flashing. She cut the call, stuffing the phone into the back pocket of her jeans. 'Come on.' Rattled, she looked shame-faced at Lena, who got up, checking she had everything, and followed as instructed, leaving Leon forlornly walking back to his family.

***

As usual, the car valet was busy, even though the dark skies of evening had descended over the streets. Droplets of rain lightly tapped the exterior of the windscreen. Dwayne stared out of the window, watching a crew of men vigorously wiping down a luxury vehicle. His phone rang loudly, interrupting his thoughts. He settled back into the cushioned seat, checking his screen. The name Lisa flashed.

'Yo, what's up?' he answered, his voice deadpan and tired. He put the phone on speaker. Lisa's voice came through, sounding sultry and relaxed. 'So… I made some stew chicken, rice, salad and a cold Guinness punch.' She spoke playfully, enticing him. 'Kai's fast asleep, and I got Netflix on pause.' She giggled, her voice low and husky.

'Hmm, sounds good to me. I'm starving.' A broad smile emerged on his face. He turned, looking out of the window; he could see Ricky walking out clutching the leather sports bag. 'Ricky's here; I'll get him to drop me.' He sat up as Ricky approached the car. 'Soon come, keep it warm,' he reassured her. 'The food or my…' She giggled seductively again before cutting the call.

Ricky jumped into the driver's seat, tossing the bag onto Dwayne's lap. 'Hold that for me.' He adjusted his seat, then started the car. 'I feel like Jason Statham, the Transporter blud!' Ricky cackled, obviously in a jovial mood. Drill music pumped from his speakers. He pushed Dwayne. 'Cheer up, nah, man!'

He laughed, checking himself in the rearview mirror, then pulled away from the car valet premises.

Dwayne turned the music down. 'Drop me to Lisa's before you get into Transporter mode.' Dwayne pushed him back, wiping the bag with his sleeves then tossing it onto the back seat. 'Don't want my prints on that, bro. Who are dem peeps?' He looked at Ricky.

'It's calm. I drop the bag off, collect the change, job done.' Ricky swerved around a double-decker bus which had pulled over to the bus stop. 'Dem rich city men want the merch; fuck I care what they do with it.'

Dwayne sat silently in his thoughts for a few seconds. 'Seen; that explains Paige, the high-class parties…'

Ricky nodded. 'But I bagged Paige from Insta. She's just a good face to get the clients in.' He sped up towards a set of traffic lights which had turned red as he approached.

'Bro, the lights are red,' Dwayne warned him, not that it bothered Ricky.

'Fuck that,' Ricky responded, accelerating across the junction, much to Dwayne's annoyance.

'Slow down, Hamilton! What's the rush?' He shook his head, dismayed.

Ricky started laughing, checking his phone as he sped through the streets.

'Fuckin' 'ell, feds behind us.' Ricky sat up, gripping the steering wheel.

'Slow down then!' Dwayne, now agitated, slid down the window and glanced into the wing mirror; he could see the blue lights flashing a few cars behind them. 'Shit,' he muttered under his breath. Ricky put his foot down and sped up, driving recklessly, cutting in front of the other cars on the road.

'Ricky, wha gwan?' Again, he pleaded with his friend.

'Fam, we can't get caught with that shit. Do you want to go back to prison?' Ricky asked, twisting the steering wheel sharply, turning the car into a side street, struggling to control it as if he was trying to rein in a wild, bucking stallion.

The car flew over road humps. Rain was splashing onto the windscreen, and the wipers swished back and forth, barely aiding the visibility. He honked the horn loudly at a crowd of people who had spilled out of a club into the road ahead of them.

Dwayne gripped the handle of the door. 'Oi, Ricks, stop man!' he shouted. Ricky still sped towards the stragglers, who all, belatedly, scattered out of the path of the oncoming vehicle. The sirens got louder, the police pursuit unrelenting. Ricky's jovial mood had disappeared; he now looked panicked, scanning the roads ahead, trying to work out his next move.

'Hang on, think I can go down here.' He spun the steering wheel again, swinging the car down a dark muddy pathway.

'Where you going?' Dwayne stretched over and attempted to grab the steering wheel, causing Ricky to veer into the bushes.

'Let go man!' Ricky panicked but still accelerated, regaining control. The blue lights of the police car were still visible, and their sirens were growing louder.

Ricky continued to drive down the hill, the wheels spinning through the mud. They passed a sign saying 'Canal Ahead', but at the speed they were driving, it had only flashed briefly in the headlights. 'Bro, just stop—' Dwayne had barely finished his sentence before the car smashed into a low concrete wall, which acted as a barrier separating the path from the dark, murky canal. The force threw them both like crash test dummies onto the dashboard console, and the windscreen shattered, peppering them with glass shards.

The police car stopped a few hundred yards behind them. Its bright headlights flashed as Ricky's car horn blared into the night. Dwayne shook himself groggily. He looked over towards Ricky, whose face was pushed against the inflated airbag, which was covered in blood. 'Ricky!' Dwayne shouted, shaking his friend, who remained lifeless.

Dwayne yanked at his seatbelt, struggling to release himself. He turned around and could see more blue lights converging down the hill. 'Ricky…' his voice trembled as he continued to shake him to no avail. He finally released the seatbelt. 'Fuck, Ricky, man…' he shouted in panic, on the verge of tears, knowing he had to make a choice there and then—either stay with his friend and face the inevitable or try to escape.

Quickly he picked up the leather bag and his own rucksack. He tried to open the door, but it was jammed. He bashed it hard with his shoulder a couple of times, grimacing as the delayed pain from the crash kicked into his body. His phone fell onto the floor, and the screen cracked through the LED lights. Finally he managed to force the door open; he stumbled out and fell into the mud. His legs were as weak as jelly.

He grabbed his phone and the bags and got up, clothes muddied. He managed to scramble to the top of the wall, then fell again, pulling the bags with him. He could see the torches of the police officer coming towards the car. He held his hands over his ears, clenching his teeth at the deafening sound of the horn and sirens.

'Arrgh fuck!' He got up and stumbled away along the canal path, the two bags weighing heavily on his already weary body, but he knew he had to find the strength to run. *Come on Dwayne, go! Fucking run!* He used every sinew he could muster and ran into the darkness with no sense of direction, away from the glare of the torches and the blue lights. The further he ran, the fainter became the sound of Ricky's car horn.

Dwayne walked slowly. He was out of breath and stopped to heave, but nothing came out. He spat out some of the blood that was still trickling from his nose. The leather bag, his rucksack, his trainers, jeans and hoodie were stained with mud as he trudged through the streets.

He constantly looked over his shoulder, making sure he was not being followed. A man walking his dog came towards him. Dwayne put his head down, shielding his face. The dog, a white and brown Jack Russell on an extended lead, came towards him to sniff before being dragged away by his owner, who offered only a deathly stare.

He eventually stopped outside a block of flats. He walked through the desolate car park towards a row of different-coloured doors. He continued until he reached a red door numbered twelve. He dumped the bags onto the wet pavement and banged on the door. He took out his phone and looked at it. A drop of blood from his nose blotted the cracked screen. He banged on the door again, agitated, sniffing up the blood in his nose, then wiping it with his sleeve.

Footsteps could be heard behind the door, followed by the sound of the lock turning. It opened. 'Better late than never.' Lisa smiled, standing in a cream silk dressing gown, diamante slippers and black lace lingerie cupping her golden-brown cleavage. Her red hair tumbled down over her shoulders.

Her smile was instantly replaced by a look of horror. 'Oh, no way.' Her romantic moment was shattered, her dinner date ruined by a dirty and dishevelled man. Dwayne picked up the bags and stumbled into the flat, brushing his muddied body past the fresh, sweet-smelling Lisa and groaning loudly from pain.

* * *

Dwayne opened his eyes, disturbed by the crack of daylight which cut through a slight gap in the curtains. He heard the sound of a child's voice counting slowly. 'One, two, three, four…' He rubbed his eyes and turned uncomfortably on the sofa, the pain from his bruised body a sharp reminder of his tumultuous night's events.

His eyes squinted, still burning from tiredness caused by minimal sleep. He adjusted his position and saw a little boy dressed in a smart green school uniform. He made out Kai kneeling next to the leather bag, taking out the cellophane-wrapped bricks of drugs and stacking them on top of each other.

'No… Kai, you can't touch them.' Dwayne slid his body down to the floor and crawled towards Kai. 'No, Kai, put it down.' He grabbed one of the tightly wrapped bricks from him. 'I counted eight.' Kai giggled, looking please with himself.

Lisa entered the room dressed in black leggings, a T-shirt and trainers. 'Kai, you ready…' Her jaw dropped at the sight of Dwayne sprawled out on the floor, still in his muddied clothes and holding the brick, with Kai kneeling beside him playfully moving the others around.

'Kai, go and get your bag.' Lisa's voice was stern. Kai got up and ran out to the hallway. She looked down at Dwayne, giving him a cold stare. 'Nah, Lisa, it's not mine… I mean it's not what you think,' he stuttered, knowing he had no feasible explanation to offer. 'We need to talk,' he continued to plead, crawling around and picking up the rest of the bricks.

Lisa backed away insulted, her expression one of disgust. 'Come on, Kai, let's go.' She left the room and pulled the door shut. 'Fuck, fuck, fuck, fuck!' Dwayne punched the wooden flooring several times before succumbing to the pain. He held his torso tightly while crouched on both knees.

Chapter Six

Missing words

Sasha sat in silence in front of a large mirror, staring at herself for a few seconds. A weary, worried expression was reflected back at her. Her hand shook as she dusted her cheeks lightly with a make-up brush. Her usual tanned skin looked paler than normal as if she was drained of energy. Deep red lipstick accentuated her mouth. Her shorn hair, which had grown out a little, was brushed back away from her face, allowing her big brown eyes, which were lined by thick black mascara, Cleopatra style, to stand out vividly.

She continued to sweep the soft brush across her face until the sound of her phone jerked her back to reality, causing her to nervously drop the brush. She was all fingers and thumbs as she picked up the phone and placed it to her ear. She didn't speak, but nodded, sighing deeply, then clicked it off, holding it against her forehead and drawing a deep breath.

Again, she stared directly at the mirror. Something was weighing heavily on her mind. She wrapped a headscarf around her head, then put on a black niqab, fixing it so it covered all of her face, adjusting the section where her eyes were visible. She stood up, grabbing her phone, keys and a black leather jacket, before leaving.

Outside was crisp, the sharp sunlight belying the frosty temperature. Ilyan sat waiting in a luxury silver Mercedes, dressed smartly in a suit, with sunglasses perched on his face. Sasha got into the sleek car without a word and sat in the passenger seat. Warm air from the heater flowed in the car, carrying a sweet vanilla aroma from the dangling air freshener which hung from the rearview mirror. She felt uncomfortable seeing Ilyan's smirk which greeted her.

Sasha shifted into position, pulling the seatbelt across her and clicking it into the socket. Ilyan was robotic, putting the car into gear and driving away. Sasha stared blankly out of the window, watching the world go by. Her eyes focused on a large digital billboard mounted on a concrete flyover advertising a theme park, depicting a happy-looking family on a rollercoaster. 'Do it for the kids' was the strapline under their excited faces.

The car sped under the bridge to the sound of Romanian folk music—Ilyan's choice of soundtrack for their journey. They drove for about an hour until they reached a tree-lined suburban street flanked by smart, detached houses. Ilyan pulled into the drive of a house which was undergoing some form of refurbishment. Scaffolding stood outside the main entrance, and a yellow skip was anchored in front of the side garage.

Ilyan switched the engine off. He looked at Sasha from behind the smoked lens of his glasses. She opened the door and stepped out of the car. Ilyan followed, locked the vehicle, fixed his shirt, then walked behind Sasha, who had already reached the front door. She fumbled in her handbag and pulled out a bunch of keys, dropping her phone on the floor, clearly still unsettled. Ilyan picked it up and handed it back to her. She took it, looking at him, her sullen eyes framed by the black niqab.

On entry, it was evident the interior was being redecorated. A large, open plan kitchen was covered in white dust sheets, amongst a step ladder, pots of paint and various power tools left on the counter. Sasha walked in slowly. Ilyan closed the door behind them. She headed straight up a black cast iron spiral staircase to the left of the kitchen. Ilyan waited at the bottom of the stairs, watching as she walked across a tiled landing towards one of the rooms.

Alone, she stood outside a dark oak door which was locked with a large metal bolt and a padlock. She took the bunch of keys, jangling it to find the right one. Movement and footsteps could be heard from inside the room while she turned the key and pulled the bolt across. She selected another key and pushed it into the lock, turning the handle slowly. She pushed the door open softly. Only the high-pitched creak of the unoiled hinges penetrated the silence.

The door opened, revealing a room of cowering children huddled together on a couple of large beds, surrounded by empty packets of snacks and empty water bottles. Instantly, the smell of urine and sweaty bodies wafted into her face. A few of the children began to cry at the sight of her figure covered head to toe in black, with just her eyes looking back at them.

Sasha stood motionless. She wanted to run but knew she was here to do a job. She pointed to two of the children, a boy and a girl no more than eight or ten years old. Their dirty faces, tatty clothes and overgrown hair signified their harrowing ordeal. They shuddered and clung onto each other, realising it was their turn to face their fate. The little girl—tiny and dusky-skinned—began to wail, shaking her head and gripping onto her friend.

Sasha stepped into the room and walked straight towards them. She prised them away from the others and dragged them out of the room. The little boy also began to cry, trying to resist, but he was too weak.

Ilyan ran up the stairs. The sight of him scared them even more. He came to Sasha's aid, grabbing them both forcefully and dragging them away. The other children watched on, all backed up against the wall, hoping that they would not be chosen next. Sasha quickly slammed the door shut, locked it, slid the bolt back across and clicked the padlock on.

The two children stood naked under a shower, crying, shivering and holding each other while Sasha scrubbed them down harshly with a large sponge. After they were washed, Sasha opened a wardrobe in another bedroom. It was full of brand-new kids' clothing and shoes. She selected a few items then turned to the two, who were both wrapped in the same towel, trembling, upset and sniffing.

After a few minutes, she walked slowly back down the spiral staircase, holding their hands. They were now dressed smartly, their hair still wet. Ilyan, waiting by the front door, gave Sasha a cold stare and checked his watch. He had taken off his designer shades and looked frustrated, his dark eyes boring into Sasha. As they walked towards him, he turned and opened the door, then led them out to the car.

After another long drive, they arrived at a posh gated house in the countryside. The earlier sun was now masked by grey thunderclouds. Gold-railed gates slowly swung open, allowing Ilyan to drive in and pull to a halt behind two parked Bentleys. The two children sat quietly in the back seat, holding each other's hands. They looked smart, almost normal, except for their spooked expressions.

On entry, they were greeted by a middle-aged Arabic-looking man with a greying beard and portly belly, smartly dressed in black trousers and a pale blue shirt. He bowed, greeted Sasha and shook Ilyan's hand enthusiastically, kissing him on both cheeks. He ushered them in, then switched his attention to the kids. His smile revealed his slightly yellowed teeth.

Sasha and Ilyan sat on a large, cream leather sofa in a spacious room with lavish furnishings, crystal chandeliers and a marble-tiled floor covered by a large Persian rug. In a modern, black-tiled fireplace, logs crackled, orange flames flickering in the background.

The two children stood side by side in front of them being inspected by the man's wife. She was younger—maybe mid-thirties—with brown highlighted hair, fair skin layered with make-up and gold bracelets stacked on each wrist.

The woman walked around, looking them up and down. She stooped down, staring adoringly at the young girl, cupping her face with her long fingers, her nails elegantly manicured. The little girl flinched, turning up her face at the touch. A smile broke across the woman's face. She stood up and turned to her husband, nodding, elated. She ran across the room and embraced him. He hugged her back, kissing her on the top of her head, and also nodded in approval.

Sasha sat motionless. Her eyes glassed over with tears as she observed the two children. Ilyan stood up, exchanged a warm handshake with the man and nodded towards his wife who was so happy. She went back to the children, taking both of their hands and leading them away.

Sasha stood up. Her heart sank watching the kids disappear into the house. The man clasped her hands, squeezing them tightly to show his appreciation. Sasha took her hands away. The man held his hands up, still smiling. He looked at Ilyan, who shrugged before following Sasha out of the house.

Music was the only sound on the drive back into the city. The tall skyscrapers in the distance cut a jagged pattern against the grey landscape, an indication of the vibe between Sasha and Ilyan.

Sasha had discarded the niqab and headscarf. She used a wet wipe to remove the make-up from her face. Ilyan reached over and touched her leg, rubbing it slowly, a curt act of reassurance. Sasha brushed it away with force. Again Ilyan smirked, continuing to nod his head to the folk music.

As the car slowed to a halt in the late-afternoon gridlock of traffic, Sasha grabbed her handbag, opened the door and jumped out of the car, zig zagging her way through the rows of static cars. Drivers honked their horns as she darted through to the safety of the pavement and disappeared into the busy side streets.

In a dingy backstreet bar, Sasha sat alone, with only a student-looking, goth bar girl for company. The black and purple décor matched her mood as she downed another tequila from a row of shot glasses lined up on her table. An old-school, thick-tubed television hung tentatively from the grimy, purple-painted walls, and a weathered pool table stood alone in the middle of the floor.

Sasha signalled to the goth bar girl to bring over the bottle for a refill. The girl, who was dressed in a dark purple, crushed velvet bustier and oversized black jeans, with pale, ghoulish make-up, rolled her eyes and came over with the bottle. Sasha pointed to the shot glasses, barely looking up from her phone as she scrolled through.

The girl huffed but did as instructed, pouring the clear potent liquid into each of the six glasses, filling them to the rim. Sasha barely acknowledged her and instead picked up one of the glasses and downed another shot. She repeated this, but the second shot caught her throat, making her choke and cough violently. She wiped her mouth, caught her breath, then tackled another, throwing it down her throat in one go.

* * *

Dwayne sat on the floor in Lisa's kitchen, dressed in only his tight black boxer shorts. He was leaning against a cupboard next to the washing machine, which was dealing with his dirty clothes. His mobile with its cracked screen was on the floor between his legs.

The whir from the machine was the only sound. Dwayne's head hung bowed; every few seconds it shook from side to side, his memory recalling the prior night's events.

The sound of the front door slamming stirred him momentarily; at the same time, his phone buzzed into life, vibrating on the tiled floor. Sasha's name blinked through the shattered glass pattern on his screen. Lisa pushed the door wide open. She stood staring at Dwayne, who barely picked his head up, distracted by his phone.

Lisa's stance was resigned, her disappointment still etched into her face. She unfurled a copy of a local paper. The headline 'Man killed in police high-speed chase' was printed in big, bold letters above a picture of the mangled car crushed into the wall.

Dwayne's gaze held for a few seconds seeing the brutal picture of Ricky's car wreckage. He stared up at Lisa, seeking some kind of refuge or compassion, but her face remained stern. She was seething inside, and he knew it. Hanging his head again, he watched his phone continue to vibrate against the floor until it stopped just as the spin cycle on the washing machine kicked in and Sasha's name faded from the screen.

Chapter Seven

Riding through the desert

A windswept rainy day greeted a hurried and flustered Cindy, who fought hard to hold on to her large umbrella as well as Cece's hand. They splashed their way through the puddles on the pavement. Cece, in her Disney Princess wellies and transparent plastic raincoat, and Cindy, in a pair of black trainers and a long cream mac, braved the elements on the journey to school. 'Cece, slow down, wait!' A frustrated Cindy yanked her back away from the kerb. 'Remember, stop to cross the road.'

A sporty red BMW slowed to a halt, blocking them from crossing. Cindy stared at the rain-stained window, annoyed at the driver delaying her progress. 'Oi, move your…' Before she could finish her sentence, the driver's side window slid down, revealing the chirpy, gold-toothed, smiling face of Leon.

'Want a lift?' His smarmy patois irked Cindy, who stepped to the side, dragging Cece with her so they could walk around the car. 'I mean it, Cind. I'll drop you,' he hollered as the impatient drivers behind him beeped their horns.

Cindy ignored him, her face screwed up due to the weather. She continued to cross the road, winding between the cars. 'Was that Daddy?' Cece asked, craning her neck to look at Leon, who by now was slowly driving away. 'Don't worry about him; let's just get you to school,' she replied sternly, marching on purposefully.

* * *

Cindy entered the plush reception area in the Schuster and Klein building. Her trainers squelched against the polished black tile floor. She pulled her umbrella closed, the droplets of water leaving a wet trail behind her.

'Morning, Miss Harper. Horrible weather.' One of the security guards did his best to greet her with a smile, although his stating the obvious to a bedraggled Cindy barely lifted her mood. She tapped her building pass onto the chrome access counter, opening the sliding glass gates which allowed her to the lifts.

Once in her office, she put the umbrella next to the coat stand and had begun to remove her mac when her desk phone began to ring. She huffed loudly, shrugging the wet mac from her arms. Leon's random appearance still rankled as she reached over and grabbed the phone.

'Good morning. Cindy Harper.' Her energetic tone was still laden with stress from the wet and blustery school run. 'Hi, Andersen. Right now? Of course.' She slammed the phone down and flung her mac at the coat stand. She kicked off her trainers, picked up a pair of black heels from under her desk and shoved her damp feet into them. Grabbing her iPad and phone, she rushed out of the room.

Cindy stood waiting for the shiny, silver-doored lift which would take her up to the Orbit, trying to fix her hair, which had been flattened by the rain. The doors opened and Lena stepped out, almost bumping into Cindy. 'Oh, hey!' Lena's appearance and loud greeting startled Cindy.

As usual, Lena was smart in her black-rimmed glasses, pinstriped business suit and immaculate blonde fringe. 'Oh hi, Lena!' Cindy was surprised to see her friend coming down from the Orbit. It was unusual for her or anyone else to be up in Andersen's office, but her mind was so scattered she didn't completely register, especially as Lena quickly embraced her with a warm hug.

'Catch you for lunch?' Lena suggested fleetingly as Cindy entered the lift. 'Yeah, fine,' Cindy replied as the doors slid shut. She turned, checking herself in the gleaming mirror, tidying herself as best she could until she heard the announcement 'You have arrived at the Orbit.' The programmed robotic female voice came through the speakers.

Cindy walked swiftly across the atrium clutching her iPad and phone to her chest, her shoes sinking into the deep carpet. She arrived at the door to Andersen's office and held her pass against the panel, which flashed a green light to let her in. She tapped on the door lightly to signal her entrance.

'Morning.' Cindy tried to sound as upbeat as she could. She poked her head around to see Andersen seated in his chair behind his large glass desk, dressed smartly in a sea-blue waistcoat and white shirt.

'Hi, Cindy. Come in; pull up a chair.' Andersen swung his eyes from his large Apple Mac screen to Cindy, who did as instructed, sitting down opposite him.

'Coffee?' Andersen asked casually, getting up from his chair and walking towards a cool looking espresso machine positioned on a glass sideboard.

'Yes please,' she answered, catching her breath and trying to compose herself, wondering about the reason for the impromptu meeting.

'Good weekend?' Andersen asked in his pronounced Dutch accent. He handed Cindy her cup of coffee.

'Was ok,' Cindy answered and took a quick sip. Her eyes were focused on Andersen, who rested back in his chair, gazing out of the window at the darkened clouds and rain lashing the glass.

'British weather…' he mused and sipped his drink. He turned back to Cindy, who was waiting on tenterhooks, ready to start typing notes into her iPad.

'Firstly, thank you for your help.' Andersen placed his cup on the table. His blue eyes smiled at Cindy. 'I'm impressed by your work,' he continued.

Cindy was flattered, nodding gratefully. 'Thank you,' she replied.

'Tell me, Cindy. How ambitious are you?' he asked, clasping his hands together, his silver cuff links glinting in the beams from the ceiling spotlights. Cindy was struck by the unexpected question, but, as always, she managed to switch into professional mode even though her mind was still racing from the morning's events.

'Very ambitious, Andersen! Can't you tell?' She cracked a smile. 'Why do you ask?' She returned the question, perked up by the caffeine flowing through her system.

Andersen offered a warm smile and nodded. 'I know you are, but what about your personal life?' He rested his chin on his hands.

Cindy's posture changed. She sat up now, intrigued, giving a supressed chuckle. 'Not quite sure how to answer that.' She looked back at Andersen, trying to work out the reason for his interest.

'Can't imagine you'd want to bring up Cece on Kingfisher Estate for the rest of her life,' Andersen said calmly, glancing towards the framed picture of his family. He picked it up, gazing at it. A satisfied smile warmed the wrinkled, freckled skin on his face.

'You know, when I met Frieda, our first place was a shared student flat.' He placed the picture back on the desk. 'Absolute shit! In a crap part of Den Haag.' He continued his personal life story. 'It gave me the drive to be successful, work hard, you know.' He clenched his fist, focusing his attention back on Cindy, who smiled and nodded in agreement.

'Now, I'd do whatever it takes to keep my girls secure and happy.' He stood up and walked over to the sofa. He sat down, crossing his legs and relaxing back. 'Come sit.' He patted the cushion beside him, beckoning Cindy.

Cindy sat on the sofa, spacing herself a cushioned seat away from Andersen. She clutched her phone and iPad on her lap.

'So, tell me. What would you do to ensure Cece's future?' he asked dryly.

Cindy paused for thought before answering. 'Everything, I guess,' she answered coyly. Her phone rang loudly, interrupting her line of thought. She glanced at the screen, It was Dwayne.

'Take it if you have to,' Andersen gestured.

'No, it's fine.' She cut the call.

'So here's the thing. I've given you a little bonus, a gesture of goodwill,' Andersen flashed a smile at Cindy, 'for helping me with…' he paused briefly, 'that thing the other day.'

'Oh no, it's not necessary.' Cindy shifted in her seat, perturbed by the conversation.

'But necessary it is,' Andersen countered firmly, only to be interrupted again by the loud ringtone on Cindy's phone.

'So sorry!' Again she looked at the screen to see Dwayne's name flashing. Again she cut the call. 'I'll put it on silent,' she huffed, smiling, trying to mask her annoyance.

'It's ok. Look, I'll cut to the chase.' Andersen sped up his speech. 'On top of your normal tasks, you'll be helping me with that little project. Discretion is still key.' He spoke now with authority, brushing his hand onto the comfortable suede cushion that separated him from Cindy.

'You can prove exactly how ambitious you are… for your daughter.' He looked at her intensely, his eyes conveying the degree of importance. The sound of a text message broke the awkwardness. Cindy checked her phone, still processing his last comments. The message appeared on her screen: 'Ricky's dead.'

For a moment, she was held in suspense, unable to fathom what she was reading. 'Everything ok?' Andersen jolted her mind back into the room.

'Huh, yep… it's fine.' Cindy tried to brush it off. 'Discretion… of course.' She smiled uncomfortably.

Back on her floor, Cindy sat on the toilet in the clean, quiet comfort of the cubicle. She had finished peeing a few minutes ago but was stuck in her thoughts. She checked the message on her phone again. 'Ricky's dead?' she muttered in disbelief. She pressed the screen, dialled Dwayne's number and held the phone to her ear.

The call went straight through to Dwayne's voicemail. 'Dwayne! What the fuck happened? Call me back, soon as….' she whispered through clenched teeth, only stopping on hearing someone entering the restroom. The sound of a pair of heels stepping onto the marble floor echoed in the silence, followed by the sound of running water.

As she exited the cubicle, she saw one of the office workers—a young, mousey-haired girl wearing a red-and-white polka-dot blouse.

'Hi.' Cindy smiled at her in the reflection of the mirror, placing her phone and iPad down on the pristine granite counter. She washed her hands, staring at herself in the mirror, her brown eyes filled with concern.

* * *

Dwayne stood outside, staring at the cracked screen on his phone. The battery icon flashed red, indicating the last bit of power was draining. His face was slightly obscured by his hoodie.

Drizzle continued to fall annoyingly as he watched the usual activity of men wiping down a row of cars on the forecourt. He looked down at the leather bag which hung from his hand, his breathing heavy.

Finally, he strode purposefully across the road towards the entrance. The men cleaning the cars all looked up and watched him. Dwayne gave them a cold stare. Undeterred, he kept walking towards a grey portacabin. He passed a window and could see Raz sitting at a desk, talking animatedly on his phone.

He approached the door, pausing for a few seconds before turning the handle and pushing it open aggressively, startling an unsuspecting Raz, who was speaking in his native tongue. He slammed his phone down on the desk.

'Who the fuck are you?'

Dwayne, unperturbed, dumped the leather bag on the table and stood menacingly over Raz. 'Ricky's dead, so I'm bringing this back.' He sniffed through his wet nostrils, patting the bag.

Raz sat back, staring with wide eyes. His mind searched for a few seconds. 'How?' he growled.

'Read the papers,' Dwayne replied huskily, wiping his nose with his wet sleeve. 'Anyway, you've got your merch back.' He turned to leave and made his way towards the door.

'My friend, where are you going?' Raz's gravel tone caused Dwayne to stop dead in his tracks. 'You now inherit Ricky's tasks.' He wheezed out a crusty cough.

Dwayne turned back to face him, his sunken eyes tired. 'Nah, I'm good,' he replied, a hint of frustration in his tone. He opened the door to leave, but Ilyan was standing there blocking his exit, his dark, chiselled features intimidating against the rainy backdrop. Dwayne backed up, reversing into the room.

* * *

Cindy paced up and down in her office barefooted, phone in hand, distracted and agitated. Her eyebrows knotted. 'Pick up, Dwayne.' She cut the phone call on hearing her brother's voicemail. Her frustration was interrupted by a tapping on the glass door.

Lena poked her head around the door. 'Hey, ready for lunch?' Her cheery disposition jerked Cindy back to reality. 'Huh?' She turned to see Lena's face radiating happiness and energy. 'I'm really sorry—would you mind if I didn't?' Cindy's shoulders sagged, and she flopped into her chair, deflated.

'Everything ok?' Lena entered and closed the door behind her. Her tall athletic figure, immaculately dressed in her fitted business suit, strutted towards her friend and co-worker.

Cindy offered a fake smile, her high cheekbones expanding, trying to mask her true feelings. 'Yeah, just been a manic day so far.' Defeated, she rested back.

Lena bent down and hugged her. 'Aw, sweetie. I'll grab you a sandwich. Chicken salad?'

Cindy smiled. 'Thanks, Lena.'

'No problem.' Lena spun around and walked out of the office, waving as she passed the glass panel.

Cindy focused on her screen. She began tapping on the keyboard to bring up the local news. 'Car crash victim named,' the headline stated. Cindy leant forward, reading the print. 'Oh my days!'

* * *

the sleek Mercedes car being driven by Ilyan, the cool breeze of the air conditioning hitting him in the face. He looked withdrawn, tired and fed up, especially with the Romanian folk songs playing on the car stereo.

'Do you drive?' Ilyan asked, slowly turning to Dwayne, steering the car through a dark country lane.

'Can't,' Dwayne replied.

'Why you can't?'

'I'm banned.'

'I'll get you a fake licence,' Ilyan said casually, turning the car into a muddy drive which led to a distant house on the horizon. Dwayne breathed heavily through his nostrils, then kissed his teeth, shaking his head.

Ilyan slowed the car to a halt on the smooth tarmac which swirled around the front of the house. It was decorated with a contemporary water feature of shards of black slate illuminated by bright blue neon lights.

'In and out.' Ilyan's robotic tone drove home his simple instructions. Dwayne turned to grab the leather bag from the backseat. He gave Ilyan a cold stare before opening the door and exiting the vehicle.

He walked quickly, the rubber soles of his dirty trainer's sticky against the black surface. Loud music reverberated from the inside as he approached the door—a glossy, black-painted, wooden one with shiny brass fixtures. He pressed hard on the doorbell several times, the annoyance at his task still smouldering.

After a few seconds, the door opened revealing a tall, mixed-race girl with curly red hair, wearing a sparkly black cocktail dress and a glittery Venetian mask. Her bright red lips parted. 'Good evening.' Her brown eyes sparkled through the gaps of the mask.

Dwayne remained calm. He could see, beyond her, people mingling, all dressed smartly and wearing different-coloured masks. 'Need to see Dietmar,' he said confidently, firming up his posture. 'Come this way.' She smiled enticingly, stepping aside to let him in.

The hallway was grand. White marble tiles with black peppercorn speckles led into a wide, open plan living room where fifteen to twenty people danced while others chatted, drinking large glasses of wine.

The girl who had opened the door played host, walking sexily in front of Dwayne as she led him through the room. He looked around, soaking in the vibe, watching middle-aged hipsters in sequinned masks socialising. No one took much notice of him as he strolled casually behind the girl.

'Wait here.' She turned to Dwayne, who stopped at her command. He watched her saunter over to a dining area where two men sat smoking cigars and talking. He stood waiting, bag in hand, while the music faded, momentarily replaced by the hum of conversation and raucous laughter.

In the restroom, a pair of manicured hands rubbed together under a running tap; a black and silver mask lay on the countertop next to a half glass of wine. The large portrait-framed mirror revealed Sasha's face. Her short dark hair was slicked back behind her ears, which were stapled with silver earrings. She stared at her reflection for a few seconds, her brown eyes framed by smoky eyeshadow and mascara. She turned off the tap, shook her hands and took a white hand towel from a silver rail.

Sasha touched up her make-up, applying some pink lip gloss, before picking up her mask and placing it back over her face. She, like the other girl, wore a sparkly black cocktail dress, which revealed a section of her rosary back tattoo. She picked up her wine glass, took a large gulp, then left the room.

A tall man—blonde, slim, clean cut, dressed in all black—walked across the room towards Dwayne. He puffed on a cigar, his expression dull until he greeted Dwayne by extending his hand for a shake.

'Dietmar,' he said with a foreign accent. German.

'I guess this is for you, then.' Dwayne thrust the bag towards him.

At that moment, Sasha walked into the living room area holding a tray of drinks. She caught sight of Dietmar and Dwayne, which distracted her so much she bumped into a man who was doing a matrix-style dance move and the tray was knocked out of her hands.

The din of glass breaking on the floor caused everyone in the room to look towards her.

'Ooh, so sorry.' The man grabbed Sasha by the arms.

'It's ok, really.' She quickly crouched down, bowing her head, and picked up the broken pieces.

Dwayne and Dietmar turned on hearing the commotion, giving her a fleeting look. Sasha kept her head down, fumbling with the broken glass, before standing up and running out of the room.

'I'll leave you to it.' Dwayne handed the bag over to Dietmar, then turned to leave, only to be grabbed by the arm.

'You're new?' Dietmar asked, speaking out of the side of his mouth as the cigar dangled. 'Stay, have a drink,' he encouraged, signalling to the curly-haired, mixed-raced girl, who quickly toddled over in her high heels and took Dwayne's hand.

'Come with me.' She attempted to pull Dwayne towards the dining room.

'Nah, I'm good.' He smiled politely, retracting his hand. 'Laters.' He backed away, retreating to the entrance, as Dietmar and the masked hostess watched on.

Sasha leant over the banister at the top of the stairs, mask still on her face, staring down at the hallway entrance. She watched Dwayne walking through the hallway and leaving. She hung her head, relieved to hear the door slamming. Droplets of blood dripped from her hand onto the white marble-tiled steps.

Chapter Eight

Farewell summer

Two years earlier.

The sun shone through the dusty windows of the minibus, which drove at speed across the sandy terrain. The driver, a man of Arab descent, mid-forties, circular glasses and a thick black moustache, chewed ferociously on some shelled pistachio nuts. He concentrated silently as the car juddered on the bumpy track.

A Gold Crown air freshener dangled from the rearview mirror, which reflected a female passenger sitting a few seats back. Large square sunglasses covered her eyes. Only a sliver of reddened white skin and stray blonde hairs were visible beyond the black scarf which covered her head and face.

She swigged on a bottle of water, gulping down the liquid. 'How long?' she asked him, barely able to tolerate the shaking drive in the heat. 'Twenty minutes,' the driver replied, maintaining his concentration on the road ahead.

Her mobile phone rang just as the driver pulled into the driveway of a guarded commune where two men in military uniform waited at a large wooden and barbed-wired gate. The woman answered. 'Hi, yes, just arrived.' After a brief conversation, she clipped the phone closed, gripping it tightly in her hand.

One of the men held up his arm, signalling to the driver to stop. Wearing dark overalls and black shades, he was reminiscent of Public Enemy's SW3s. He walked towards the car and the driver wound down the window. He began to speak to the guard in Arabic. A short, animated conversation took place before the guard walked around the minibus, checking it out, observing the sign boldly stencilled on the side panel. 'United Orphanages Aid' it read under a film of dust. He continued his inspection until he reached the window on the side where the woman sat.

The guard peered into the vehicle. Returning his stare, she wound the window down, his reflection prominent in her shades and her reflection in his. After a few seconds, he turned away and yelled to the other guard. On command, he unlocked the gate and waved them through. The driver stepped on the gas and drove them into the commune.

Down a sandy pebbled track appeared what looked like an old, disused, whitewashed brick church. It had a worn wooden door set on crumbling concrete steps, stark against the background of rubble and rusted steel frames that were once the supports of surrounding buildings.

The driver checked again in the rearview mirror as the woman fixed her headscarf before letting herself out of the vehicle. Her tall frame, cloaked in black, strode towards the entrance and up the steps towards the door, which was ajar. The sound of children playing and crying greeted her as she pushed the door open, the high-pitched creak from the rusted hinges cutting sharply across the cries and giggles.

She stood in the doorway surveying the old church hall, which was sparsely furnished, lined only with parallel rows of single beds. Young children were either running around playing or lying crying on the slim mattresses. She loomed in the doorway, the sun behind her exaggerating her already imposing silhouette as she removed her sunglasses.

She was met by a short, elderly woman wearing a white smock, a white headscarf and a cross on a gold chain. She tottered forward, taking pigeon steps with an unsteady limp.

'As-salaam-Alaikum,' she grumbled, bowing her head. 'Wa-Alaikum-Salaam,' the woman in black replied softly, bowing her head in return. A little girl aged no more than four or five, with black, curly, bedraggled hair and a dirty grey Mickey Mouse T-shirt, ran up to her and tugged at her cloak, pulling her into the airy room. The driver of the minibus came in behind them, struggling under a stack of boxes labelled 'Schuster and Klein Pharmaceuticals'. He dropped them off into a corner and puffed back out.

The two women walked around slowly, viewing each of the children, boys and girls, who looked back at them, all desperate for attention. One particular boy stood on the bed, boisterously jumping around on the mattress.

The old lady uttered a few words in Arabic to him, making him immediately sit down in a huff. As they continued walking around the room, the lady in black pointed towards a handful of children including the little girl in the Mickey Mouse T-shirt. The old lady clapped her hands, getting their attention, then instructed them to stand at the end of the beds.

The children all stood fidgeting, waiting uncomfortably while the woman walked slowly past each one, inspecting them. She stopped at the little boisterous boy, who offered her a cheeky smile. She tapped him on the head then continued, staring at each child warmly. She stopped at the little girl with the dirty grey Mickey Mouse T-shirt, crouching down to her eye level.

The girl gazed back demurely, gently brushing away the strands of fair hair that protruded from her headscarf. The woman put her sunglasses back on, unable to continue her eye contact. She stood up and patted the girl on the head before turning to the old lady. She pointed randomly at three more children, then walked hastily out of the room into the sunshine.

The driver emptied a small pile of pistachio shells from the car ashtray onto the dry, sandy ground. He knocked the ashtray against one of the tyres, making sure it was clean. He stood up slowly, lighting a cigarette and peering into the minibus at the woman who was now seated in the front passenger seat, staring pensively ahead.

After a few minutes, the old lady hobbled down the steps flanked by five of the children, including the boisterous boy and the little girl with the Mickey Mouse T-shirt. The driver walked around the side, slid back the door and watched as the high-spirited children climbed into the vehicle. He shouted a few choice words at them in Arabic, slammed the door shut and took a few last draws on his cigarette before climbing into the driver's seat.

The long drive took them across potholed paths and dangerous bumpy tracks with views of bombed-out buildings where there had once been small towns and villages. The sun had dipped, reduced now to just a large orange glow on the horizon.

The children, knocked out from the journey, were all sleeping in the back seats. The driver continued to concentrate, puffing on a cigarette which was wedged in the side of his lips, while negotiating the treacherous roads. The woman sat, her head leant back and tilted to the side, staring out of the window. Little beads of sweat formed on her forehead and dribbled into the black cloth which still covered most of her face.

'Two minutes,' the driver said. The woman nodded, glancing at the miniature Gold Crown air freshener which swung from side to side hypnotically as the minibus's tyres fought with the uneven surface.

Eventually, they pulled into a disused industrial area, a prehistoric graveyard of stark metal frames of old warehouse buildings and broken-down vehicles succumbing to the elements. The woman flicked open her phone, dialled and placed the phone to her ear.

After a few seconds, a man's voice answered. 'We're here,' she said, her tone flat, understated. She clipped the phone closed and turned around to see all of the children sleeping except for the little girl in the dirty grey Mickey Mouse T-shirt, who stared back at her, rubbing her eyes before breaking into tears.

Shortly after, an old truck raced towards the parked minibus, bright headlights beaming through the windows, reflecting off the woman's large, square sunglasses but catching the whites of the driver's eyes as he gazed with trepidation. The truck skidded to a halt, the noise from the brakes waking up the other children, sparking a frenzy of cries and moans. The woman opened her door, stepped out and slammed it behind her.

A short, stocky man dressed in a black baseball cap, T-shirt exposing his tattooed arms, and matching black combat trousers exited the truck and walked towards the woman. It was Raz, his grizzly features unmistakable, even in the early dusk. He talked to the woman for a few seconds, peering over her shoulder at the children who were all staring out of the window, watching on anxiously.

Raz walked over to the minibus and slid open the door. 'Out now,' he ordered. The children recoiled and began to cry, intimidated by his presence. A couple of men jumped down from the back of the truck and came over. They began grabbing the children, roughly pulling each one out until they were all standing in a huddle in the direct beam of the headlights.

The woman got back into the minibus. She could only watch on as the children were dragged away and put into the back of the truck. She could see the little girl in the Mickey Mouse T-shirt bawling and looking back at her.

The truck reversed at speed, jerking her little body backwards so she fell onto the other kids. The woman let out a small yelp, choking back tears as she watched the truck swivel around and roar off into the distance.

'Take me to my hotel.' Her voice trembled, and she held her head in her hands. The driver responded to her request, pulling away back down the deserted path, the red brake lights leaving an elongated trail in the dust.

The sound of a shower mixed with sobs broke the silence in the hotel room. A tall oscillating fan stood next to the bed where the black sunglasses, cloak and headscarf had been discarded, strewn across the flowered blanket. On the floor were shoes and items of underwear leading to the bathroom.

The woman sat crouched in the foetal position on a white and blue mosaic-tiled floor, her pale skin wet from the jet sprays and long blonde hair matted to her back.

She raised her head with the palms of her hands covering her face, continuing to cry. She wiped away the tears from her eyes, revealing her identity. Lena, her blue eyes staring skywards, let the warm sprays of water funnel down her reddened cheeks onto her chest. She pulled her hair back, wringing the water out, her naked body shivering uncontrollably.

Chapter Nine

Never is a promise

Brown autumn leaves blew across the lawns of the cemetery. Some loose leaves had been sucked into the grave that housed the wooden coffin containing Ricky's remains. Lumps of dirt landed on top, scattering on impact across the silver plaque inscribed with his name and dates.

Wailing from Ricky's sister Charmain pierced the sombre quietness. Dwayne stood respectfully a few yards away, hands dug deep into his pockets, still dressed in his black hoodie, tracksuit bottoms and muddied trainers. He sniffed, partly from the cutting breeze and partly from trying to hold back the tears at his friend's demise.

The small gathering of friends and family members dispersed, a few making a point of acknowledging the pastor, who clasped his hands around the thick black Bible. Out of the corner of his eye, Dwayne noticed Paige; he nodded towards her. She returned a pained smile; her black attire reflected her mood as she dropped a single red rose into the grave.

Dwayne trudged slowly over to the grave. He bent down on his haunches, staring deep into the ground at the coffin. The rose dropped by Paige lay angled, amid the crumbled dirt thrown in.

He pinched the top of his nose between his eyebrows, halting the flood of tears that eventually breached the barriers of his eye ducts. He shook his head in disbelief, recalling that fateful night of the car crash and the events which led up to it.

'Dwayne.' A deep voice vibrated behind him. He felt a heavy hand on his shoulder, snapping him out of his sad funk. Dwayne sprang up to face the person behind him. 'Trevor.' He cleared his throat, wiping away the tears from his face. 'Sorry, bro.' He thrust out his hand for a shake.

Trevor was Ricky's elder brother—tall, serious, imposing, cornrowed hair, his broad shoulders constricted by the tight black polo-necked sweater and blazer he wore. He stared sternly at Dwayne for a few seconds before offering his hand and gripping Dwayne's tightly.

'Walk with me.' By the tone of his voice, it was more an order than a request, one which Dwayne followed, carefully treading across the muddy peat to the path where the other mourners walked ahead in dribs and drabs.

'What happened?' Trevor asked, rubbing his black leather-gloved hands together in front of him. Dwayne shrugged, digging his hands further into the pockets of his tracksuit bottoms. 'Dunno, man; just heard about the crash.' Dwayne shrugged again, his body tensing up in the cold breeze. Trevor nodded, yet his face remained unconvinced.

'So when did you last speak to him?' Again Trevor probed, his words digging into the consciousness of an already fragile Dwayne. 'I… I saw him a few hours before,' he stuttered, searching in his mind. Trevor rubbed his bearded face. 'See, thing is…'

He paused. 'I can't understand why my brother would just crash his car into a wall next to the canal. Like, what was he doing there? Who was he running from?' His inquisition continued. 'You're his bredrin—he must have said suttin.' He pointed his finger at Dwayne.

Dwayne's heart pounded. He turned, ashen faced, his eyes still glassed over with tears. 'Trev, if I knew anything, standard I would tell you.' His impassioned plea did little to dent Trevor's suspicions. He blew into his gloves then continued to walk.

'I'm gonna keep digging. If you hear anything, shout me,' Trevor said gruffly, his heavy, paw-like hand patting Dwayne on the back, before he walked ahead, leaving Dwayne alone on the path with the fallen leaves swirling around his muddied feet.

* * *

The bright laptop screen beamed into Cindy's face. She sat at her dining table, transfixed by the information on the screen, which read 'Transaction received **£10,000**'. The figure stood out starkly against the rest of her usual incomings and outgoings.

A single candle burned on the windowsill, illuminating her glass which was half-filled with red wine. She held her head in her hands for a few seconds before returning her gaze to the screen.

'This is unreal,' she whispered under her breath, trying not to wake Cece, who had crashed out and was sleeping snugly on the sofa across the room. She clicked off the banking screen, revealing an open page advertising a new building development:

The Hive – New Residential Apartments. A high-spec picture showed the interior of a plush designer showroom.

Cindy picked up her glass and took a small sip. She stood up and walked towards the balcony door. She opened it quietly and stepped out into the cold air. For a while she stood, arms wrapped around her body, glass in hand, looking out to the other blocks which made up the rest of Kingfisher Estate.

Under the stars and glow of the orange streetlights, anyone would think that Kingfisher was an attractive place of residence, but Cindy knew from her years of being placed there after Cece's first birthday that in the cold light of day it was far from that.

Her yearning for more had been the fuel that fired her career aspirations, leading her to land the job at Schuster and Klein; now, maybe keeping Andersen's little secret could actually help her to take the next step.

* * *

A warm reggae bassline reverberated in the car, breaching the silence of late evening. Leon exited the vehicle. He slammed the door and unwound his tall frame. His dreadlocks were tied into a large bun on top of his head, and his dark silhouette, clothed in a long black coat, leant on his unmistakable fire engine red BMW.

He took a large drag from his spliff, blowing a plume of smoke into the chilly night air while staring upwards at the high-rise tower block where Cindy lived. His eyes, squinting from the smoke, gazed ominously at the balconies, each one lit up from the internal lights.

His loud ringtone distracted his trance-like state. He pulled his phone from his pocket and answered. 'Yeah, pick up some milk? Cool, see you soon.' His voice was deep and low. He clicked the call off and took another large drag of his spliff before throwing it to the ground.

Leon sat back in his car, resting in the reclined seat, high from the weed. He slid open his phone screen and began to go through his photos, stopping on a picture of him holding a baby Cece with a younger-looking Cindy standing happily next to him.

Dwayne trudged slowly back into Kingfisher Estate. He was drained, his feet barely able to make the next step along the pavement. He was in a world of his own, his mind still fuzzy from all the recent events, the raw, painful reality of Ricky's death now kicking in.

The roar from the engine of Leon's BMW, which flashed past in front of him, shook him into life. The driver had avoided hitting him by a few inches. 'Fucking prick,' he muttered, shaking his head, as he continued towards the lift entrance.

As usual, L Boi and his cronies had congregated in the stairwell a few yards away, huddling away from the cold. They all stared at him while he waited. 'Yo, fam, heard about ya boy. So sad,' he shouted, a sarcastic, childish edge to his remark, making a point of winding up Dwayne.

Dwayne looked over at him; his tired eyes stared coldly in defiance. 'You'll keep, fam,' he said in a deep, husky voice. The smell of weed floated in the air around him before the lift doors opened.

L Boi cracked up, laughing hysterically. 'You'll keep,' he mimicked, followed by cackles from his bunch of sidemen. Dwayne paused as the lift door creaked open. He felt a strong urge to engage, the rush of pent-up adrenaline coursing through his body, but instead chose to just step into the lift.

As the dirty metal box rose past each floor, Dwayne skulked angrily in the confined space. 'Fucking pussyhole!' he shouted, slamming his hands against the rugged metal, tearing the skin from his knuckles and drawing pellets of blood, which dripped onto the dirty floor.

He managed to fight back the tears, suppressing his turmoil by making high-pitched squealing noises. The door slid open. Dwayne wiped his face with his bloodied hands, inhaling deeply to compose himself before stepping out.

Cindy downed the last of her wine, plonking the empty glass onto the table. She continued gazing at the plush new properties on her computer screen, clicking into each gallery picture and checking out the rooms until she was interrupted by erratic banging on the front door.

She jumped up quickly, checking on Cece, who stirred, adjusting her body but not waking even as the banging continued. Cindy opened the door, about to start cursing whoever it was, but stopped short on seeing her brother in a beleaguered state. They stared at each other for a few seconds before Cindy stepped forward and embraced him. He melted into her arms, letting out a whimpering cry.

* * *

'Where are you? Why is your phone switched off?' Sasha moaned in frustration. She threw the phone onto the sofa and paced around in her lounge wearing only a cropped white vest and black knickers.

Her right hand was covered with a large pink plaster. For once, her beauty was somewhat jaded, her usually tanned skin now pale and pasty, with dark patches lurking under her eyes. She flopped onto the sofa, grabbing a box of cigarettes from the table. She placed one of the sticks between her lips and lit up, kicking her feet up onto the table. Once again, she picked up her phone, checking for any sort of response, but nothing.

* * *

Andersen was undisturbed by the intermittent squeaks from rubber trainer soles, fleet-footed against the beechwood flooring of the squash courts. He sat in the sports bar, in white kit with a towel wrapped around his neck, sipping from a bottle of an isotonic energy drink.

His racquet balanced across his knees, he sat catching his breath. He glanced over to the bar where a young girl—brunette, smartly dressed in black uniform—smiled back at him while she tended the bar in front of a large-screen television displaying the latest news bulletins.

After a few minutes, he was joined by his squash partner, an athletic bearded man, who plonked himself on the chair opposite him. 'Next time I'll let you win,' he crowed, taking a bottle of water from his sports bag. Andersen shook his head, unimpressed by his friend's gloating. 'I'm getting a drink; fancy one?' He brushed off the smug comment, standing up and making his way over to the bar.

He sat waiting patiently, staring ahead at the large screen. 'Breaking news – The body of a child has been found in a shallow grave.' The words appeared in bold, bright red across the ticker. 'Excuse me, can you turn this up?' Andersen's interest was piqued by a news reporter standing in front of a police cordon, while police in bright yellow hi-vis jackets mulled around behind him.

'*The child, who is thought to be no more than eight or nine years old, possibly a migrant or a refugee, was spotted by a local dog walker…*' The words rattled into Andersen's consciousness. He stared, haunted by the images on the screen, prompting him to tap into his mobile phone.

The bar girl came over and handed him two tall glasses of beer. He nodded, acknowledging her, and put the phone to his ear. 'It's me… Have you seen the news?' he said in a low voice, then paused. 'Better not be one of ours.' He ended the call, gripping the device tightly in his hand.

* * *

Raz, wearing a white vest and shorts, sat phone in hand on a large black leather sofa, accompanied by his wife, who laid her head on his chunky, tattooed shoulder. Two children played energetically in front of them, running around screaming.

'Remote control,' Raz growled at his wife, making her surrender it to him. He pointed it at the television, switching the channel to catch the breaking news. He sat forward on the edge of the seat, shrugging his wife to the side, much to her disgruntlement.

'Ssh... Quiet!' His commanding voice stopped the children in their tracks. Raz stared engrossed as the news reporter continued to divulge the latest findings of the case. He gesticulated to his wife to leave the room.

She acted as instructed, calling the children and leading them out, leaving Raz to absorb the information on the screen. He rubbed his face with his beefy hand. A mask of worry crept across his face. He sat back, the wind taken out of his sails. For the first time, he looked defeated.

Chapter Ten

Affirmative action

Low music played in the background. 'Cry for You' by Jodeci was juxtaposed with the rapid squeaking of the coiled springs of the mattress that was being tested by the bouncing and gyrating of two bodies.

A sweaty, naked female—chocolate-skinned, ample breasts, with black saucer-shaped nipples—ground hard on the muscular male body beneath her. She held up her black and gold-highlighted braids with a black bandana tied around her eyes, mouth agape, sucking for air as she breathed rapidly from her exertions.

The male below her gripped her waist, pulling her into him, causing him to groan loudly from each thrust, his face also obscured by a black bandana tied around his eyes. They continued to indulge aggressively, both nearly reaching the point of no return.

The music faded out, leaving just the sounds of the rapid, high-pitched squeaks from the bed and their heavy breathing and groaning until a mobile phone vibrated loudly on a glass bedside table next to a couple of empty wine glasses and discarded condom wrappers.

'Don't you fucking stop,' the female ordered, licking her lips while she cupped her breasts, speeding up her motion and grinding her body harder, building herself up to a climax. The phone continued to vibrate violently. On the screen it read 'Unknown caller', rattling each time it rang.

'Maybe… you… should…' The man barely got his words out before his mouth was covered by her hand over his face 'Shut up!' she screamed at him. At the same time, she began to orgasm, jerking her body rigid multiple times until she flopped onto his torso.

The phone stopped vibrating. She lay on his chest for a few seconds, catching her breath, until the phone began to vibrate violently again. 'Fuck's sake.' She stretched out her hand, fumbling with the phone, until eventually she picked it up and answered it. 'Bree Archibald,' she said breathlessly.

'What?' She pulled the bandana from her head, revealing her light brown eyes under the dimmed lights. 'Ok, be there soon.' She tossed the phone back onto the table, then pulled the bandana onto the forehead of the male, who blinked, adjusting his sight like a newborn baby. 'I'm outta here.' She planted a kiss on his cheek, then sprang up, catapulting her naked body from the bed.

* * *

'Took your time.' A scruffily suited man, balding with grey stubble, wearing silver spectacles and a police lanyard dangling around his neck—Darren Nolan, the senior investigation officer—greeted Bree in the corridor. Bree strolled casually in her brown chequered tweed trench coat and Doc Marten boots, her long braids swinging from side to side.

'Yeah, was getting my brains fucked out.' She smirked knowingly, but Nolan held his hand up. 'TMI, Bree, TMI. We're in the incident room.' He walked away ahead of her, laughing and scratching his head.

The images of the young girl found in the woods were displayed on a large screen in front of a handful of other detectives. Her frail body lay limp amongst the dirt and bracken, which hardly shielded her from the elements.

The dirty grey Mickey Mouse T-shirt was twisted on her small body; her face looked as if she were sleeping peacefully. 'It's our belief she is part of a child trafficking ring. The problem is which one?' Darren Nolan spoke with authority but no conviction.

Bree sat silently, viewing the pictures of the dead girl on the screen. She interrupted. 'There's more; got to be.' Not renown for her subtlety, Bree Archibald was brash, no-nonsense and, quite frankly, grating to anyone who encountered her but respected as a detective. Her methods were questionable but always yielded results. Once she had a grip on anything, she would not let go until she got to the truth.

'So, what's your thinking?' Nolan asked hopefully as the others in the room waited with bated breath for her response. Bree tapped her silver-ringed fingers on the table for a few seconds, gathering her thoughts. 'Looks like I'll need to go undercover, see what's the word on the street, but… Let's wait for forensics.' She clasped her hands together.

The others, including Nolan, all nodded in agreement. She pushed her chair back, got up from the table and walked towards the large screen, staring trance-like at the image of the dead child. 'What's your story?' She touched the screen with her hand, placing it on the pixelated graphic, putting her face nose to nose with the glaring screen.

Chapter Eleven

Can I live?

Life in the Harper household was back to normal. Well, as normal as things could be for the two siblings, who both harboured dark secrets. The grief of Ricky's death still sat deep in Dwayne's psyche, along with the debt bequeathed to him from Raz in Ricky's untimely absence.

Cindy, stoic as ever, continued with her life, no fuss. She remained focused in her job, loving her role as Andersen's PA and mystery account secretary, but the paranoia over the thought of Leon's next random appearance gnawed away in the back of her mind, giving her more than a few sleepless nights.

The only real winner was Cece, who seemed very happy having her uncle back in her life, walking her to school every day. 'Uncle Dwayne,' she asked, 'did you know it's my birthday in…' She began counting with her fingers. 'Fifteen, sixteen days!' she exclaimed.

'Well done, my Cees. What do you want for your birthday?' Dwayne asked, looking down adoringly at his niece. 'I want a scooter, a bright red one like Daddy's car,' she enthused. Dwayne stopped suddenly. 'What did you say?' He stared at her. Cece smiled cheekily, giggling. 'Why did you say that?' he asked her again. Cece said confidently, 'Because Daddy has a red car.' Dwayne took her comments on board, digesting them silently, another thought in his already messed up mind.

As they approached the school gates amongst the gaggle of parents seeing their kids off, he saw Lisa, who spotted him through the ruck. Dwayne crouched down to kiss Cece before ushering her through the crowd into the school gates. 'Have a good one.' He waved her off before turning to catch up to Lisa, who had walked away hastily, arms folded, tucked into her black bubble goose coat. The red dye in her hair barely masked her black roots. Dwayne jogged lightly behind her. 'Hold up a sec, Lisa,' he hollered in vain. Lisa forged ahead, head down, ignoring his pursuit.

Eventually he caught up to her, yanking her arm. 'Lisa, man, jeez.' He spun her around, much to her annoyance. She shrugged him off.

'Cha! Get off me, Dwayne. I ain't got nuffin to say to you.' Lisa batted away his hand. Her expression exuded the raw hurt that ate away deep inside her. 'I don't want nothing to do with you.' Her brown eyes burnt into him; the cold air slightly reddened her nose. 'Leave me alone, Dwayne.' This time she whispered, conscious of the other nosey parents who, by now, were peering slyly towards them with interest.

'Can't do that, Lisa,' he responded adamantly. Lisa stood defiantly, looking him up and down.

'Chat then,' she demanded, pointing her finger towards him.

Dwayne threw his hood over his head. 'Not here; let's go to the park.' His demeanour changed; he became more assured, angry even. He tucked his hands into the pockets of his jacket and walked ahead, leaving Lisa stewing for a few seconds before she reluctantly followed.

They sat in silence on a park bench, watching a flock of pigeons pecking away at a discarded bag of chips from the night before. Autumn had stripped the trees of their leaves, which were now scattered like a large ripped-up brown paper bag across the frost-topped lawns.

Dwayne hunched over; head hung low. 'Sorry about what happened. Shit just went mad that night,' he began his defence, slowly sniffing in the cold air. 'Ricky was on a madness; he didn't even tell me.' He spoke to the floor, unable to look Lisa in the eyes.

'Was you there when he…' She paused, watching the pigeons fluttering their wings, frantically pecking the grass, and allowing a couple of joggers to run past out of earshot before continuing. 'The crash. Was you…' Finally, she turned to Dwayne. He stared back, his eyes sombre from his mental recollection. He shivered.

'He just told me to take the bag. Feds were on us. I just ran. I couldn't get caught and go back to prison.' His voice croaked with emotion, dry from the morning air. 'That was the night I turned up at yours.' He shook his head, looking away from Lisa, ashamed.

'So you brought drugs to my yard. To Kai.' Her voice rose, the thread of anger still strong. 'Left your friend to die because you couldn't face…' Dwayne turned to her, feeling the pressure.

'No! You got it twisted. The situation is fucked. I didn't mean to!' He pulled his hood tightly over his head, rocking back and forth and groaning.

Lisa watched him, a grown man, emotionally broken, riddled with guilt and grief. She felt her anger dissipate slowly, replaced by a flood of sympathy. She inhaled deeply, rolling her eyes towards the overcast sky, placing her hand on his back and rubbing it slowly.

'Allow it, man; it's too early for all this stress.' She tried to inject a dose of jest into the bleak situation. 'I dunno what you want from me, but I can't be having this stupidness in my life.' She continued patting him on the back.

Dwayne lifted his head. He rubbed his face vigorously, his knuckles still scabbed. He peered through his fingers at Lisa. 'Just need you to have my back,' he requested, sniffing again. 'And don't say nothing to anyone.' His eyes were wide between his fingers as he spoke.

Lisa nodded with more than a hint of reluctance. 'Just don't bring no fuckery to my door again,' she answered vehemently, ensuring Dwayne was clear on that. He nodded. Lisa stood up, causing the pigeons to flap eagerly. 'Got to go; I'll call you later.' She zipped up her jacket and walked away, leaving Dwayne to his feelings.

* * *

Repetitive banging on the door interrupted an already moody Sasha, who was in the middle of getting dressed. She quickly threw on a hooded top over her bra and dashed to the door. 'Alright, I'm coming!' she shouted. The banging continued, constant heavy thuds one after the other. She turned the lock and pulled open the door.

'Where the hell have you been?' Her first reaction was to shout, expecting to see Dwayne, but was gutted to see the figure of Ilyan standing there smirking, wearing a long black coat with black leather gloves and leaning on the frame of the door.

'Surprise,' he said dryly, giving her a fake smile. 'Expecting someone else?' he asked while trying to look beyond her into the house. Sasha's face dropped, her disappointment obvious.

'What do you want?' She stood in the doorway, arms folded, blocking his entrance.

'We need to go to the house,' he said robotically. 'Now!' He reached forward, squeezing her cheeks, the smell of the leather and his woody musk invading her nose. She managed to push his hand away.

'Fuck off!' She stepped back, annoyed, watching him leer at her. 'Wait downstairs.' She slammed the door in his face, then leant her head against it, trying to suppress her anguish.

* * *

'Have you not seen the news?' Ilyan asked directly while keeping his eyes on the dark roads in front of him. The windscreen was being splattered with tiny raindrops, the wiper swiping it clean every few seconds. Sasha sat in silence, still simmering internally that Dwayne had not been in touch and not really paying attention to the words coming out of Ilyan's mouth. 'They found the girl,' he said, almost in staccato, knowing it was his negligence that had created this mess.

Sasha turned her head towards him slowly. She stared for a few seconds, allowing the information to process before turning her head back towards the passenger window. 'Your brother is going crazy.' For once, a slight tone of concern was detected in Ilyan's voice. 'Hey! This is serious!' He grabbed her arm, causing the car to swerve dangerously close to the trees which flanked the road.

Sasha resisted. 'Serious for you because *you* fucked up!' She pushed his hand away and began to laugh, chuckling to herself. 'You're pathetic. My brother's lap dog, big man Ilyan, fucking up the plan.' Her remark was met by a sharp stinging backhand to the face, leaving her skin reddened and blood trickling from her nostrils.

Sasha wiped away the blood, smearing it across her cheek. 'Bastard.' Her eyes cut a look of disgust towards Ilyan, who was fuming, his breathing heavy and his lips pursed. 'Raz will kill you,' Sasha continued, smiling wryly, putting her head back against the headrest.

* * *

Cindy stood over the cooker stirring a large pot of stewed chicken, the spicy aroma filling the kitchen, amongst the other foods she had prepared—plantain, vegetables and a large saucepan of rice and peas.

She hummed to herself, enjoying her moment. Dwayne and Cece messed around in the other room. She could hear Cece's high-pitched shrieking and giggling drowning out Dwayne's silly monster impression.

'Oi, you two, dinner's ready. Lay the table,' Cindy ordered, smiling to herself. Her mood seemed to have lifted, especially now that she had made peace with Dwayne; her home seemed a much happier space.

They all sat around the table in silence, munching down on the mini feast. Dwayne chewed a large mouthful, savouring the flavours. 'Hmm, you know how much times I dreamt of a meal like this when I was…' Cindy stared at him, clearing her throat to interrupt him, diverting her eyes towards Cece, who was happily oblivious; she was chewing on a chicken drumstick, her long braids tied with pink and red baubles dangling into her plate.

'Don't speak with your mouth full.' Cindy imitated him, puffing her cheeks and making a chewing motion. Dwayne ignored her, tucking back into his food. 'Mummy, Dwayne likes Kai's mum. Is that your girlfriend?' Cece looked at Dwayne. 'Kai said you came to his house,' she continued, chewing down on the bone.

Dwayne stopped chewing, not knowing where to look. 'Is that right?' Cindy put down her knife and fork and wiped her mouth daintily with a napkin. 'Ok, spill.' She sat forward, eager to hear from Dwayne, who playfully pushed Cece in the head.

'Big mouth.'

'Oww,' Cece laughed, hitting him back.

'Nah, just bucked her at the school gates innit,' Dwayne answered bashfully. 'Know her from time,' he continued, shoving another forkful of food into his mouth.

Cindy sat back in her chair, eyebrows raised in surprise. 'Chatting up mums on the school run now, huh?' She shook her head. 'Shameless.' She picked at some food in her teeth and burst out laughing. Dwayne couldn't help but laugh along, finally appreciating an injection of humour into his world. Even Cece joined in, not really knowing why she was laughing, but for Cindy, who looked on, it was nice to see her family all getting along for once.

A heavy-handed bang on the front door interrupted their moment of togetherness. Suddenly the mood changed. Dwayne's expression turned serious. 'Expecting anyone?' he asked Cindy, who shrugged, getting up from the table and walking across the room to the hallway.

The banging continued, each thud getting louder. Dwayne had also got up from the table, following Cindy into the hallway. 'Sis, wait, let me answer it.' He stepped in front of her wedging his broad frame between her and the door. He opened the door. Leon's tall, lean frame fell into him. The stench of weed and alcohol hit Dwayne's nostrils as he held back a drunken Leon. 'Yo, what the fuck?' Dwayne lifted him, grabbing his neck and aggressively pushing him back.

'I want see my daughter.' His Jamaican patois was slurred, and his arms were flailing, trying to wrestle Dwayne off him.

'Back off, Leon!' Dwayne jerked him backwards with force, causing him to stagger back outside onto the landing.

'Don't get involve, rude bwoy; it's me and her,' Leon spat. As he spoke, his lips wet with saliva, he pointed at Dwayne, the bling on his jewelled fingers and wrists shining under the lights.

Cindy stepped forward, trying to get past her brother. 'I'll call the police if you don't leave!' she shouted, her slim frame held back by Dwayne. Leon sneered, rushing forward and aiming a wild kick at Dwayne, who retaliated, aiming a straight punch into Leon's face.

'I told you, back off, Leon!' Dwayne's temper ramped up so much that he shoved Cindy back into the house.

Cece came to see what the commotion was and caught a glimpse of her drunk father holding his face after Dwayne's sharp jab to his eye. 'Daddy!' Cece tried to run forward but was scooped up by Cindy. 'Go back inside,' she instructed, her voice strained, as Dwayne continued to grapple with Leon, attempting to pick him up off the floor.

Cindy's neighbour Barry came out of his flat to intervene and dragged Dwayne off of Leon. 'Oi, pack it in or I'm calling the old bill!' he shouted, managing to separate the two. Cindy came outside and pulled Dwayne back into the house. 'I'll do you for stalking, you freak!' an angered Cindy spouted at Leon, who remained crumpled on the floor, looking sorry for himself. 'I'm so sorry, Baz,' she said to her neighbour, who backed away, shuffling in his sheepskin slippers to his doorway.

'I'm coming for my daughter, you bitch. I want my daughter!' Leon got to his feet, bedraggled and wiping his lip. '*And you*,' he said, pointing towards Dwayne. 'We nah done. Watch your back.' He fired off his threats before staggering away.

Dwayne stood, pumped up, watching him leave, 'Get inside,' he instructed Cindy brusquely.

'Damn man.' She clenched her teeth, hands on hips, turning to go back into the flat.

Cece stood in the hallway, tears running down her face, shaking with fear. She gave a long, drawn-out scream before running into Cindy's midriff and hugging her tightly. Dwayne slammed the door. 'Jeez, man, what was that?' He stood vexed, staring back at Cindy.

Chapter Twelve

Rain on me

Day ones – Cindy BC (Before Cece)

New Year's Eve 2012 was the night when a younger Cindy and her then best friends, Jade Pearson and Maria Bennett, were getting ready to go to the Island Bar to see the New Year in. Sitting in Jade's kitchen having a few pre-drinks was nothing but jokes.

They had known each other from Our Lady's Convent School. Jade, being the most extrovert, was doing a crazy butterfly dance to a dancehall song that pumped from the radio. She was big-boned, with corkscrew hair, pretty brown skin and green eyes; she was dressed in tight, red, shiny pants and a black and gold fitted Versace T-shirt. Jade was always the loudest but funny at the same time.

Maria was more sensible, kind of the prude, which was obvious by her shamed expression as she watched Jade exert herself. Ebony-skinned, reserved, in a loose-fitting black jumpsuit, she rolled her eyes, nudging Cindy, who stood holding a champagne bottle ready to pour.

Cindy was everything then—smart, focused, funny and pretty. Her hair was longer with a fringe—Cleopatra style—

mascara accentuating her almond-brown eyes. She wore a pair of white designer jeans printed with the word 'Moschino' all over the legs, with a simple black ruffled blouse.

They were all hyped up and ready to hit the club, already a little bit tipsy from the bubbles. 'Where's this cab, man? I'm ready to shock out.' Jade, breathless from her dance workout, took a gulp of her drink.

Maria leapt up and looked through the curtains. 'I think he's here,' she confirmed, smiling.

'Ok, girls, before we go, let's have a toast.' Cindy brought them all together for a hug. 'Hope the new year is a wicked one for all of us and tonight we meet the man of our dreams!' She chinked glasses with Maria and Jade, who looked at each other.

'Why you got to fuck the last bit up?' Maria asked dryly.

'Come on, man, let's go!' Jade, ever eager, picked up her jacket and switched off the radio.

The Island Bar was a ghetto fabulous club in the depths of North London, not quite classy like a club in the city but a good spot where the vibe and music were usually good, even though it was a bit of a meat market with all the usual local road men lurking.

Being New Year's Eve, it was heaving, packed with party goers enjoying the end-of-year festivities. Cindy, Jade and Maria were at the bar trying to shove their way to the front and get the attention of the under-pressure bar staff.

'I'm next!' Jade pushed forward, arm raised in the air as if she were waving down a taxi. Maria and Cindy shuffled their way out of the crowd, turning towards the dance floor, which was packed. The music, a mix of hip-hop and reggae, vibrated loudly. 'Bloody hell, it's madness in here!' Maria fanned herself with a flyer. 'Yeah, but let's just enjoy it!' Cindy leant in, shouting into her ear to be heard above the din.

Finally, the three of them found a place on the dance floor, drinks in hand, to get ready for the countdown as midnight crept nearer. They were all having fun dancing but were getting bumped about by the other drunk party goers.

'Who's ready for 2013?' the DJ screamed excitedly. A hearty roar went up. Jade was yelling loudly, hand in the air, holding her glass up. Maria laughed at her antics, while Cindy was doing her own little dance.

The countdown began: ten seconds until the new year. The girls all huddled together, Jade taking pictures on her Blackberry phone. 'Three, two, one, Happy New Year!' the DJ shouted, and gave a blast on an air horn. Gold balloons and streamers descended from the ceiling, and party poppers exploded everywhere. 'Whoo!' the three of them screamed, hugging each other, and jumping up and down as the next tune kicked in—a heavy bass reggae tune.

Cindy danced with her eyes closed. She felt merry from the liquor and was having fun in her own world, swaying to the beat and doing a little two step. 'Happy New Year.' A deep voice close to her ear interrupted her moment. She opened her eyes to see a tall, dark man in a white Yves Saint Laurent T-shirt laden with a thick gold chain.

His dark skin was highlighted by the multicoloured spotlights which flashed on his face. 'Thanks, same to you,' she replied politely, smiling. 'Drink?' He held up a bottle of champagne, smiling to reveal gold teeth which glinted under the lights. 'Ok, why not?' Cindy held out her glass while he poured the gold liquid in. She looked around, but Jade and Maria had disappeared into the crowd.

'Cheers.' The man held his glass to hers. 'Leon. What's your name?' He leant in close to her ear, his breath warm, reeking of alcohol as he spoke, his sweet aftershave wafting into her space. Cindy looked him over. *He's alright looking,* she thought. *Not bad.* She was already feeling tipsy. She cracked a smile. 'Cindy. Happy New Year.' She raised her glass to his, smiling shyly.

That was the start of it all—the charm offensive that swept Cindy up into Leon's world. At the time, all she was doing was working as a receptionist in a dental clinic so the distraction of going on weekend picnics, fun nights at the bowling alley and dates to the cinema seemed like the normal things a young woman of her age should be doing.

Seated in the busy, noisy barber shop which doubled as a nail salon was the perfect place for Cindy to fill Maria and Jade in on all her dating news.

'So he took me shopping the other day,' Cindy cooed wistfully.

'Hope you took him to the cleaners,' Jade chimed in, watching the young Korean girl applying a layer of nail varnish to the tips of her fingers.

'I just got some shoes; don't need no man buying me stuff,' she replied, asserting her independence.

Maria nodded in agreement. 'Hmm, that's true,' she concurred. 'Anyway, forget all that, is there magic in the bedroom?' Maria tilted her black Nike baseball cap up, staring impatiently at Cindy for her answer.

'Yeah, come on, can he do the ting?' Jade snapped with all the subtlety of an elephant on ice skates.

'Shush man.' An embarrassed Cindy turned around to make sure no one else had heard Jade's crude question.

'We're taking it slow,' Cindy answered in a hushed whisper.

'Boring.' Jade's brashness made Maria burst into laughter. 'You need to loosen up that ting, hun. Must be dry under there,' Jade continued, cracking up with Maria, much to Cindy's disgust, even though she eventually managed to see the funny side and break into a laugh.

Leon was a cool, calm character, although his aesthetic told a different story. He drove a black Mercedes convertible and wore a good amount of jewellery around his neck and wrists. He was not really Cindy's type; she preferred a more refined man, but through misty eyes in the Island Bar, he hadn't seemed that bad. She liked his coolness, but there was always an edge.

He would come to pick her up from work at the dental clinic unannounced. He didn't seem to get that it was her place of work, and on one occasion, he came in agitated, pacing around the lobby area and cursing under his breath while the last of the patients were waiting in the seating area.

Cindy felt uncomfortable; he could be crass, shouting into his phone with no respect for her professional space. The other side of him was charming; he had the chat and the jokes and knew how to treat her when he was ready. And that was the side that she eventually fell for.

It had been a few months into their relationship when Cindy decided to spend more time staying at his flat. Her little brother Dwayne, protective as ever, was not taken by him, especially when he came to their mum's house to collect her, thinking he was some kind of don.

'He's a bit off-key for me,' Dwayne said, leaning his mountain bike against the wall of their front garden as Cindy waited for Leon to pick her up. She sighed heavily.

'You just don't know him. He's alright if you give him a chance,' she answered defensively. She was holding a large sports bag and wearing jeans, a plain white, fitted Versace T-shirt, flip flops and shades as the sun was beating down on the street. 'Just be nice,' she warned Dwayne, who kissed his teeth as he perched against the bike.

The sound of a heavy bass line could be heard, getting louder as Leon's car drove closer. 'What a prick,' Dwayne said, watching Leon's car rolling slowly towards them.

'Look, I'll be back Sunday night. Stay out of trouble.' She quickly gave Dwayne a hug. 'Laters.' She made her way to the edge of the kerb, watching Leon slow to a halt.

Leon nodded to Dwayne, who gave him a scornful stare before nodding back. 'Wha you ah say, big man?' Leon asked Dwayne, grinning, his gold-braceleted arm hanging out the window.

'Looking good, babes.' He licked his lips watching Cindy walk around the car. Dwayne watched on, unimpressed, as his sister threw her bag into the back of the car, jumped into the passenger seat and was consumed by a hug and kiss from Leon. He turned to Dwayne, grinning smugly again, before accelerating away. Dwayne jumped onto his bike and followed them, pedalling fast until they disappeared ahead.

* * *

Cindy lay on her back, eyes closed, enduring Leon's third round of intercourse, his sweat dripping from his head and chest onto her. She enjoyed sex with him, but by now she felt sore down below and frankly wanted it to hurry up and end. Still, she did her best to entertain her ravenous boyfriend, who continued to hammer away as if his life depended on it.

This was now what her relationship with him was all about—no more going out to the movies and nice picnics in the park; just staying at his for the weekend, morning sex, after lunch sex and, especially when he'd had a drink and a few spliffs in the evening, which she hated, more sex.

The charm mask had slipped far enough to reveal his real face: the mood swings, drunken rambles, flagrant disregard for her feelings. She had become one of those girls she always swore she would never be, the type she frowned on. Just with him for his fancy car and sporadic gestures of decency.

Cindy washed her skin in the bath, scrubbing away the smell of Leon's sweat and cologne while he sat in the front room with a gang of his friends watching the football, acting as if she didn't exist. She was now a mere accessory, nothing more. To make things worse, she was late and had been feeling unwell for a few weeks but never got the chance to tell him.

Once she'd emerged from the bathroom, she was confronted by another one of his demands, showing off in front of his friends. 'Yeah, Cinds, bring us some ice for this whisky.' He now shouted his orders, not even looking at her anymore. It grated on her soul. She felt too scared to confront him, especially in front of his friends; it never seemed to be the right moment.

Whenever they did have time alone, Leon would be drunk, high and not a nice person to be stuck alone with. She had endured enough and began to spend less time at his place. She never felt like her normal self and sought solace with her girls, Jade and Maria.

An evening at Jade's house was the time she found out she was pregnant. She came down the stairs from the bathroom, tears streaming down her face. Jade and Maria were standing at the bottom waiting, and as soon as they saw her face, their reactions said it all.

'Shit, Cinders, nah man!' Jade, as ever, shooting from the hip.

Maria calmly waited until she reached her, then gave a warm embrace. 'It's ok, babe.'

'What am I gonna do?' Cindy blubbed.

'Get rid of it, man.' Jade's brashness didn't help the situation. Maria frowned at her.

'I can't do that,' Cindy sniffed, numbed by the realisation that she would soon be a mother.

Leon's reaction was as expected; he accused her of sleeping with someone else, calling her every derogatory name under the sun, which was ironic. Cindy had heard from Jade that a girl she knew from another part of London was also pregnant by Leon and about to have his child. Cindy was completely broken. Dwayne had warned her and was fuming, seeking retribution from Leon.

Their parents had just relocated back to Jamaica, so Cindy did not even have her mother to support her. She felt disappointed in herself. She was supposed to be the smart one, the one that was going to have a career. Miss Independent, the one that made educated decisions and focused. Instead, she was about to be a single mother by a man who had intoxicated her with his potion of charm, false promises and imitation.

She felt humiliated and retreated inside herself for a while. The hurt of knowing she had fallen for a man like Leon dug into her gut more than the twinges and kicks she got in her belly from the baby growing inside her.

Jade and Maria stuck by her side. At least she could laugh through her pain, knowing the only good thing to come from New Year's Eve at the Island Bar was the determination she now had to be the best she could be for her soon-to-be-born child.

Chapter Thirteen

Don't cry for me

Dwayne sat on the floor, back against the wall, in the corridor outside Sasha's apartment, his legs stretched out across the tiled surface. He checked his phone. 2:30 am displayed on the scratched, cracked screen. He had returned from another run for Raz; same set-up but a different party. This time, a location in the Docklands. Another rich client taking a bag of drugs to share with his affluent friends.

Dwayne thought of Ricky every time he did a run. How did he get into bed with Raz? He could see the benefits, his own pockets now swollen with wads of cash, payment for a month's worth of drops, but he didn't want to be in it. To him, the risk was far greater than the reward. Ricky's crash etched that into his brain.

His eyes were getting heavier by the second. He dozed off momentarily until he heard the lift doors slide open. The sound of high heels clopping against the tiled floor roused him enough to make out the figure of Sasha returning. 'Bout time,' Dwayne said calmly, wiping his face, his voice low and tired. He hung his head, checking the time on his phone.

Sasha's shorn hair was now grown enough to be swept back a la Brigitte Nielsen. She was dressed in a black leather jacket, ripped jeans and black high heels. She looked down in surprise. 'The wanderer returns.' Her sultry voice was hoarse. She dug into her handbag and took out her door keys.

Dwayne dragged himself up from the floor. He stood in front of Sasha and went in for a hug, but she resisted, still prickly at his previous absence. 'What, no love?' He playfully grabbed her waist, much to her annoyance; she pushed him aside and put the key into the lock. 'No love.' Dwayne rolled his eyes, stepping aside to let her get past into the apartment.

Sasha lay stretched out on the soft cushions of the sofa, eyes closed, still dressed in her jeans and a T-shirt. Dwayne was in the kitchen. He lit some tea-light candles, lining them up along the marble island counter. 'Tea?' he asked calmly as if he owned the house. Sasha didn't respond. Instead, she placed her hand across her forehead. She was stewing, remaining silent despite Dwayne's best efforts.

He came into the room and sat beside her, edging his beefy body next to hers. 'Hey.' He took her hand, noticing the reddened scab from the cut. Tenderly he touched it. 'What happened here?' he asked, rubbing his own scabbed knuckles slowly across the scar.

Sasha pulled her hand away. 'Why do you care?' Again she responded angrily, the hurt still apparent in her voice. Dwayne shook his head, sighing.

'You're confusing me, man. What do you mean?' He tried to stay calm; he was too tired to be drawn into a late-night argument. Sasha opened her eyes. A tear trickled down the side of her face. She wiped it away defiantly, sitting up to face Dwayne.

Dwayne cradled her up onto his lap, his strong arms holding her close, and rested his forehead against hers. They gazed at each other for what seemed like an age. Only the flickers from the candle flames behind them revealed their expressions. He could feel Sasha's body shaking.

'I needed you. I tried so many times. Where were you?' She tried to stay strong and articulate her feelings, but her tiredness and emotions got the better of her. She ran her fingers through Dwayne's curly hair, her brown eyes glassed over. 'What have you been doing?' Her question was so direct it took Dwayne a few seconds to register the right response.

'Look, I've had a shit time. One of my friends…' He stopped, pausing to allow a gulp of saliva to drain down his throat.

Sasha cupped his face, the cool of her rings pressed against his skin. 'Talk to me.' She held him. Dwayne stared back. He was not used to opening his heart to anyone. He always kept his emotions guarded, but for some reason, in that minute, staring back at Sasha, he was overcome. The chemistry was undeniable.

'My best friend died… and I don't know what to do.' He began to shake, crumbling into her chest, unable to hold back his tears. Sasha wrapped her arms around him and held him tightly.

'It's ok, let it out.' Her husky voice cracked with emotion as she comforted him.

* * *

They sat in silence, still intertwined. Dwayne had managed to compose himself, feeling a sense of relief after letting out the delayed wave of emotion from the depths of his soul. 'I've had a pretty shit time too,' Sasha blurted out, sniffling. She managed a restrained laugh. Dwayne looked up at her.

'Now it's your turn. Talk to me.' He also managed a smile, wiping his eyes.

Sasha sat reflecting. She lifted Dwayne's chin, raising his face to her eyeline. 'Come away with me,' she said softly.

'What?'

'Let's go together... Somewhere away from this.' She was serious. Hopeful even. Suddenly she straightened, still clutching Dwayne's face tenderly. 'I have money. We can go wherever. Somewhere far, hot, start a new life.' She became excited by every word that tumbled from her mouth. 'Let's do it, me and you.' She nodded, a smile breaking across her face.

Dwayne's expression changed to one of confusion, his eyebrows inverted and knotted. 'Whoa, wait a sec,' he said, but Sasha continued babbling, charged by her suggestion.

'Nah, I can't...' His reply stopped her in her tracks. 'I can't just leave.' His reaction pierced her bubble, deflating her desire and causing her shoulders to drop. 'What about my sister? Cece? Nah, I can't.' He shook his head, removing her hands from his face. Sasha leapt up from his lap.

'Don't you understand? We *have* to go!' She stood above him, animated, her shadow projected onto the white wall behind her. 'I have to get away, and you, you're in danger...' She stopped mid-sentence, covering her mouth with her hand, realising she'd let slip her knowledge of Dwayne's involvement with Raz.

'Wait! What are you talking about?' he asked, raising his voice a few decibels. 'I said, what the fuck are you chatting about?' Dwayne stood up.

Sasha stood motionless. Her bold, strong, sexy persona dwindled to vulnerable, fragile and scared. 'Just come; we can do anything,' she pleaded.

'Wait a sec. Nah, like who are you?' He walked forward, pointing his finger at her.

Sasha stood defiantly, eyes bulging with fear. 'I am...' She paused, lips trembling. 'I am ...' Again she paused, struggling to get her words out, trying to hold back.

'Tell me!' Dwayne roared, his frustration soaring. He grabbed her arms. 'Tell me!' He gritted his teeth, squeezing her limbs tightly.

Sasha stared back terrified, trying to wriggle free of his grip, but her indomitable spirit, unwilling to ruin any chance of a future, defiantly led her to spurt out, 'I am... in love with you.' She sucked up the oncoming tide of emotion, bottling it up so much her body shook and her nose ran.

Dwayne let go of her. He spun around even more confused. 'What!' He did a little skip as he turned back to face her. 'Nah, you said I was in danger. In danger from what?'

Sasha coolly walked forward, stretched out her hands to his, interlocked her fingers and pulled him towards her. 'I meant in danger of losing me,' she said in a hushed whisper.

She moved in and kissed him passionately, rocking him back onto his heels. At first he resisted but realised in his clouded state of confusion that he truly couldn't resist her. His posture softened, melting his body against hers. He let go of her hands and swept her up. She clasped her legs around him.

They continued to kiss, devouring each other. Dwayne grabbed her head, scrunching her hair. He walked her over to the bedroom, kicked the door open and stepped into the darkness. Only the sound of their kisses and gasps for breath could be heard, followed by a thud as he threw her onto the bed, her squeal and then silence.

* * *

The shards of daylight cutting through the vertical blinds of the large window and the sound of the early birds chirping woke Dwayne. He tossed and turned in the bed, pulling the sheets over him. He reached around, feeling for Sasha, but felt an empty space.

Eventually, he opened his eyes, shielding them from the light. That confirmed that Sasha was not there. He sat up, rubbing his face and yawning, still tired from the previous night's exertions. He drew his body out of the bed, scratched his bare torso and shuffled into the kitchen area.

The tea light candles were now burnt out, but the foil cases had been positioned in a heart shape on the countertop, with a note and keys placed on top of it. Dwayne yawned again, making his way over. He smiled on seeing the heart shape, picked up the keys and read the note, which, by the style of handwriting, had been scribbled in a hurry.

You are the only person I have ever said those words to in my life. I love you but I have to leave. I want you to understand, even though I know you won't.' Dwayne became more confused and disappointed with every word he read. *'It hurts me that I can't tell you why. Don't try to call me. I will call when I'm safe. Use my place when you need to but please be careful. Sasha x.*

Dwayne stood motionless, gripping the keys in his hand. He scrunched up the note and threw it down. He leant on the counter, mumbling under his breath. He felt as if the wind had been taken out of his sails. He shook his head, still processing everything, staring at the keys in his hand, then looked around at the plush apartment, his mind completely lost.

Chapter Fourteen

Sweet serenade

'Can't you at least change this music?' Dwayne shook his head, fed up with the Romanian folk music which played through the car speakers.

Ilyan turned to Dwayne with a crooked grin on his face. 'What, you want that jungle music your people play?' He burst into a laugh. 'No way, I like traditional music.' He continued to drive, swaying his head to the acoustic guitar and bad vocals, much to Dwayne's annoyance.

'How many more of these do I have to do?' Dwayne stared ahead, watching the faint drizzle spit against the broad windscreen, only to be wiped away by a large wiper.

'Until I say so,' said Ilyan, his voice deadpan, not even turning to acknowledge Dwayne, who was slumped back in his seat scratching his hair.

'Dietmar must be moving serious weight. We've been to his nuff times now,' Dwayne mused. 'Who is he?'

A now agitated Ilyan pressed hard on the brake, making the tyres screech against the wet tarmac before the car came to a halt. He turned to Dwayne, his dark eyes staring intensely.

'Why you like to ask so many questions?'

Dwayne shrugged. 'Just asking, innit. Ricky never mentioned him.' He looked at Ilyan, who was now wound up.

'Ricky did his job; he wasn't a chatterbox.' Ilyan gripped the steering wheel, his chunky watch glinting in the dark. 'All you have to do is learn to drive and do the drops!' he ordered, cursing under his breath in Romanian. His foot pressed hard on the accelerator, jolting the car forward.

'I hate this shitty area.' Ilyan spat out his disgust as they approached the dark streets which led to the bleak towers of Kingfisher Estate, which were just visible below the gloomy, dank horizon.

'Someone's got to live here. You can drop me on the corner if you're too shook to drive in,' he suggested sarcastically, knowing Ilyan's ego would be dented.

'Fuck you,' he replied, accepting the challenge and navigating his way into the maze of side streets which led directly into the car park.

They both sat in the car observing L Boi and his small crew in action. They were busy serving the late-night fiends, zipping up and down the pavement on e-scooters and generally being a menace to anyone who walked past. 'See. Fucking little parasites,' Ilyan remarked, watching their antics through his windscreen. He took an envelope out from his inside jacket pocket.

'For tonight's work.' He passed it over to Dwayne, who took it and opened it, counting the layers of notes.

'Just making sure you don't bump me.' He smirked while handling each note separately. 'It's all good.' Dwayne tucked the envelope into his jeans front pocket. 'Peace, out.' He opened the door and stepped out of the sleek vehicle. Ilyan nodded. No words as the door slammed shut. He watched Dwayne walk towards where L Boi and his crew were active. The folk music continued to play on his stereo.

L Boi noticed Dwayne coming from the side. He looked over to Ilyan's car, clocking him, barely making out his face in the driver's seat. Dwayne walked confidently, paying attention to the youths, who began circling him on their bikes and e-scooters. 'Mind out, innit,' Dwayne told them as they cut across his path. L Boi, smoking on a spliff, walked towards him. 'Working with the feds now, snitch?' He glanced over to Ilyan's car just beyond Dwayne.

Dwayne laughed, approaching L Boi, who seemed high, hyper and confrontational. 'Bro, piss off,' Dwayne responded, pushing L Boi to the side as he tried to get past the young pup, who was intent on testing his resolve again. L Boi staggered back from Dwayne's hefty push.

'Big man, you ready for me now!' An angered L Boi came bucking back aggressively, getting in Dwayne's face.

The rest of his crew quickly blocked Dwayne's escape, surrounding him, ready to act on their leader's command. 'Likkle man, get the fuck out of my way.' Again Dwayne pushed him back, but as he did, L Boi produced a large-bladed knife from inside his waist.

'Ready for you now, big man!' he shouted aggressively, lunging forward, aiming a swipe with the blade at Dwayne, who instinctively pushed his arm out to defend himself. The blade cut into the material of his puffer jacket, which stopped it from slicing into his skin.

Dwayne saw red. He'd had enough of L Boi—the constant comments, sly digs and now this. His mind went black. All he could think about was surviving what was now a direct attack. He spun around, glaring at each of L Boi's crew members, who were poised to strike.

'Come on then!' Dwayne got himself ready into a combat stance. He knew now he had to kill or be killed, no matter what. L Boi again came forward, plunging the knife into Dwayne's upper thigh, just below where the envelope of money was tucked into his pocket.

'Arrgh fuck!' He buckled slightly as the searing pain shot across his leg but didn't have time to even process the feeling before he was attacked from all sides by the crew of youths like a pack of lions all hungry for their feed.

Dwayne did his best to fight back, getting a couple of digs in, but was overwhelmed by the masses of limbs kicking and punching him. L Boi was hyped up, screaming, 'Yeah, pussy. Yeah, fuck him up!' He jumped around like a crazy chimpanzee, waving the knife above his head and screaming, his voice twisted with evil rage. Dwayne buckled, falling onto the dirty, wet pavement, leg bleeding, trying to fend off the crazed youths, who continued to pound and stomp on him while shouting obscenities.

Ilyan watched on for a few seconds before opening his glovebox and taking out a shiny silver revolver. 'Fuck this,' he muttered, opening the car door, the folk music still playing out into the night. He stepped out and walked quickly towards the attack on Dwayne. Dressed in black as usual, he raised the gun as he approached. 'Leave him alone.' His robotic voice rose above the din. By this time, curtains were twitching in the windows of the blocks as the residents could hear the commotion.

L Boi carried on screaming at his boys, 'Fuck him up, man. Let me get him!' He muscled in, pushing his boys aside, and stood over Dwayne, who was coiled up on the floor trying to protect himself.

L Boi had raised the knife, ready to make a decisive blow, when the loud bang from Ilyan's gun rang out, echoing into the night. Another shot rang out, scattering the youths, who fell over their bikes and scooters in their attempts to run away.

Dwayne looked up to see L Boi, knife in hand, spinning into freefall. His jacket had been pierced by the bullets and feathers from it floated into the air. Dwayne turned and saw Ilyan standing menacingly, still aiming the gun at a stricken L Boi, who fell slowly to the ground against the backdrop of Romanian folk music.

'Ilyan! What the fuck?' A dazed Dwayne managed to stagger to his feet. He looked around, vision blurred, just making out the once-brave youths all scattering in different directions like cockroaches into the dark crevices of the blocks. He turned back and saw L Boi lying motionless, blood seeping onto the wet concrete.

Ilyan quickly retreated to his car, jumped in and reversed at speed out onto the road, spinning around and driving off into the distance. Everything seemed to happen so fast, yet Dwayne's mind replayed the stages of the incident in slow motion. He could hardly fathom what had happened. He looked up towards the windows where he could see the silhouettes of residents.

He started to panic, touching his leg and covering the palm of his hand with blood. 'Shit man.' His leg stiffened, the sting of the wound throbbing. Dwayne limped away, hearing sirens in the distance. He looked down at L Boi. He was dead, flat on his back, eyes still half open as if the impact of the bullets had shocked him. A pool of blood surrounded him, a cherry tide which expanded around his body like a silk sheet unfurling.

Dwayne clutched his thigh, dragging his leg along the ground, as he made his way to the lift. Then he turned towards the stairwell and grimaced as he limped his way up each step.

It took him what seemed like an age, but Dwayne finally made it to the floor where Cindy's flat was. The sound of multiple sirens was now closer than before. Out of breath and sweating, he managed to stagger to the door. He banged hard, trying to cover his wound with his other hand.

Cindy opened the door, wearing her fluffy towelled robe and matching fluffy slippers. Her face dropped at the sight of her brother, who wasted no time in barging into the flat. 'Close the door!' he demanded. Cindy did as she was told, slamming the door shut, then looked at Dwayne.

'What's happened now?'

'Ssh!' Dwayne put his finger to his mouth. 'Keep your voice down.' He beckoned her into the front room. Cindy stared at the blood seeping through his jeans, her eyes wide. She covered her mouth to stop herself screaming. She did as he said, following him into the front room.

'Whatever happens, I was here all night. Never left the house, ok?' Dwayne sniffed up a load of snot, wiping his face with his bloody hand, which shook uncontrollably. Cindy was trying to digest everything, not registering Dwayne's words. 'Sis, did you hear me? I was here with you all night, ok?' he repeated through gritted teeth, mindful to not wake Cece or allow the neighbours to hear. Cindy nodded, still in shock.

'Gonna get myself cleaned up.' Dwayne went towards the stairs.

'What happened to your leg?' She blocked him, staring down at the wound. 'We need to get this seen to.'

'It's cool. I beg you, sis, just act normal. Put a movie on or suttin.' He moved past her and disappeared up the stairs.

* * *

Bree Archibald lay on her back, legs astride, on a massage-type table covered in a layer of white tissue paper. Her eyes closed at the sound of a strip being torn off. She grimaced, groaning loudly, and bit her lip.

A woman dressed in a white uniform smiled down at her. 'Just a little bit left,' she said. Standing to the side of Bree, she prepared another waxing strip. 'Ok, we are ready.' The woman held the strip in her hand, wearing protective latex gloves.

The scene was interrupted by Bree's phone, which buzzed loudly. She sat up, taking the phone out of her bag. 'Bree Archibald,' she answered, lying back down. 'Yeah, go ahead, Sarge.' As the woman ripped another strip off, Bree grunted loudly. 'No,

I'm ok. I'm on my way.' Her face screwed up as another ripping sound was heard. 'All done.' The woman smiled down at her, tossing the strip into a bin and removing her gloves.

Shiny black Doc Marten boots trudged through the puddles of rain. Bree stepped deliberately, determined to survey the carnage of the shooting on Kingfisher Estate. Already there was a crowd of police, emergency service workers and nosey neighbours. The area in front of the lift was cordoned off with police tape. Bree arrived, flashing her badge at the policewoman in hi-vis yellow who stood steadfastly guarding the scene. She nodded back at her, lifting the tape, allowing Bree to duck under.

A small white and yellow tent had been constructed over L Boi's body, protecting him from the rain. A couple of forensic men dressed in white overalls gathered evidence, shining small white torches in and around the tent.

'What's the score?' Bree chimed in.

'Two gunshots, wounds to the chest area,' one of the men replied, his voice gravel-toned as if this was just routine to him.

'Any ID?' Bree continued her line of questions while her eyes scoped the many windows of the flats which overlooked the scene.

'Nope, just the knife it looks like he was holding. And some wraps of coke,' the man responded. Bree walked away, her gold and brown braids getting soaked from the incessant drizzle. She pulled her green parker coat tightly around her, folding her arms and walking back to the policewoman guarding the cordon.

'Witnesses?'

'A couple of neighbours over there gave a statement. Said there was a fight between youths; then they heard the gunshots.' The policewoman shrugged. 'Not much else, ma'am.'

Bree observed the couple before being joined by Darren Nolan, who held a large black umbrella above his head. His black creasy rain mac, unbuttoned, showed his untucked white shirt.

'What a fucking mess,' he exclaimed grumpily.

'No, it's a beautiful mess,' Bree countered, once again checking all of the windows above. 'Get some uniformed officers; we need to do door to door.' She continued surveying.

'Got the autopsy back on the little girl.' Nolan's hushed statement instantly perked up Bree's attention. She diverted her gaze towards him.

'Well?' she asked impatiently. Nolan looked around him before leaning in towards Bree sheepishly.

'Hypothermia and malnutrition. Wherever she'd been, she had been exposed to the elements for a while,' he said from the side of his mouth, aware of prying ears. 'Let's deal with this shit show first,' he continued before walking away.

Heavy thuds rattled Cindy's front door. She was still dressed in her fluffy robe and slippers, even though she knew that at some point she was due a visit. The constant banging shook her to the core. Dwayne limped down the stairs into the hallway with his thigh heavily bandaged, a spot of blood visible on the white strapping. 'Remember what I said,' he whispered to her as she approached the door.

Cindy stood behind a slightly ajar door, clutching her robe tightly around her neck, faced with Bree and another uniformed officer. 'Hello.' Cindy tried to stay calm as she stared back at Bree.

'Hi, we are investigating an incident that took place tonight. Did you see or hear anything out of the ordinary?' Bree fixed her gaze on Cindy, who shook her head in reply.

'No, sorry, I didn't,' she said softly.

'Gunshots?' asked Bree, trying to look past Cindy into the house.

'No, I'm afraid not,' Cindy replied.

'Anyone else live here who might have heard or seen anything?' Bree continued, unconvinced by Cindy's nonchalant responses.

'Just me and my daughter. She's been asleep, sorry…'

Bree stared at her intensely, trying to read her, her face still gleaming with a sheen of raindrops. She broke into a cheesy smile. 'Thanks. If you do remember anything,' she dug into her overcoat pocket and pulled out a card, 'give me a call.' She pushed the card into Cindy's hand. 'Ok, will do, thanks.' Cindy slammed the door, barely able to continue. She took a deep breath, leaning back onto the door. 'You better start talking,' she snapped at Dwayne, who sat on the stairs, returning a look of defeat.

* * *

'Fuck sake, bruv, when are you going to grow up?' Cindy planted her head in her hands, shaking it in disbelief. 'Who shot him?'

She peered through her fingers in his direction, hoping that he made the right choice in his answer.

'Dunno. Might have been a rival or suttin. I was too busy getting stabbed and beaten.' Dwayne scrunched his hair, his leg stretched out, thigh wrapped in bandage stained with an expanding patch of blood.

'I warned you before, didn't I?' Cindy was still in shock, angry and disappointed in her brother. 'You can't stay here. The police, that woman…' She paused recalling her encounter with Bree. 'She's gonna be watching us.' Cindy's paranoia levitated her from her seated position. 'Jeez, I hope none of the neighbours saw.' She paced around the room, her mind racing ten to the dozen.

'Look, I've got somewhere to stay. I'll kotch there for a bit.' He rested back in the chair, wincing as he moved his leg. 'I'll duck in the morning.' He shook his head just as a text message came through on his phone. He looked at the cracked screen; it was Ilyan. 'Raz wants to see you now!' it read.

Dwayne threw the phone onto the dining table. 'Who was that?' a still-jumpy Cindy asked. Dwayne looked up at her, the blood draining from his face, unable to hide his stress levels.

'No one; just some girl bothering me.' He closed his eyes, his chest rising from the heavy breathing kicking in.

'Kai's mum was it? Well, going bed. Some of us have work in the morning.' Cindy's throat tightened, her voice cracking as she left her parting shot, leaving Dwayne alone once again to stew in his own juices.

Chapter Fifteen

Only if you knew

Cindy stood alone in the plush, shiny restroom in the Schuster and Klein building. She spoke into her phone, which was on speaker, as she applied the last bits of make-up to her face. She looked gorgeous in a slinky black off-the-shoulder dress, with sparkly earrings and her hair styled in a short bob like Halle Berry in *Swordfish*.

'Make sure you behave for Uncle Dwayne, ok?' She ran the lipstick across her lips, a deep red accentuating her already plump pout.

'Yes, Mummy; we are at a big, nice house,' Cece replied, sounding excited and happy.

'Oh really, who's house is that?' Cindy quizzed.

'It's an Airbnb.' Dwayne's voice echoed through the room.

Cindy sprayed some perfume onto the base of her neck, leaving a sheen. She checked herself out, fixing her dress, distracted only when Lena entered the room. 'Oh hey, how come you're not ready?' She looked at Lena, who came in wearing a heavy overcoat, her face ashen as she blew her nose into a tissue.

'Sorry, I feel so ill. I came to say have fun.' She snuffled into the tissue and wiped her nose.

'Mummy, I'm watching Moana,' Cece's voice interjected loudly.

'Ok, darling. Bye, love you.' Cindy quickly disconnected the call and turned to Lena, pulling a disappointed face.

'Ahh, babe, you were meant to be my wing woman.' Cindy stood hands on hips. Lena stuck out her bottom lip, expressing her sadness. 'I know, but you go have a great time. I'm sure Andersen will look after you.' She made a heart-shaped gesture with her hands. 'Call me tomorrow. I want the goss,' she said, her voice hoarse, and blew Cindy a kiss before leaving.

Cindy sat at Andersen's desk. She typed the word 'Complete' into the mobile phone and pressed send. She watched the screen until the confirmation of the message being received appeared. She switched it off and placed it back in the bottom drawer. She checked her phone; 18:21 the time read.

She sat back, her black dress shimmering under the spotlights. She studied the pictures on his desk; then, for some reason, her curiosity got the better of her. She sat forward and pulled open the other drawers of the desk. She checked through a few files: nothing major, just business reports. She carried on delving until she saw a brown leather diary. Intrigued, she picked it up and unclipped the small, buckled strap which held it closed.

Cindy flicked through a few pages until an old photograph fell out onto the floor. She leant forward and picked it up. In the picture, she saw a younger Andersen with his wife Frieda and two teenagers, a boy and a girl. They were standing in front of a marina. It looked as if they were on holiday. She flipped the picture and saw writing on the back, but it was hard to read as the ink had blurred, but she could make out two words, 'Monaco' and 'Lena'.

She flipped the picture again and studied it. Sure enough, the young girl resembled Lena—blonde, tall, goofy, awkward. Her gaze was interrupted by her mobile phone ringtone. 'Shit.' Cindy fumbled, picking up her phone from the desk. 'Hello,' she answered.

'Miss Harper, your car is downstairs,' the voice responded.

'Ok, thanks.' She cut the call, her eyes still lingering on the photograph.

* * *

Dwayne lay spread out on the long cream sofa, staring at the artificial flames from the fireplace, still nursing the stab wound, which was now covered by a large plaster just visible under his shorts. Cece was on the floor sleeping on a pile of plumped-up cushions, worn out from her day. The place was quiet.

It had been just short of a month since Sasha had disappeared. He took a deep breath, reflecting on the recent events, until loud banging on the front door stirred him into action. He sat up quickly, checking on Cece.

'Who the fuck?' he muttered, dragging himself up and limping towards the door. He could hear someone shouting from the other side and kicking the door.

'Sasha, open the door!' The voice sounded strangely familiar, robotic, aggressive and foreign.

Dwayne looked through the peep hole. 'Shit!' He was taken aback to see the image of an angry Ilyan stepping back and launching another kick at the door. Dwayne ducked down and away from the door. *Shit, what's he doing…?* The banging continued.

'Sasha, you bitch, I know you're in there!'

Dwayne's mind was racing, his heart beating hard and fast. *Why is he here? Asking for Sasha? How does he even know her?* He stayed crouched low, the multiple questions overloading his mind. He was hoping Ilyan would go away, but the banging continued. He crawled painfully on his hands and knees back to the front room, panicking that the noise would wake Cece.

After a few minutes, the banging and shouting stopped. Dwayne sat on the floor next to Cece, who continued to sleep, only stirring to get more comfortable. He watched her, patting her softly on the back, ensuring she was not disturbed.

He grabbed his phone and scrolled through until he found Sasha's number. He hit the call button, placing the phone to his ear. 'Come on, Sasha,' he whispered, but the call didn't connect. The line was dead. 'Fuck, man. What's going on?' He tossed the phone to the floor, searching in his mind for answers only Sasha could give him.

* * *

Cindy walked hastily through the lobby of a plush hotel, her faux fur jacket slung over her forearm. She looked stunning, yet inside she felt nervous. She hated going to these work events alone; also, her mind was still scrambled by the photograph she had seen in Andersen's old diary. She knew she would have to park her thoughts for the next few hours and put a brave face on as she entered the lounge area where the event was taking place.

On walking in, she looked around the room. She could see some of the Schuster and Klein personnel mingling and sitting at tables. It was a black-tie event, so everyone was dressed up in smart suits and slinky dresses. A waitress approached her holding a tray of champagne in tall flutes. 'Madam?' she offered. Cindy smiled back at her while taking one of the flutes. 'Thanks,' she responded, smiling. She took a sip then walked confidently into the room.

Andersen was seated at a table with a few of the other directors and clients. He spotted Cindy and stood up. He looked dapper in a full tuxedo. 'Cindy, over here,' he invited, waving her towards him. Cindy took a deep breath, smiling, but inside, her stomach churned with butterflies.

'Good evening; you look amazing! No Lena?' Andersen greeted her, ushering her to a seat next to his. Cindy smiled. 'She's not feeling well,' she replied, trying to sit down elegantly. The others at the table, mainly middle-aged men and women, smiled politely as she joined the table. 'You all know my PA, Cindy Harper.' Andersen's relaxed European style always put her at ease.

The waiters brought over plates of food—fresh salmon, rump steak with fondant potatoes and a range of vegetables. Wine was poured into large glasses. Cindy did her best to enjoy the meal, although it wasn't her culinary style, while everyone around her talked business.

Andersen winked at her, nodding his head and chewing on a piece of steak. 'All good?' he asked. Cindy nodded, understanding that he wasn't talking about the food. 'Yep, all good,' she replied, her eyes watching the others at the table, hoping they didn't pick up on anything.

After the meal, most of the table, including Andersen, dispersed, leaving Cindy talking to one of the other directors who was waxing lyrical about how much he appreciated her in-depth reports. She was actually tired and bored to tears with constantly 'talking shop' when Andersen came back to the table to save her. 'There's someone I'd like you to meet,' he whispered in her ear. 'We'll be back,' he signalled to his colleagues, taking Cindy's hand and helping her up from her seat.

Andersen, as always, was calm, smiling and waving at some of his employees as they made their way to the bar where a man stood alone, puffing on a cigar. He was blonde, tall, and dressed in a black velvet blazer and black roll neck.

'Cindy, this is Dietmar. Dietmar, please meet Cindy.' Dietmar turned to Cindy and smiled. He was handsome, with blue eyes and dazzling teeth, and refined. He held his hand out for a shake.

Cindy was captivated by him. So much so she forgot to reciprocate. 'Oh, I'm sorry.' She thrust her hand out. 'Hello.' Her voice quivered; she was unable to hide the pleasant feeling which ran through her in that moment.

'Right, I'll get some drinks.' Andersen patted them both on the back before turning to the bar.

'Smoke?' Dietmar offered a cigar but Cindy shook her head in disgust.

'No thanks, I don't smoke.'

'You're right; awful habit.' He removed it and stubbed out his own smouldering cigar in an ashtray.

His accent was familiar, German. He sounded like Lena when he spoke. 'Here we are.' Andersen returned with a couple of whiskeys and a cocktail for Cindy.

'So, do you work in medical research?' Cindy asked Dietmar. He raised his eyebrow looking directly back at her.

'No, I'm into export.' He smiled and took a healthy sip of his whiskey.

'We met a long time ago in Germany. A friend of the family,' Andersen interjected, swirling the cubes of ice around in his glass. Cindy's mind flashed back to the photograph in the diary, but the alcohol she'd consumed had her feeling tipsy. She was just trying to stay composed. 'Excuse me.' Andersen placed his glass down on the bar and walked away after seeing someone else who wanted his attention, leaving Cindy alone with Dietmar.

Cindy giggled shyly after listening to another charming story from Dietmar. She found him intriguing and was enjoying his company. It was as though it was just the two of them in the room. He was a fascinating character.

'I'd like to see you again, Cindy. Dinner maybe?' Dietmar leant forward, his warm whiskey breath drifting to her nose. Again she giggled, holding her hand over her eyes while she digested his request. 'Ok yeah, that'll be nice,' she replied, disbelieving her response.

'Can I have your phone?' Dietmar asked confidently. Cindy was putty in his hands. Her walls were down, her head dizzied by his flattery. She slid her phone over to him and watched as he put his number into it. His blue eyes looked up and connected to hers.

'Let's do this again in more intimate surroundings.' He gave her back the phone. She was enticed by his assuredness. She sipped slowly on her cocktail, taking a moment to swallow before replying. 'Yeah, why not.' She burst into a laugh. 'You're dangerous.' She wagged her finger in his face playfully. Dietmar raised his glass, grinning back at her.

Chapter Sixteen

Who will save your soul?

Condensation left streaks down the steamed-up windows of the greasy spoon where Bree sat mopping up the remains of the bright yellow egg yolk with the last quarter of her toast. Nolan sat watching, sipping a mug of black coffee. 'Wish I could still do that.' His eyes looked on enviously as she stuffed the last bit into her mouth.

'Not my fault you got a dodgy ticker and a fat belly,' she snorted, cheeks bulging, chewing savagely. 'I don't have a dodgy ticker.' Nolan's rebuttal was defensive as he patted his paunch. 'Anyway, forensics confirmed a hair was found on that little girl's clothing and it's not hers, as well as fibres from a car boot,' he said, chuffed with himself.

Bree washed her food down with the last of her tea. 'What type of car?' she continued.

'Not sure yet,' he answered. 'Poor sod. You know she shat herself?' Nolan mused, rubbing his creased forehead. 'Soiled her knickers, dear God …' He pursed his lips tightly, allowing the thought to sit in his mind.

'Tell forensics to run that hair through the European database.' Bree finally cleared the food from her throat. 'If she's been trafficked, my bet it's a foreign gang.' She rested back, satisfied.

'No flies on you.' Nolan gulped the rest of his coffee and slammed his mug on the table.

'And I bet there's more kids holed up somewhere.' He wiped his mouth, staring at Bree.

'We'll find 'em, the kids and the gang.' Bree pushed her chair back and stood up, giving a thumbs up to the café owner, who was looking bored, leaning on the till. He reciprocated the gesture as they left.

* * *

The heat in the portacabin was stifling. The sweat which trickled down Dwayne's forehead indicated how high the setting of the fan heater behind Raz's desk was. Raz sat wearing a tight black vest which revealed his inked arms—mostly faded military tattoos which had greyed into his hairy skin.

Dwayne sat stiffly in a chair, a gun pressed against his temple, ensuring his movement was limited. 'Ricky never gave me any trouble,' a downbeat Raz grumbled, picking meticulously through a pile of pine nuts. He raised his eyes to Dwayne. 'Tell me, what happened with Ilyan?' His voice was barely above a mumble.

Dwayne stared ahead, eyes bulging with fear, as a tall, slick, ponytailed gunman called Jorgi kept his long arm outstretched, holding the muzzle of the gun steadily against his head. 'I didn't know he was gonna shoot.' Dwayne grimaced, feeling the tension.

Raz cracked another nut between his teeth. 'Hmm, so...' he casually replied.

'So I was attacked by some youths from my ends. Next thing I know, shots went off. I swear I didn't even know he was gonna do that.' The fear made his trembling voice rise an octave.

Raz remained brooding, unimpressed by Dwayne's tale. He looked up and nodded towards his gunman, who finally removed the tool from Dwayne's head. Raz sat back, nibbling on a nut. He looked rough, his jaw outlined by dark salt-and-pepper stubble, his facial skin rugged and creased.

'Ilyan has disappeared, probably for the best,' Raz grumbled, chewing on the side of his mouth. 'But I have a problem now. Also, my sister Sasha disappeared too.' He tapped a nut on the table.

He gave Dwayne a cold stare. Dwayne did his best not to react on hearing the name Sasha, although his mind was now speeding faster than the bullet that had hit L Boi in the chest, realising the reason Ilyan had turned up angrily at the flat.

'You now have extra work. On top of the drops, there's something else I have in mind.' Raz's voice was still barely audible. He nodded at Jorgi, who put the gun back to Dwayne's head. 'You go with Jorgi,' Raz ordered. Dwayne froze although the heat in the room was causing him to sweat buckets, the fluid dripping down into his bushy beard.

* * *

A bright young saleswoman, perky and smartly dressed, chattered away, clutching an iPad in her hand. Her long blonde ponytail swung from side to side as she walked Cindy and Cece through the show home plot of the plush residential apartments called The Hive. 'Now here is the master bedroom.' She walked into a spacious room decked in sleek modern furniture, with brightly coloured bedding and plumped-up pillows.

'Also has its own en suite.' She opened another door which revealed a modern, spa-like bathroom with shiny grey tiles. Cindy's eyes sparkled in awe as she surveyed the space. 'Oh, this is lovely,' she cooed, checking out all the shiny taps. 'Mummy, can I see my room?' Cece asked, tugging her mum's hand.

'Sure, do you want to come with me?' The saleswoman stuck out her hand for Cece, who eagerly clasped it. 'I'll let you have a look around, then I'll show you the garden.' Her bright blue eyes gazed back at Cindy before she walked away with Cece.

Cindy walked around holding a glossy brochure to her chest, her eyes lighting up on seeing the beautiful modern kitchen and large glass patio doors, which looked out onto a lush green turfed garden. She sighed heavily, hope and anticipation overwhelming her soul. This was a world away from Kingfisher, and as her eyes scanned around, she envisioned herself happily cooking and watching Cece play in the garden.

It felt as though all her hard work and achievements were coming to fruition at the right time, regardless of what she had to do to get there. Cindy knew she deserved it all. Cece came running back, a big smile on her face, with the saleswoman in tow. 'Mummy, I like my room. Can I get a puppy too?' She hugged Cindy tightly.

Cindy rolled her eyes, laughing. 'We'll see. What are they like?' She shook her head, staring at the saleswoman, who stepped forward and offered her hand to shake. 'Take your time. Here's my card.' She placed a business card in Cindy's hand.

'Give me a call. I'll leave you to have a couple of minutes.' Her perky sales patter subsided into a more personal, compassionate tone. 'Goodbye, Cece. So cute.' She rubbed Cece's back, then swivelled on her heels and walked away, allowing Cindy and Cece to soak up the rest of their time.

* * *

Jorgi had driven Dwayne to a dark, dank, crumbling housing estate on the other side of London. The heavy clouds introduced another chilly evening as they pulled up among the almost derelict, graffiti-riddled buildings. They walked through a narrow corridor, the old worn lino-tiled flooring stained and littered with cigarette butts, empty lager cans and decaying food in takeaway boxes. Dwayne limped behind Jorgi, turning up his nose at the stench.

They reached the end of the block and came to a flat that had no front door, just a metal grate with a padlock. Jorgi pulled out a bunch of keys. He looked at Dwayne, smirking, as he selected the key that unlocked the padlock.

'Yo, what are we doing here, bro?' Dwayne could sense that whatever was behind this door was not going to be anything good.

'No questions, just work,' Jorgi replied dryly. Dwayne tucked his hands into his jacket pockets, bracing himself for whatever was about to come.

The sound of the door creaking behind him sent shivers through Dwayne as he stood in the hallway of the run-down flat. Jorgi switched on a dim light, revealing a neglected interior—peeling wallpaper, damp mould creeping down the wall like blotted ink on dirty paper, worn stained carpet and grime on the walls. Jorgi nudged Dwayne in his back, forcing him towards a closed door at the end of the hallway.

Dwayne stepped forward apprehensively. 'So what's really going on?' he asked Jorgi, who remained serious, focusing ahead and prodding Dwayne in his back. They reached the door. He could hear the sound of a TV in the background. Jorgi tapped on the door lightly and waited, his tall frame towering above Dwayne.

The door opened slowly, revealing a short, tubby woman dressed in black, with a floral headscarf wrapped tightly over her head. Her wrinkled face was reddened by the numerous capillaries on her cheeks. Jorgi mumbled something in his native tongue before bending down and kissing her on both cheeks. She grumbled, then opened the door, ushering them into the room.

The room was sparsely furnished—a small, battered, black leather sofa, thread-bare carpet, a small, glowing electric heater and a mattress on which sat the last of the children, four boys, all huddled together in tatty clothes with bare feet.

Each of them looked dirty and gaunt. Their big eyes stared up anxiously towards Jorgi and Dwayne, whose own eyes widened dramatically on seeing the state of them. Dwayne actually choked back puke in his mouth while trying to hold his composure on realising the scale of the situation he was in.

* * *

It felt as if they had been driving for a few hours along the motorway, the orange street lights flashing past at speed. Dwayne struggled to keep his eyes open, disturbed only by the sound of one of the young boys whimpering in the back seat behind him. Jorgi was slumped back in the driver's seat, relaxed, cigarette dangling from his mouth, staring at the road ahead. He never spoke, apart from shouting at the children, which angered Dwayne.

The blue motorway sign read 'Sheffield'. That was the only indication of direction. Dwayne's anger had subsided, but inside he was still fuming, questioning all of the decisions and signposting every turn that had got him into this position. The moments flashed through his mind faster than the white lines on the tarmac ahead. His thoughts were interrupted by his phone buzzing in his pocket.

Dwayne checked his phone and saw a text message from Lisa. *'Hey where are you? Had some bad news could do with some company…'* He sighed deeply, rubbing his forehead, before replying, *'Out of town be back tomorrow. Call u then.'* Jorgi turned his head to check on Dwayne but said nothing. Instead, he pressed down on the accelerator and turned the steering wheel, veering off the main road into a slip road.

Chapter Seventeen

The man with the child in his eyes

Dwayne sat on the edge of the bed bare-chested, in dirty jogging pants with his legs outstretched, barefooted. On the floor by his feet was a half-empty bottle of Wray and Nephew rum nestled amongst a cluster of fifty-pound notes scattered around in front of him. His eyes were tired, reddened and glassed over with teetering tears. He sniffed up his runny nose and looked around him at the clean, spacious, contemporary apartment bequeathed to him by Sasha. He chuckled but out of pain, not laughter; it was almost a choke rather than a full chuckle.

His brown chest was covered with wispy, curly hair which he scratched aggressively, agitated. He picked up his phone and stared at the screen, burping loudly, then coughing hoarsely. His fingers fumbled around with the screen buttons; he shook his head, sniffing loudly again.

Sasha's name lit up on the screen with the word 'Calling'. He held the phone to his ear, swaying back and forth. There was the dead tone, followed by the message 'The number you are calling is unavailable.' Dwayne threw the phone to the floor angrily.

It bounced among the litter of bank notes on the floor before spinning off to the side.

He leant forward to grab the bottle to prevent it from falling onto the floor amongst the crisp notes. His built body rolled around, unstable. He unscrewed the top, then poured the remains of the coarse liquid down his throat, spilling most of the contents out the side of his mouth until he began to choke, coughing vigorously again.

The sound of a message ping from his phone jolted him. He began to heave as if he was about to vomit, turning his head towards the discarded device. The screen flashed a message from Cindy. 'Don't be late for Cece's birthday party I need your help to sort things x'. He stared at it until the message faded.

* * *

Ilyan's mugshot was projected onto the widescreen. His face stared back ominously, the glare from the screen the only light illuminating Bree's face. She sat alone in the darkened room, crunching loudly on a crisp Granny Smith apple, staring back at the visual.

Ilyan looked slightly younger, his black hair tidy, combed over slickly. He wore a T-shirt—black, military style, the short sleeves revealing his inked, muscular arms. His eyes, though, were dark, cruel and deathly, signifying a cold personality behind the chiselled features. Bree sucked the juice from the apple before taking another large bite as she continued to stare into the light of the screen.

* * *

The electronic sound of a message came through on a mobile phone on the glass-topped bedside table. Cindy rolled over, keeping her scarfed head on the pillow. Her eyes opened slowly as she reached for the phone. She tilted the screen towards her, seeing a message from Dietmar: 'Are you free for dinner Sat night?'

Cindy broke into a sleepy smile. Yawning at the same time, she rubbed her face before eagerly tapping a reply. Another smile crept across her face. Her moment of indulgent bliss was soon interrupted by an excited Cece, who burst into her room wearing a Lisa Simpson onesie and a big smile on her face.

Cece jumped onto the bed. 'Mummy, it's my birthday!' she exclaimed, showering Cindy with kisses. 'I know, babes, coz it's your party later!' Cindy hugged her tightly, then began to tickle her, making Cece burst into a high-pitched squeal of laughter and roll around, attempting to escape the clutches of her mother.

* * *

Dwayne sat outside a well-known coffee shop in the middle of a busy shopping mall. He downed an espresso shot in an attempt to inject some energy into his weary state. He was surrounded by a variety of retail bags and a large silver helium balloon in the shape of the number nine.

He lifted a small white paper bag and took out a brand-new boxed phone. He eagerly removed the packaging then removed it from the box, ogling the shiny new screen, very different from his old scratched and cracked one. He emerged onto the streets, bags hanging from both hands and the balloon floating behind him in the wind. The fresh breeze hit him, stiffening him up as he made his way through the crowds.

His mood had lifted slightly, the effects of the alcohol diminishing, returning some sense of normality to his mind. He was dressed smartly; a new grey tweed trench coat covered his hench frame, worn with black ripped jeans and soft grey suede loafers.

He was filled with anticipation. He couldn't wait to see Cece's face when he handed her all her gifts, even though he had to try and push the truth to the back of his mind about how he had earned the money to afford it all. He felt a shiver run through his body, the fight with his conscience conflicting.

As Dwayne continued to walk, musing at the hi-tech window displays, the reflection of a silver Mercedes could be seen crawling along the road. At the sound of the car horn, he turned and saw Trevor, Ricky's brother, gesturing to him to come to the car.

Dwayne's heart sank. He stood for a second, contemplating, before making his way over. He leant down to the window, which slid down until the scent of apple vape drifted past his face. 'Put that shit in the back and get in.' A few words from Trevor were enough to force Dwayne into action.

Trevor drove slowly away from the busy shopping area, leaning back in his seat. A black New York Yankees baseball cap, worn low, covered his eyes. One hand was on the steering wheel; the other held the small black and chrome vaping device his thick lips tugged on. He blew out another plume of smoke, which was quickly sucked out of the half-opened window.

'How you been, Dee?' he asked, without even turning to look at him. Dwayne shrugged, trying to stay calm. 'Been ok, same old,' he replied. Trevor nodded slowly, his mouth upturned, mulling over his answer and staring into the rearview mirror at the silver balloon, which wiggled from side to side in the jet stream.

'Man's splashing the cash, yeah?' Again he tugged on the vape, inhaling deeply, allowing a few seconds before blowing out the smoke. Dwayne smiled wryly, scratching his head. 'Yeah, my niece's birthday, so just thought…' he continued, only to be interrupted by Trevor. 'That's some nice clobber too, bro. Man's balling out here.' Trevor brushed the shoulders of Dwayne's tweed coat, letting out a deep belly laugh which caused his whole muscular torso to shake in the cream leather seat.

'What's really good?' Trevor's tone took a serious detour from being jovial and cordial to being direct and threatening. 'See, remember that chick Paige?' he asked Dwayne as he steered the car into the winding runway of an empty multi-storey car park.

Dwayne steeled himself, scratching his head, the nerves kicking in as he observed the sparse concrete asphalt in the middle of nowhere, overlooking a spaghetti junction below. 'Yeah, course. Have you seen her?' His reply was rhetoric, merely a search mechanism for where Trevor was navigating this conversation to.

'Lovely girl, Paige; she proper loved Ricks.' Trevor smiled, staring upwards towards the heavens as he reflected on his brother.

'Yeah, he was punching though.' Dwayne tried to bring a dose of humour to the tense tête-à-tête, but his attempts were thwarted immediately by a vexed Trevor, whose mood switched from calm to angered.

'She came to see me, Paige, yeah. Told me about Ricky's little hustle.' He leant over towards Dwayne, with his plump face and sleepy eyes, his breath pungent with apple vape. 'She said you knew what he was on. Who he was working with.' Trevor prodded Dwayne's shoulder hard with every word, hard enough for him to feel the tip of his chunky finger through his coat.

Dwayne leant his head back onto the headrest. He tried to keep himself together, but he had the feeling that at any moment, his last vision on earth would be a derelict car park and the grey skies which loomed above them.

'He never told me nothing; just said he had a little side ting.' Dwayne closed his eyes. As he spoke, a flash of the car chase and crash caused him to blink back to reality. 'Told him I didn't want to know coz I just got out,' he said calmly, trying to veil the truth.

Trevor leant back away from Dwayne, peering into his soul. 'Who's this Sasha girl?' he asked. Paige said you two linked up.' He flicked a lever which squirted water onto his car windscreen, causing the wipers to flick into action.

'Sasha?' Dwayne pretended to search his mind as if the name was new to him. 'Oh yeah, that ting from the party, same one where I met Paige.' He nodded, acting out his recollection. 'Nah, don't really know her; just a beat after jail.' He shrugged causally but inside feared there was more to come from Trevor's inquisition.

Trevor continued to watch him, giving himself a few seconds to digest the information before projecting his arm quickly and grabbing Dwayne around the neck. The grip from his chunky hand constricted Dwayne's throat.

'My brother is fucking dead, bro! He was alive until you came out. I know you're fucking lying!' He continued to squeeze with force, shaking Dwayne to his posh suede loafers. Dwayne grabbed Trevor's hand, trying to pry it off his neck. He choked, his eyeballs bulging out of his skull as he stared back at Trevor, whose nostrils flared as his aggression intensified.

The struggle continued for what seemed like an age until Trevor finally released his grip. 'Don't think I won't duppy you as well,' he snarled, sweat seeping from underneath the rim of his hat. Dwayne coughed, crouched over in his seat, sucking in air. 'Tek your tings and get the fuck out my car,' Trevor ordered. Dwayne tried to catch his breath, fumbling with the handle of the door.

'Swear down, Trev, I don't know any more,' he wheezed, pushing the door open, allowing cold air to sweep through the sweaty vehicle.

Dwayne grabbed his bags and the balloon then staggered back away from the car, which sped away with a wheel spin, careering back down the broken concrete ramps. Dwayne dropped onto his haunches, spitting out bloodied phlegm. He gasped in the fresh air. Left alone in the middle of a sparse, deserted landscape, holding onto the number nine silver balloon, his recovery was interrupted by the joyous ringtone from his new phone.

* * *

Cindy walked hastily across the wooden boards of a small community hall which had been decorated with balloons and streamers. She held a pile of plastic plates and cups in her hands while tilting her head between her shoulders, holding the phone. 'Dwayne! Where are you man? Could do with some help here.' Although she was dressed nicely, her make-up and hair done, her expression was frazzled as she rushed to finish the final bits before the guests arrived.

Lena came inside the hall from the garden which housed a large Disney *Frozen* bouncy castle. She was dressed casually in jeans and a sweat top, her face flushed from her exertions. 'I don't think you're going to get Cece away from that.' She caught her breath, laughing, seeing a busy Cindy running from table to table, laying out the plates and cups. 'What can I help with?' Lena placed her glasses back on her face and stepped in to assist her friend. 'Just need to get the crisps. Oh, and put the ice cream in the freezer,' Cindy replied frantically.

Cece came running into the hall in her socks, wearing a pink jogging suit with a silver sash across her reading 'It's my birthday'. Her hair was braided with her bright pink baubles dangling. 'Mummy, I'm thirsty.' She ran towards Cindy throwing her arms around her.

At that point, a few parents began to show up with their children, stepping tentatively into the hall. Cece turned to see some of her friends. 'Amy!' Cece was distracted. Her excitement at seeing her friends arrive diverted her attention from her thirst as she ran over to greet them.

Cindy smiled, watching her, while waving to and welcoming the other parents as they began to trickle in. Amongst the gaggle of people entering were Lisa and her son Kai. Lisa's bright red hair flowed over the shoulders of her black puffer jacket. Kai was dressed smartly, his face lighting up on seeing the colourful decorations and tables laid out with bowls of sweets and crisps.

Lisa looked around, hoping that Dwayne would be there to greet her but was only recognised when Cece spotted Kai and shouted his name. 'Hello.' She politely waved at Lisa before grabbing Kai's arm and dragging him away.

Cindy looked over to Lisa, noticed she was slightly out of her comfort zone and came over to greet her. 'Hi, you must be Lisa. Kai's mum, right?' She smiled warmly, giving her a friendly hug. 'I'm Cindy, Cece's mum.' She smiled again.

'Hi, nice to meet you,' Lisa replied nervously.

'Dwayne's not here yet. Come in—can I get you a drink?' Cindy asked. She was in full hostess mode, walking Lisa over to where Lena was seated.

Most of the parents were gathered in the community hall talking amongst each other while the kids were mostly in the communal garden, playing and jumping on the bouncy castle. Lisa sat alone sipping on a drink, politely smiling fleetingly at the other parents whom she recognised.

Lena and Cindy were standing in the kitchen area of the hall preparing some sandwiches and various bitesize snacks. 'So… I kinda have a date on Saturday.' Cindy could hardly contain her excitement, nibbling on a piece of cheese as she continued to prepare the food. Lena became equally excited, nudging her.

'Oh really! Who?' Lena pinched a piece of cheese and tossed it into her mouth, smiling back at Cindy.

'Hmm, can't say yet. I just want to see how it goes; it's nothing serious,' Cindy replied coyly, shrugging it off and blushing. 'I suddenly feel hot.' She started to fan herself with her hand, laughing.

'Come on, you can't hold out on me.' Lena squeezed her arm, begging for a piece of juicy gossip, but Cindy was keeping her secret suitor to herself.

Dwayne had finally arrived. His entrance was somewhat subdued and underwhelming, except for the silver helium balloon, which caught everyone's attention when he walked into the hall, especially Cece's.

'Uncle Dwayne!' she screamed, running towards him, barely giving him time to put the bags down. Her moment of elation drew the attention of the others in the room. Dwayne scooped her up and hugged her tightly. He let out a huge sigh, which evaporated into laughter, the woes of his last few hours dissolving in his niece's warmth. 'Is all this for me?' She leant back, grabbing the balloon.

'All for you, Cee.' Dwayne kissed her on the cheek before letting her down.

'Took your time. Where was you?' Cindy sauntered over, tapping her wrist with Lena in tow. Dwayne puffed out his cheeks.

'Last minute shopping.' He picked up the bags, showing her all the things he had purchased.

'Hi, I'm Lena.' A perked-up Lena stretched her hand out, her eyes scanning Dwayne through the lenses of her glasses.

'Ahh, the famous Lena! I hear about you all the time.' Dwayne took her hand and leant forward, giving her a kiss on the cheek. Lena's face went red.

'Am I famous?' she shrieked in surprise, flattered.

'Come on, you two.' Cindy stepped between them, picking up the bags. 'Your friend Lisa is here too.' She nodded over to where Lisa was sitting alone watching on. Dwayne made a beeline over to her.

'Hey, thanks for coming. Sorry I'm late. Was running around, last bits...' He went in for a hug which, at first, Lisa shunned.

'Had me sitting here on my ones like a saddo.' She gave him a death stare, her brown eyes watching his expression as he hung in suspense. 'You're lucky it's a kid's party.' Lisa finally relented, breaking into a smile. Her diamond tooth glinted, receiving his embrace.

'Jeez, man, such a hard nut,' he joked, giving her a big hug. 'You smell nice.' He sniffed in her perfume as he let her go. 'Where's Kai?' he asked. Lisa pointed out to the bouncy castle where they could see the kids all jumping around enjoying themselves.

'Stop staring at them.' Cindy pushed Lena playfully as she gazed towards the table where Lisa and Dwayne sat.

'Sorry, but he's hot,' Lena declared in a heavy accent.

'Excuse me!' Cindy laughed. 'Help me to get this cake ready.' She shook her head, retreating into the kitchen, leaving Lena, who continued to gaze in their direction.

'Glad you came. So you've met my sister then?' Dwayne asked, chomping on a sandwich while looking at Lisa, who had now removed her puffer jacket and was more relaxed.

'Yeah, she's cool, and at least Kai's enjoying himself,' she replied, pointing at the kids running in and out of the hall.

'What about you?' Dwayne wiped the crumbs from his mouth with a tissue napkin.

'What about me?' she replied, flicking her red mane away from her face.

'Are you glad to be here?'

'With you and a bunch of screaming kids? It's alright.' She shrugged.

Dwayne rested back in his chair, sensing Lisa's vibe was off. 'Suttin up?' he asked. Lisa brushed her legs with her hands, her red-painted fingernails stark against her black jeans. She seemed moody, unwilling to really talk, but knew she had to.

'I text you, I got air.' She stared at him. 'Heard some bad news, family stuff.' She tried to palm it off but was really seeking a way to open up.

'Yeah, sorry, was busy, but tell me.' Dwayne boldly took her hand, holding it gently.

Lisa bowed her head for a few seconds, then looked back at Dwayne, her eyes searching. 'My cuz got killed few weeks back. Shot on your estate. Surprised you didn't hear,' she whispered.

'Lyall, they called him L Boi. He wasn't no angel, but still…' She shook her head. 'He was only eighteen…'

A rush of heat surged through Dwayne's body. He dropped her hand, resting back. 'Shit! Yeah, my sister mentioned something had happened. No way, that's… your… cousin. Wow, sorry to hear that.' His act was dramatic yet believable. He knew the truth, his mind racing back to Illyan's moment of madness. He rubbed the wound on his leg through his jeans. It itched at the realisation of Lisa's connection.

At that moment, an excited Cindy came over. 'Come on, guys, we're gonna do the cake. Dwayne, go outside and get Cece and the rest of them.' Her instructions were a welcome interruption.

'Yeah, ok.' He got up, trying to disguise his shock. 'Give me a sec.' He looked at Lisa, who nodded back solemnly with a half-smile.

'You alright?' Cindy put her hand on Lisa's shoulder. 'Come on, you can help me with the cake.' She ushered Lisa to her feet, escorting her over to the kitchen where Lena stood nibbling on some pretzels.

Dwayne came rushing back into the hall with worry etched on his face. He dashed across the pine floor, the rubber soles from his suede shoes squeaking as he darted in different directions. He looked around, frantically checking all the other kids before turning and rushing into the kitchen where Cindy, Lisa and Lena stood chatting and laughing as they made the last preparations for the grand entrance of the cake.

'She's gone.' He stared, wide-eyed, at Cindy.

'Who's gone?' Cindy replied, her smile quickly disappearing on seeing Dwayne's face.

'Cece. She's not outside in the garden.' He pointed towards the door, agitated.

'No, she must be in here somewhere.' Cindy broke into a nervous smile, dropping the packet of candles on the counter. 'Come on, let's find her. I'm sure she's just being cheeky, hiding…' she said, more in hope than certainty.

A hum of chatter filled the room as the other parents watched with concern as Cindy, Dwayne, Lena and Lisa rushed around, looking in every nook and cranny of the hall. Lisa took Kai's hand and crouched down to his eye level. 'Did you see where Cece went?' she asked calmly. Kai's body language became awkward. He squirmed; his smart clothes slightly bedraggled from his exertions. 'She went with her daddy in the red car,' he said softly, almost reluctant to tell in case he got into trouble.

'Ok, when?' The urgency in Lisa's voice upped a level. She caressed Kai's face. 'When, darling?' Kai shrugged.

'I dunno.' His little face looked confused.

'Ok, come.' She stood up clutching his hand, and rushed over to Cindy, who was looking increasingly worried.

'Cindy.' She hurried towards her. 'Kai said she left with her dad?' Cindy's heart dropped.

'Oh my God, Dwayne!' Her pained scream horrified everyone.

Dwayne came bounding towards her. 'What's happened?' He looked flustered and was sweating as he approached his sister.

'It's Leon! She's gone with Leon!' Cindy began to shake with emotion, the reality of the situation hitting her in the gut, her pretty face now creased and riddled with fear.

* * *

Cece sat quietly in the back of the car, engrossed in a hand-held computer game. A large red balloon with the words 'Happy Birthday' spelt out in silver was anchored down by a small pile of wrapped gifts.

Leon drove at speed, puffing on a cigarette. The radio played in the background—an upbeat disco tune. He flicked his eyes up to the rearview mirror. The reflection showed jagged red lines in the whites of his eyes. He grinned as he looked back at Cece, who was content playing her new game, still wearing her pink jogging suit with the silver birthday sash across her body.

Chapter Eighteen

Wandering romance

'When are we going back to my party?' Cece sat slumped on a small sofa, now fidgeting and agitated. She pulled her birthday sash over her head, dumping it next to the pile of discarded wrapping paper and gifts, including a new pair of trainers which were set on top of the box.

Leon peered anxiously out of the window of a high-rise block from behind stained net curtains. 'Just be quiet, Cee.' The blue smoke from his cigarette which smouldered in an ashtray on a wooden table wavered in the air.

'I want to go back to Mummy now.' Cece's voice quivered as she watched her father frantically staring out of the window then pacing up and down the small, sparsely furnished room.

'Shut up, Cece... doing my head in now!' he snarled aggressively, tugging hard on his cigarette, his cheeks inverted as he drew the smoke deep into his lungs, and flicking his locks out of his face. Cece folded her arms, sulking, fighting back the tears, her bottom lip curling as she looked back at her erratic father.

* * *

Dwayne sat alone on the bouncy castle. He looked lost, staring ahead at the huddle of police officers standing around questioning Cindy and Lena. Lisa walked over to him with Kai in tow delving into a packet of sweets. She gave Dwayne a paltry smile, doing her best to reassure him but knowing inside the turmoil he was feeling.

'Are you alright?' she asked. 'Dumb question, I know,' she added, taking a seat beside him and pulling a weary Kai between her legs. Dwayne scratched his head.

'How can this happen? It's her birthday, for fuck's sake.' He aired his feelings—raw and unapologetic—although Lisa nudged him, covering Kai's ears because of his language.

'Sorry,' he acknowledged. Lisa rubbed his back tenderly, a sign of her compassion towards a troubled soul.

'It's mad, but they will find him.' She looked over to the police.

'Fuck dem feds! I don't want them involved,' Dwayne spat out, his frustration boiling over.

'Oi!' Again Lisa nudged him, casting her eyes towards a sleepy Kai.

A distraught Cindy made her way over to Dwayne. 'They want to ask you some questions.' She sniffed back her tears, motioning to Dwayne, who was unmoved by her plea.

'Got nothing to say, sis. I didn't see anything.' He was ardent in his reply.

'Please, Dwayne, they're trying to help!' Cindy wiped away a solitary tear which rolled down her cheek, her normal chilled persona broken. 'I'm worried. Leon's a loose cannon.' Her urgency caused her to shake.

Lena put her arms around her to console her. 'Let's all try and stay calm.' Her pragmatic German approach quelled the heightened emotion between the siblings.

'Kai, did you see what Cece's daddy was wearing?' Lisa gently asked her son, trying to pry some useful information from him. Kai shrugged, offering nothing, while popping another sweet into his mouth.

A female officer approached the group, her hi-vis jacket over her uniform and utility belt bolted with various contraptions weighing her down as she waddled towards them. 'Miss Harper… Sorry to interrupt, but we need you to come to the station.' She paused. Her rosy cheeks glowed. 'To make a formal statement.' She cleared her throat before nodding and retreating respectfully.

Dwayne stood up and walked away in a huff without saying a word, throwing his jacket on and brushing past the gaggle of officers still milling about. 'Dwayne!' Cindy shrieked, causing the police team to turn and look over at her. Dwayne continued to walk away, leaving a distressed Cindy to wilt into Lena's arms.

* * *

'Happy birthday to you… a happy birthday to you!' Leon stepped out of the small cubicle of a kitchen holding a tiny pink frosted cupcake with a mini number nine candle on top of it, the flame flickering with each step that he took.

Another cigarette dangled from the corner of his mouth, just showing glints of his gold teeth. Cece sat watching him, unimpressed, her face glum even though she had been showered with gifts. 'I want to go back to Mummy,' she said slowly, her tone layered with disappointment.

'Come on, my darling. Blow the candle; make a wish.' He grinned, the grey ash from his cigarette flaking to the floor. Cece stood up and considered the cupcake, the flame illuminating the crystal glints of teetering tears in her eyes, which she swung to Leon.

'No!' she shouted, sweeping the cupcake onto the floor. She ran to the bathroom, slamming the door behind her, leaving Leon flustered and fumbling around on the floor, doing his best to stop the flame from burning the carpet.

* * *

Lena and Lisa sat next to each other on the uncomfortable blue plastic chairs in the waiting area of the police station. A musty smell, mixed with the clinical stench of disinfectant, hung in the air. The two strangers sipped weak tea from plastic cups as they waited for Cindy or any news. Kai stretched out across the seats next to them, fast asleep.

The events of the last few hours had drained the energy out of them, to the point that the effort of conversation was not even entertained. The only noise came from a cleaner wheeling a squeaking trolley full of products along the corridor.

Lisa checked her phone when the ding of a message alerted her. She read it, then turned to the main entrance to see Dwayne leering in from outside. She motioned for him to come in, which he eventually did, after a few seconds of contemplation.

He strode purposefully, with his head down, trying to avoid the internal CCTV cameras. 'What's happening? Where's Cindy?' he asked directly.

'She still in there,' Lisa answered, sounding fed up.

Dwayne paced around in front of them. He looked at Lena, who could only return a slight smile. 'I can't be in here,' he muttered to himself, raking his hands through his hair. His histrionics were interrupted by Cindy's reappearance. She looked drained and worried.

'Sis, what's the deal?' Dwayne rushed towards her. 'Have they found her yet?' he continued, holding Cindy by the arms.

'Dwayne, get off.' She shrugged him off, leaving him standing as she sat next to Lena, resting her head against her shoulder.

As they all congregated in the waiting area, mulling over their plan of action, Bree stepped through the entrance doors. Her eyes were immediately drawn to Cindy. She stopped in her tracks, her memory recall kicking into gear on clocking her familiar face. Bree reversed, stepping back out of sight, but continuing to watch. 'What's she doing here?' she muttered to herself, peering at Cindy and the others.

'I've got to get him home.' Lisa looked down at Kai, who had flaked out from his day's exertions. 'I'll get an Uber.' She pulled out her phone, ready to make a booking. Dwayne came and sat beside her, still in a huff.

'Thanks for staying. I'll give you some money,' he said, still in a frustrated growl, digging inside his coat to pull out some cash.

'Nah, I'm good.' Lisa looked fed up, her patience with Dwayne running out.

'Look, I'll come to yours after, once we find her.' He lowered his tone, realising his manner was irking Lisa. He placed his hand on her leg, rubbing it tenderly, only to be stopped abruptly by Lisa pushing his hand away.

'Bro, you're bare confusing. Decide what you want this to be, innit.' She stood up and reached down to pick up Kai.

'Cindy. Was lovely to meet you. I hope they find her soon. Bye, Lena.' Lisa smiled sympathetically at a deflated, forlorn-looking Cindy, who was still nestled into Lena's shoulder. Lisa turned to Dwayne and gave him a reluctant hug. 'Call me later.' She let go, turning to Kai. 'Come on, Kai, wakey wakey. We're going home.' She shook Kai, who fidgeted, barely woken from his slumber.

Bree stood outside in the car park leaning on a wall, her long black leather coat open, revealing her bleached ripped jeans and black Che Guevara print T-shirt. She causally pretended to look at her phone screen until she saw Lisa step outside, dragging a sleepy Kai behind her.

'Aww, poor thing, he looks knackered.' Bree made a random comment towards Lisa, who looked over at her.

'Trust me, been a long day,' she replied. Bree made her way towards her, bending down to Kai.

'Hello, I'm Bree. What's your name, then?' Her long braids dangled down like doorway beads. Kai looked back at her, his face glum, still acclimatising to the chilly outside air.

'He's not in a sociable mood.' Lisa rolled her eyes, ruffling Kai's hair.

'Everything alright? I mean no one visits this place voluntarily.' Bree stood up, staring back at Lisa, who by now was more than ready to go home.

'Tell me about it,' Lisa replied. 'My friend's niece has gone missing. Think her baby father took her, on her birthday as well.' She continued checking her phone. 'Where's this Uber man?' She paced around with Kai clinging to her leg.

'Oh swear?' Bree acted surprised. 'God, hope they find her,' she continued, pretending to be concerned. 'Look, I can drop you; them cabs are long,' she offered. Lisa checked her phone again.

'Ok, if it's alright? I'll cancel. They're saying another twenty minutes.' Lisa made the decision, her mind firmly on just getting Kai home.

Bree smiled, stretching out her hand towards Kai, who recoiled grumpily, clinging tightly to his mum's leg. 'Ok, mummy's boy, I see.' She moved her hand away. 'Come on, I'm parked over here.' Bree pointed the way, striding forward, followed by Lisa and Kai.

* * *

The bland police reception room was still the uncomfortable location where Cindy, Dwayne and Lena sat waiting. Every minute that passed was unsettling for Cindy as the early evening drew into night. Dwayne sat forward, head bowed, his eyes looking towards his suede shoes. He rubbed his hands nervously. 'Wait till I get my hands on Leon; that fucker's dead,' he growled, only to be nudged in his ribs by Cindy. 'Oi, that's not helping.' She lifted her head from Lena's shoulder, shooting an infuriated look at her brother.

A female officer came from a room behind the reception desk, her black shirt and trousers tightly fitted on her hefty body and her shiny black boots squelching across the polished floor. 'Miss Harper.' She came towards Cindy, who stood up on hearing her name. 'What's happened? Don't tell me she's…' An air of panic set in as the officer neared. 'No, please give me a second.' The officer tried to calm down a worried Cindy.

'We've had a phone call from Leon's partner; she heard on the radio.' She held Cindy's hands, drawing breath. Her cheeks reddened, blue eyes showing a glint of optimism. 'She's provided us with an address, and our units are on their way now.' She smiled. 'Hopefully, we will find her safe and well.' Her tone was promising.

Lena put a supportive arm around Cindy. 'It will be ok.' She did her best to reassure her friend.

'So where is it? Come, we go,' Dwayne chipped in, unable to contain his anger. 'Well? Where is it?' he shouted angrily at the officer.

'Sir, I need you to calm down.' Her tone was now firm, keeping an amped-up Dwayne in check. 'Like I said, our units are on their way.' She was interrupted by the funky ringtone on Dwayne's new phone. He pulled it out of his pocket and saw Jorgi's name on the bright screen.

'What?' he answered angrily, walking away from Cindy and Lena. 'I can't come now,' he said aggressively, this time in a more hushed tone. 'I'll get back to you.' He looked back at Cindy, who was barely able to fight back the tears, her pretty face etched with worry lines.

* * *

Bree steered her car into the dimly lit car park outside Lisa's block of flats. 'This is fine,' Lisa said. 'Now to get sleeping beauty out and up to bed.' Bree cranked up the handbrake.

'Aww, bless him.' Her empathetic act continued. 'Hey, we should link up, swap numbers?' Bree put on an enthusiastic performance, attempting to convince Lisa that she needed a new friend, but Lisa, being streetwise, was not exactly reciprocating the energy.

'You know what, thanks for dropping us home, but I don't really know you,' she responded.

'I'm not a serial killer!' Bree laughed, her eyes staring wildly at Lisa like a deranged serial killer. 'I'm new around here; would be nice to have a friend.' She continued her charm offensive, taking her phone out and pushing it towards Lisa, who couldn't help but laugh.

'Ok, keen bean,' she relented, taking Bree's phone and tapping her number into it.

'We'll do something fun. I'll call you,' Bree continued.

'Alright then, goodnight, Miss Bree.' Lisa smiled, got out the car, and went to the back door, opening it to take out Kai. She dragged him out of his seat, straining to pick him up. 'See you later.' She slammed the door and walked to her flat as Bree watched on.

'Yep, Lisa, we are gonna be *good* friends,' Bree said aloud, watching as Lisa disappeared into her flat.

* * *

A frantic Leon kicked the bathroom door hard, each kick making a loud thudding noise. 'Cece, open the damn door. I'm not joking!' His face was screwed up, sweat running down his forehead.

Cece sat on the toilet shuddering, her hands clasped tightly over her ears. She was whimpering, jumping out of her skin each time Leon booted the door.

Leon was manic, darting back and forth from room to room, his locks dangling over his face. He kept rushing back to the window, peeking out through the curtains. He could see the flashing blue lights of a convoy winding its way through the grid-like streets below.

'Bloodclart!' He scampered back to the bathroom. 'Sweetie, come on, Daddy needs you to come out now.' His voice simmered to a calmer, caring, although sinister tone. 'Cee, open the door.' He tapped lightly with his dry knuckles, trying to coax Cece into unlocking the door as the sound of sirens got louder.

Cece trembled, sniffing up the tears. She finally stood up, taking a few unsure steps towards the door. The sound of light tapping on the other side continued as Leon's muffled voice vibrated through the wooden door. 'Come on, Cee. I ain't got time for this.' The volume of his voice rose again as the kicking of the door resumed, making Cece jump back and retreat.

Leon was frantic now. He knew he only had a small window of opportunity to wrest control back and grab Cece before the arrival of the police. He stepped back, flinging his dreadlocks away from his sweaty face, took a deep breath and ran, throwing a big kung fu-style boot to the door, which came away from the hinges.

A high-pitched shriek sounded as Cece backed away, cowering in the corner between the sink and the bath. Leon's face of rage suddenly altered into a calmer, kind expression. 'Now come on, darling, I told you to let me in.' He stepped in with his arms outstretched. His tall, lean figure cast a dark shadow across Cece's small frame.

'Open the door!' a loud sergeant major-type voice bellowed from behind the front door. 'Open up or we're coming in, Leon!' Leon flinched momentarily, holding his arms tightly around Cece, the whites of his sunken eyes barely visible behind his tangled locks.

Cece tried to stabilise her breathing, but she was strangled by fear. The sound of the door being smashed open was followed by a stampede of feet and barking voices as a flurry of men dressed in bulky riot gear bundled their way in, shining torches into the flat.

Chapter Nineteen

Numbers on the board

'Where's Sasha? She's not been here to see the kids lately.' Raz's wife fussed around the long glass dining table, placing bowls of cereal down for the kids, who sat fidgeting in their smart school uniforms.

Raz sat sipping on a mug of coffee, half dressed in a pair of shorts and a black vest, watching the large screen TV. He shrugged, eyes trained on the on-screen news. 'Have you heard from her?' she asked again, sitting down, taking a minute to scoff some toast. Chewing, she stared at Raz, awaiting his answer.

'No!' he responded, a veiled tone of frustration in his voice. 'Maybe she ran away with Ilyan.' He slammed his mug against the glass surface. His wife shuddered then quickly turned her attention to the kids. 'Ok, come on, hurry up or we'll be late.' She instantly got up from the table, taking a quick sip of tea, flustered by his reaction.

Raz's phone buzzed on the table. His daughter, a cute-faced child not much younger than the girl in the Mickey Mouse T-shirt, grabbed his phone and handed it to him. 'Daddy, here, it's for you.' She smiled, handing him the device. 'Thank you, bubba.' His face broke into a smile. He aimed a kiss at her, causing her to giggle, before he answered the call.

'Yes, hmm… Ok.' He cut the call and pinched the bridge of his nose, digesting whatever had been said, only to be interrupted by his children rushing to give him hugs. 'Bye, Daddy,' they said in unison, before running towards their waiting mother. 'Bye.' His wife grabbed their school bags and her keys and left, slamming the front door behind her. Raz sat alone, his head leaning against his fist, staring blankly at the TV.

* * *

Cindy lay on the sofa, snuggled up with Cece, stroking her head gently, while Cece watched Moana on her iPad. Dwayne's heavy footsteps could be heard as he came down the stairs and into the front room.

'You guys ok?' He came in wearing sliders, tight black shorts and a T-shirt.

'Yeah, we're fine.' Cindy looked up at him, giving a warm smile. Dwayne went into the kitchen. The sound of him clanking around, opening and closing cupboards, was a source of comfort for Cindy after the traumatic events with Leon.

'So, when you going back to work?' Dwayne reappeared, stuffing his mouth with a custard cream biscuit.

'Hmm, dunno. Andersen's cool, no rush,' she replied, turning her attention back to Cece.

'Wanted to ask.' He paused, giving himself time to swallow. 'Lisa asked if I would look after Kai tonight. Was thinking he could sleep over?' He popped another biscuit into his mouth, crunching down as he waited for Cindy's answer.

'Yes! Kai can come; we can play!' Cece answered.

'You turn babysitter now?' Cindy quipped sarcastically, looking Dwayne up and down, slightly bemused.

'Well, she wants to have a night off and she was supportive…' Dwayne continued to plead Lisa's case.

'Alright, I get it. Wow!' Cindy rolled her eyes. 'I'm having a night off too,' she confirmed, getting up from her comfy position on the sofa, her baggy grey tracksuit crumpled.

Cindy's attractive features reflected a weariness, the strain of Cece's abduction still affecting her. She yawned, her mouth gaping.

'And you're going where?' Dwayne looked down at her with an almost fatherly look. Cindy playfully pushed him to the side.

'None of your business.' She disappeared into the kitchen, leaving Dwayne hanging, the crumbs from the biscuits gathered in the corners of his mouth.

* * *

The deep blue chassis of an executive Mercedes E-Class looked out of place parked amongst the disused coaches, which were dated, rusted shells of their former selves, housed in a vast, metal-fenced mechanical graveyard.

Andersen's golden hair could be seen through the smoked tint of the driver's window. Inside, he sat calmly checking messages on his phone until disturbed by the glare from an oncoming vehicle. It drove into the yard and trundled across the uneven gravel surface.

The van, a dirty, dark brown transit, pulled up slowly next to his car. The words 'Lunge Ltd' on the side door could barely be made out beneath the grime. Andersen put his phone between his legs and pressed a button which slid down his window. He saw Raz do the same, rolling down his window.

'Kept me waiting,' Andersen grumbled, leaning his elbow out onto the door frame. His silver cufflinks twinkled under the night sky. 'The kids?' he asked, in his business tone, direct, dry and straight to the point.

Raz stared back at him, his gaunt face grizzled by fresh salt and pepper stubble, which he scratched rapidly, musing on Andersen's question. 'Where are they?' an agitated Andersen repeated.

'Don't panic. They've gone, out of the way.' His deep Romanian growl was barely audible, and he wiped his nose with the sleeve of his leather jacket. Andersen rested back, his eyes staring skywards. 'My friend, we need to bring more. The clients are waiting…' Raz sniffed up a hog of phlegm and spat it out onto the ground.

'You got to be joking right?' Andersen's Dutch accent came to the fore, hinting at his raised temper. 'No more! Not while one of your crazy men is wanted for the murder of a child, dammit!' He wiped his hand over his mouth to restrain his anger. 'We lie low until this mess is cleaned up,' he said more softly, giving Raz a side-eye stare before sliding the window back up and accelerating away. The thick tyres spun against the broken concrete. Raz slumped back in his seat, tilting his head to watch Andersen's car disappear into the night through his dusty wing mirror.

* * *

Dwayne stood outside the red door of Lisa's flat. He zipped up his black bomber jacket against the nip of the evening cool. Lisa opened the door. She was obviously rushing to get everything together, dressed up in a shimmery black blouse with tight stretch leather pants, her red hair curled and flicked, much to Dwayne's surprise.

'Jeez! Look at you.' A wide smile appeared on his face. 'What's his name?' he asked, his curiosity leaking from his mouth.

'It's a *her* actually.' She poked her tongue out at him.

Dwayne stepped in bravely, pulling her towards him. 'Hmm, you smell wicked as well.' He looked down at her, his eyes lusting towards her cleavage.

'Kai!' Lisa shouted, pushing him away, then bending down to pick up Kai's rucksack and shoving it into Dwayne's midriff. Kai came running through the hallway. 'Yes, Mummy,' his little voice shouted back. 'Here's your date for the night,' she said with a laugh as Kai held Dwayne's hand. 'Have fun!' Lisa continued to tease.

While Dwayne said his goodbyes at the door, Bree slowly drove towards the flats. She watched on, holding her phone out in front of her and recording Dwayne, while slowing the car to a halt. Bree watched on curiously through the screen of her phone as he and Kai walked away from the flat and got into a waiting cab. 'Who are you?' she whispered to herself, stopping the recording. She waited until the cab drove away before driving into the car park outside the row of flats.

Bree called Lisa, putting the volume on speaker. The ringtone rang loudly for a few seconds before Lisa's voice came through. 'You here?' she asked, sounding flustered. 'Yes, babe, I'm outside!' Bree faked an excited girlfriend ready to party before cutting the call, her facial expression switching back to deadpan, her black lipstick reflecting her intention.

* * *

The sound of laughter from Dwayne, Cece and Kai could be heard coming from the front room as Cindy stepped elegantly down the stairs, her red strapped high heels sinking softly into the carpet on her descent. She looked stunning. Her fitted black dress draped her body, a glimpse of gleaming brown leg revealed through a slit on the side.

Her feathered hair framed her gorgeous cheekbones. She opened the door to the front room to see all three of them under a duvet on the floor watching *The Incredibles* on the large television screen. 'Glad to see you all having fun.' She gave a warm smile at seeing Dwayne sandwiched in the middle. 'Wow, you are so pretty, Mum.' Cece turned to admire Cindy.

Cindy knelt to plant a kiss on Cece's forehead. 'My ride is here. Be good.' She stood up, checking her phone. 'Don't stay up too late,' she warned before grabbing her clutch bag and heading out. 'Laters, sis,' Dwayne bellowed, stretching his big arm and offering a tired wave.

The scene was ironic—Cindy looking glamourous, standing in her finery in the small, corrugated metal box of a lift which stank of piss, old cigarettes and cheap disinfectant which did nothing to mask the rank odour. She squirted some perfume onto her neck as the squeaky door retracted, allowing her to step out into the cool night air.

A sleek black BMW 5 Series stood out majestically amongst the crumbling concrete blocks which towered over it, the tints of the orange streetlights reflecting off the glossy roof. Cindy stepped confidently towards the vehicle. The driver opened the door and stepped out wearing a black suit, smart and official, except for his smile, which warmly welcomed her as she walked closer.

'Good evening. Allow me,' he said and efficiently opened the back passenger door. Cindy bent down to peer in and saw Dietmar sitting relaxed with his leg crossed, as always, his blonde hair combed back perfectly. He wore a black suit with a black shirt and shiny leather shoes.

'Hiya!' Cindy could hardly contain herself, blurting out her greeting nervously.

'Hiya,' Dietmar responded, using the same phrase with a polite little wave. He smiled. 'Get in,' he said, beckoning her.

Cindy sat in the cushioned leather seat, the butterflies in her stomach misbehaving. A fusion of her sweet perfume and Dietmar's sharp, fresh fragrance hung in the air.

They were both quiet. Cindy felt slightly awkward, trying to stay composed, but felt the need to break the ice. 'So, where are we going?' Her eyes twinkled as she turned to him. He turned to face her, those blue eyes mesmerising her, just like the first time she saw them.

'I told you last time, dinner in an intimate setting.' He smiled back at her, placing his hand on hers confidently, an act of reassurance which Cindy needed. It helped to settle her nerves but made her blush. She had never expected to feel this way in his presence. He was young and handsome and had an air of confidence that Cindy found comforting.

* * *

A packed dance floor energetically swayed and gyrated in time with the thumping bass and melodies of Afrobeat's. Bree held Lisa from behind, playfully pretending to spank her bum. They sang along to Burna Boy's latest hit. 'Yeah, yeah, yeah,' their voices screamed in unison. They were enjoying themselves like two excited teenagers, downing shots of tequila and raising their hands in the air.

Finally, they made their way back to a booth, laughing and out of breath. 'Jeez, you can dance, girl.' Lisa took her seat, huffing and puffing.

'You too,' Bree responded, dabbing her forehead with a tissue. 'I need a water; can't drive like this.' Bree signalled to a member of the bar staff who was clearing the table next to them.

'Can I get a bottle of water and another shot of tequila…'

Lisa interrupted. 'No! No more for me, thanks. I'm already feeling quite waved.'

'Ok, two waters,' Bree instructed the barman.

Lisa checked her face on her phone, fixing her hair. 'State of me! I ain't done this for a long time.' She applied some lip gloss.

'It's good to let your hair down,' Bree encouraged, sitting back on the black velvet seat, her tight white-and-blue-patterned top accentuating her breasts, which her long braids dangled over.

'I thought we were going for a quiet drink,' Lisa slurred, laughing, still preening her red hair as the barman brought over the bottles of water. 'Thanks.' She grabbed a bottle, twisted the cap and guzzled down a large mouthful. 'Ahh, needed that.'

Bree had moved closer to Lisa; the boom of the music meant they had to cosy up on the soft cushioned seats to have a conversation without shouting.

'I saw a guy leaving your flat when I came to pick you up… Is that Kai's dad?' Bree looked directly at Lisa, searchingly. Lisa began to laugh.

'No, he's just a friend, kinda,' she responded with a cheeky smile.

'What does that mean?' Bree raised her eyebrow. 'Tell me more.' She leant forward eagerly.

Lisa, still more than tipsy, broke into a laugh. 'I'm just saying, innit.' She became bashful momentarily, glancing over towards the dance floor, gathering herself. 'I mean Dwayne, he's an old friend,' she slurred.

'So, his name is Dwayne?'

'Yeah, Cindy's brother. Our kids go to the same school.' Bree took another mouthful of water, intrigued by the information.

'Anyway, what time is it?' Lisa quickly changed the subject, closing off the potential of further interrogation from Bree.

'It's nearly twelve. Shall we get out of here?' Bree realised she could push no further, but the names of Dwayne and Cindy were locked into her memory bank.

* * *

A female pianist sat at a white grand piano, daintily tickling the ivories, on a white marble plinth above the handful of diners who sat in the exquisitely decorated dining room of a high-class hotel. Cindy sat nervously, nibbling on fancy hors d'oeuvres. 'Hmm, I think this one is smoked salmon.' She chewed slowly, enjoying the taste. Dietmar bit into his, nodding in acknowledgement as the taste kicked in.

'So, do you come here often?' Cindy looked around at the splendour. She chuckled to herself. 'Can't believe I said that.' She covered her mouth, stifling her laughter. Dietmar saw the humour in her comment; a broad smile emerged on his face.

'No, but this is a special occasion,' he said calmly, raising a glass of red wine towards her.

After the meal, they sat talking. Cindy spent most of the time giggling like a schoolgirl; she was enjoying every moment of the experience. It had been a very long time since she had allowed herself to indulge in male company.

'I grew up in Berlin, then spent some time in Holland.' Dietmar pushed back his immaculate blonde hair while sharing his backstory with Cindy.

'Oh, my friend at work is from Berlin too!' she squealed, the wine beginning to kick in as the evening drew on.

'It's how I met Andersen, and then I met you.' He smiled again, boldly touching her hand. Cindy looked down, blushing, reciprocating. The moment felt right.

'So we owe Andersen?' she joked. Dietmar nodded his head, laughing.

'Ya, I owe him,' he concurred.

* * *

Bree switched on the engine after seeing a tipsy Lisa enter her flat safely. She picked up her mobile and made a call, putting it on speaker. The ringing continued for several seconds before someone could be heard shuffling around after picking up. 'Nolan,' the groggy voice answered.

'It's me. I might have a lead on that shooting.' Bree's intoxication had dissipated. She was clear-minded, much more so than the craggy-voiced Darren Nolan, who stumbled around coughing.

'Bloody hell, do you ever stop?' he asked, much to Bree's amusement.

'Brush your teeth and meet me in twenty.' She cut the call and put the phone between her legs.

Bree flipped down the interior visor, which had a small, square mirror. She dug in her bag and pulled out a small packet of wipes. She used one to wipe the make-up off her face, getting rid of the black lipstick and dark eye shadow. She slid the window down and tossed the damp rag onto the tarmac before reversing out of the car park.

* * *

Lena was sitting up in bed, her shoulder-length blonde hair tied into two pigtail plaits. The glare from her large iPad was reflected by her glasses, which framed her pale face as she sat engrossed, watching an episode of *Bridgeton* on Netflix.

The doorbell rang once to begin with, which shocked her out of her trance. She pressed the screen, pausing the show, listening intently, her eyes searching. Again, the doorbell rang but now multiple times, making her finally jump out of bed. She grabbed her black silk dressing gown to cover her white nightie, which was covered in pink Hello Kitty logos.

'Ok, I'm coming,' she called breathlessly, her bare feet prancing across the pine-tiled floor like a contemporary dancer. She looked at a small security screen and could make out the image of a man resembling Andersen standing outside. She picked up the handset. 'Hello,' she gasped, her heart beating fast, surprised by his late-night visit.

Andersen stepped into the room. Lena had left the front door slightly ajar so he could let himself in. She stood, arms folded, a few feet away from the door. Still dressed in his business suit,

Andersen paced up and down the spacious mirrored hallway lined with tall house plants in blue mosaic pots.

'Need you to keep Dietmar away from Cindy,' he ordered, raking his fingers through his hair. For the first time, his body language showed anxiety.

'Dietmar? Cindy? What do you mean?'

Andersen looked up at her, raising his head. 'I mean they're dating, getting too close,' he said, aggrieved. He walked past her brusquely towards the open plan kitchen, the row of motion spotlights in the ceiling activating as he walked into the room.

Lena leant on the kitchen counter holding a cup of coffee, almost in too much disbelief to drink. 'She told me about a date, but Dietmar?' She shook her head, her two little plaits swaying.

'I suggest you get in touch with him,' Andersen groaned, seated at a circular glass table on a chrome chair from which his blazer hung. He leant forward, both elbows on the table, the beginnings of a twelve o'clock shadow on his chin. Deep worry lines were engraved across his forehead.

Lena put her cup down. She took her glasses off, rubbed her eyes and took a deep breath. 'I haven't spoken to him since...' She paused. 'Well, you know,' she continued, her voice diminishing to a whisper as she recalled whatever memory her last meeting with Dietmar evoked.

'Maybe I can speak to Cindy?' she asked, dragging an empty chair and sitting opposite Andersen.

'No!' His ice blue eyes stared wildly at her, the hostility in his voice a warning. Lena recoiled, putting her glasses back onto her face slowly. She surrendered.

'Ok, I'll try… But you know Dietmar.'

It was strange seeing Andersen rattled. He was usually calm and collected in any situation, but as Lena watched him slurp down the last of his coffee, she could see his mask slipping a few inches as he rubbed his weary face. 'Ok, I'm going.' He got up, grabbing his jacket. 'Goodnight.' He kissed the top of her head, breezing past and back down the corridor, leaving Lena in the backdraft of his Tom Ford fragrance.

Chapter Twenty

This can't be life

The sun shone brightly like the yolk of an egg against the clear blue sky. The aqua-coloured sea reflected the bright sheen. In the distance, speedboats glided across the surface against the backdrop of rugged mountains as the calm ripple of waves washed onto the shore.

Footprints in the sand led to a woman sitting alone, staring into the distance. Her peroxided hair flowed down her back, her dark roots exposed. As the breeze blew it, parts of a rosary tattoo were revealed on her tanned back.

A straw beach bag with a bottle of water protruding from the top lay next to a copy of *The Art of War* by Sun Tzu and an unopened packet of cigarettes. The woman held a large-screen mobile phone, which she fiddled with for a few seconds, scrolling through some pictures. Images of sunsets and waves crashing against rocks and a few silhouetted profile selfies against different landscaped backdrops.

Her long, tanned fingers and freshly manicured nails with deep plum nail varnish slid each picture slowly across the screen, only stopping when the image of Dwayne sleeping in bed appeared. She paused on that picture, removing her large sunglasses and putting them to the side on the sand.

She enlarged the image, staring at it longingly. Above the sounds of the waves she could be heard sniffing. A teardrop blotted the screen, the liquid running down the glass across Dwayne's peaceful face. She reached for the packet of cigarettes, placing the phone in her lap.

She ripped the plastic packaging, opened the box and took off the protective foil, revealing the stack of pale orange filter-tipped sticks. She pulled one halfway out then stopped. She swiped the screen again. The next image revealed an ultrasound scan with the shape of a baby. She screwed up the packet of cigarettes and threw it towards the sea. A whimpering cry could be heard, along with snivelling. Her two fingers pressed tenderly against the image for a few seconds.

She stood up and packed her belongings back into the straw bag, except her sunglasses, which she placed back on her face, covering her teary eyes, the dried stains of her tears still evident on her cheeks. As she turned to walk away, her red bikini allowed a small, rounded baby bump to bulge out from her feline figure. She touched it tenderly with the palm of her hand, caressing her belly slowly as she began her journey across the golden sand.

Chapter Twenty-One

Sleep to dream

Cindy commanded attention in the monthly sales and reporting presentation; her aura was different after all the tension of the previous weeks. She seemed confident, assured and happy standing in front of a full room of suits including Andersen and Lena, who exchanged awkward looks across the large table during Cindy's perky, almost weather girl, report analysis.

After the meeting, the room emptied, leaving only Andersen, Lena and Cindy, who began to clear away sheets of paper and pens. 'How did I do?' She looked up at Andersen, who was still seated, making some notes on his tablet. As usual, he was dressed casually smart in a white open-necked shirt with a cream waistcoat. 'Very well,' he responded, not looking up from his device.

Lena gave her a silent thumbs up before darting out of the room. 'Is there anything else…?' Cindy asked, sensing the normally positive feedback from Andersen was missing. She stood dutifully, clutching the paperwork to her chest, her smile fading every second. Andersen ignored her, staying silent.

He pushed his chair back and stood up, picking up his tablet from the table and finally looking at Cindy. 'Nope.' He offered a protracted smile, his blue eyes lacking their usual sparkle. He quickly left the room, leaving Cindy alone with her thoughts—a mixture of confusion and disappointment at his response.

About twenty minutes after the meeting, Cindy sat alone in the canteen playing with her bowl of Caesar salad with a see-through plastic fork. Her mind was consumed by what had just happened in the meeting room and also her date night with Dietmar. Lena joined her, her striking figure accentuated by a slick black two-piece business suit and her high heels elevating her already towering height.

'Hey, why didn't you call me?' She sat down, holding a tray with a brown seeded bap and a bottle of green healthy juice.

'Sorry, just needed a few minutes. Is Andersen ok?'

Lena fixed her black-framed glasses. 'I think so. Why?'

'Dunno, he just seemed distracted.'

Cindy managed to stuff a mouthful of assorted green leaves into her mouth. Lena looked down, picking up her bap. 'He's a businessman; they are always distracted,' she reassured her. 'Anyway, no work talk on lunch. Tell me about your date.' Lena cleverly changed the direction of the conversation, her eyes widening with anticipation, waiting for Cindy to spill.

A smile crept across Cindy's face as she chewed slowly, recollecting. 'It was so good,' she gushed, swallowing quickly so she could talk. 'He was a gentleman,' she continued.

'He? What's his name?' Lena butted in. 'Give me that at least!' She matched Cindy's enthusiasm.

'Well, let's just call him Mr D.' Cindy winked at Lena coyly, reluctant to share too many details, much to Lena's disappointment.

PAPER TRAIL

* * *

Bree's face was a picture of concentration as she stared intently at the computer screen, her cheek bulging from a large lollipop wedged into her mouth. She made frequent sucking noises as she clicked through file after file. Darren Nolan strode into the office, his paunch obvious as the buttons on his white shirt barely held. He wore a black suit, tie loosened, and carried in a brown McDonald's takeaway bag.

'Still at it?' he asked, slumping into a seat opposite her.

'Yeah…' a focused Bree answered, not taking her eyes off the screen but taking the bright red lolly from her mouth and pointing it at Nolan.

'So, I've been through the electoral register four times. The only Cindy I can find is a …' she leant forward, checking, 'Harper. Cindy Harper, 72 Gordon House on Kingfisher Estate.' She leant back, slurping the lolly back into her mouth.

Nolan bit into a large burger and stuffed some chips into his mouth, then spoke with a full gob. 'Must be her then.' His muffled comment gave Bree her confirmation.

'Yeah, I swear her door number was 72.' She tapped the lolly against her teeth.

'Right, let's see who Cindy Harper is then.' She tapped on the keyboard eagerly.

'Chip?' Nolan thrust the small red pouch of French fries towards her. Bree shook her head, too engrossed in her search to entertain fast food. 'Was she alone when you did door to door?'

Again, Nolan swayed her concentration, munching down on his burger and wiping his mouth with a white serviette.

'She was, but I know this Dwayne dude is her brother.' She sat back, crunching down on the remainder of her lolly. 'She's got nada. No socials, no online profile at all.' She sounded defeated, her teeth grinding down the remains of her sweet.

'Let's check him then.' Nolan put his burger down and flipped up his laptop. 'Dwayne, you said?' he asked rhetorically, tapping the keyboard and adjusting his silver-rimmed spectacles as he scrutinised the screen.

After a few seconds, he stood up, scooping up the laptop and making his way around the desk to Bree. 'Is that the *dude?*' He mocked Bree's choice of words while spinning the screen towards her. It showed an image of a slightly younger Dwayne's mugshot.

'Fuck yes! That's him.' Bree's eyes lit up at seeing Dwayne's face staring back at her.

'He's got a record; done time.' Nolan handed her the laptop. 'Possession, robbery… assault.' Bree smiled, poking her red-coloured tongue out as she looked up at Nolan.

'One of the neighbours gave a statement saying there was a fight before the shooting.' She stood up excitedly, still reading the information on the laptop and walking around the table to Nolan, who by now had sat back down and was tucking into his burger again.

'We need to get the neighbour to ID him.' She put the laptop down on Nolan's desk, shoving aside his meal.

'Tread carefully,' a wise-sounding Nolan warned her, lowering his specs and eyeballing her. Bree tilted her head, frowning at Nolan.

'I always do.' She smirked as she stared back at Dwayne's face on the screen.

* * *

The usual mixed gaggle of parents stood chatting outside the school gates, awaiting the inevitable horde of excited kids streaming out of the classrooms. Dwayne stood beside Lisa, hands tucked into his Nike tracksuit pockets, shivering in the late autumn chill. Lisa stood impatiently waiting and staring ahead. Her red hair, tied back into a tight ponytail, dangled on her tight shiny black puffer jacket, which was zipped up tightly so the hood circled her head.

'How was your date night?' Dwayne asked, reluctant to hear her answer.

'Who said it was a date night?'

Dwayne stood rigid, nodding his head, trying not to show any emotion. 'So…' He kept fishing.

'It was a girl,' Lisa responded, staring up at Dwayne, holding back her laughter at watching his reaction as he digested her statement.

'Seen, it's like dat.' He shrugged, just as the first set of kids began to appear from the building. Lisa chuckled to herself quietly.

The usual walk towards the park was silent apart from the sound of Cece and Kai squabbling over the events of their school day. The skies had turned a dense charcoal colour, signalling the threat of rain.

'My cousin's nine night tomorrow,' Lisa casually mentioned, her black leather boots rustling amongst the brown leaves which swept across the pavement. 'You coming?' she asked, more in hope than anything else.

Dwayne contemplated for a few seconds, keeping his eyes on Cece, taking his time before answering. 'Can't,' he finally responded. 'Working.' His answers were curt on purpose.

'Cool... it's all good,' Lisa replied, but with a hint of disappointment in her voice, not knowing the real reason Dwayne had to swerve the invitation.

She turned back to face him. 'You know what? You're moving funny.' She pointed her finger in his face. 'One minute you wanna hug me up; next minute you don't even wanna support me when I need you to,' she ranted.

Dwayne stopped dead in his tracks, shocked by Lisa's outburst. 'Come on, Kai.' Lisa commandeered Kai, stomping off across the park.

'Wait, hold up!' Dwayne tried, but Lisa kept walking, ignoring his call.

'Bye, Kai,' Cece called, waving to her friend, then skipped over to Dwayne. 'Uncle, can I get some sweets?' She held his hand. 'Come on, let's go shop.' She pulled him out of his funk as he watched Lisa trudge away in the distance.

* * *

The end of the working day edged closer. Cindy sat at her desk finishing up some emails. She could hear the hum of excitement from the other workers gearing up to leave and saw them walking past the glass partition of her office.

As always, Cindy made sure she stayed focused on completing her work before getting ready to leave. It had been a strange day; she was still a little confused by Andersen's behaviour earlier but tried to put it to the back of her mind.

Before leaving, Cindy clicked on the website for The Hive, the new housing complex she had visited with Cece. She clicked through the gallery, checking out the pictures. She gazed fancifully, knowing that soon this could be her reality. A far cry from the crumbling towers of Kingfisher. She checked the information section. 'Deposits from £25 000' it read. Cindy rested back in her chair, mulling it over.

A knock on her door interrupted her flow of thought. She turned to see Andersen staring through the clear glass. She smiled, beckoning him in. Andersen stepped in, holding his overcoat and leather laptop case in his hand. 'Just wanted to have a quick chat before you go.' He entered, closing the door behind him and checking that no one else was close by.

'Sure, what is it?' Cindy took a deep breath, locking her screen, then turning to face a standing Andersen.

'Good one today, thank you,' he opened. Cindy let out a sigh of relief.

'Thank you, I was wondering…' She was interrupted by a conflicted-sounding Andersen.

'That other thing,' he said quietly, his demeanour shifting. He became uncomfortable but looked directly at Cindy. 'We need to put it on hold for a while.'

'Ok.' Cindy's quick-fire response was high-pitched, a mixture of surprise and obedience. Her eyes widened along with her smile, which was a disguised grimace.

'I'll let you know when things change.' He half-smiled before turning away to exit the room.

'Ok, see you tomorrow.' Cindy's perky tone masked her disappointment; she was relying on the financial bonus to help her get the house of her dreams. She turned back to her screen and unlocked it, revealing the images of The Hive again. She puffed out her cheeks, slumping back into the chair, staring at the computer screen.

Chapter Twenty-Two

I'm working

Dwayne placed the quilt gently over a knocked-out Cece, who was silently in the land of nod. He bent over, kissing her tenderly on the forehead. His grey sweat shorts revealed the raw scar on his thigh from his fight with L Boi.

The sound of the front door slamming alerted him as he tiptoed out of the room. Cindy had arrived back from work; she was later than usual, but it was still early evening. Dwayne descended the stairs to greet his tired-looking sister. 'You alright?' he asked, staring down at Cindy, who removed her black heels and overcoat.

'Shit day,' she responded, sounding despondent.

'Well, you don't need to cook. Miss Cece wanted Chinese, so there's takeaway.' He tried to cheer her up, but Cindy stomped into the kitchen without a word. 'Ok then, gonna shower, got work,' he shouted, retreating up the stairs and out of Cindy's way.

* * *

Cindy sat at the table staring blankly out of the window towards the brutalist blocks opposite her balcony. She had hardly touched her noodles and was, instead, in deep thought, distracted only by Dwayne's entrance into the room, preceded by his strong, dense, woody musk.

'Sis, what's up?' He strode forward, rubbing lotion into his hands, now fully dressed in his usual black hoodie and jeans.

'What do you *actually* do?' She turned and looked at him; her normally attractive face was dour. 'I mean you leave at night, don't come back for days.' She shrugged, still rankled by her earlier interaction with Andersen.

'I'm a courier,' Dwayne answered, sitting down to put on his trainers.

'Courier? You mean like Deliveroo?' Cindy asked, intrigued, stretching out and putting her feet up on a chair. Dwayne cracked up laughing.

'Deliveroo! Nah, not even.' He stuffed his foot into one of his training shoes.

Cindy continued to stare blankly at him, staying silent for a few seconds. 'Elaborate then.' She jutted out her hand, palm upturned. This caused his laughter to dissipate. He began to tie his laces, looking up towards Cindy, who still had her arm projected outwards.

'Jeez, man, must have been a really shit day at the office.' He stuffed the next foot into the other trainer. 'Serious, sis?'

'As cancer,' she answered, her expression unfailing, waiting for him to reply.

'I have to go.' He stood up, fixing himself.

'I bet. Go on, then, Mr Courier.' She waved him away.

Dwayne stood imposingly in front of her. 'Spit it out then, I know suttin's up.'

'You're running around all night, new clothes, new phone,' she moaned.

Dwayne shook his head, turning away. 'Ain't got time for this.' He started to walk towards the hallway.

'Nah, you never got time, Dwayne.' Cindy spat out her feelings, causing Dwayne to turn back to face her.

'Ok, you've obviously got an itch to scratch, so let's have it,' he responded, still with a half-smile on his face, trying not to take on Cindy's mood.

Cindy turned her face away again, staring out towards the dark, towered landscape of Kingfisher. 'I hate it round here,' she said, still looking out into the late evening skies. 'I've busted my arse for eight years and I'm still stuck in this place.' Her gaze reverted to Dwayne, who cut a confused figure.

He rubbed his chin, nestling his fingers in his beard. 'So…?'

'So you come and go as you please, cut on the leg, new phone, clothes, and yet you're just a courier?' Cindy was fed up, the news from Andersen still simmering beneath the surface. 'Don't take me for a fool.' Her normally happy-focused psyche had been punctured.

Dwayne walked across the room to the balcony. He opened the door and stepped outside. 'Need some air, man,' he mumbled, as Cindy huffed, watching his movements before standing up and following him out into the evening chill. Both stared ahead, observing the separate blocks which were like jail bars which housed them away from the freedom of normality.

'I want more.' Cindy's voice was calmer as she and Dwayne leant on a black metal railing set into the brick wall. 'I know you're up to something. I know you, bro.' She nudged him in his ribs. Dwayne shook his head.

'Sis, the less you know the better, trust me,' he responded, still staring ahead, unable to look her in the eyes.

His mobile phone rang loudly, the funky melody breaking the awkwardness of their conversation. Dwayne removed the phone from his pocket and saw the name Jorgi flash up on the screen. 'Need to take this.' He put the phone to his ear, much to Cindy's disapproval. 'Yeah, I'm coming.' Dwayne clicked off the phone and placed it back in his pocket.

'Time to deliver is it, Mr Courier?' Another cheap-shot response from a disgruntled Cindy.

* * *

Bree and Darren Nolan sat in the car looking out towards the block on Kingfisher where Cindy lived. Nolan had just received a phone call and was listening intently while Bree tapped her silver-ringed fingers impatiently against the steering wheel.

'You sure it's him?' Nolan asked, unbuckling his seatbelt and turning towards Bree. 'Grand. Great work, Steve. Will touch base later.' He gave Bree a broad smile. 'They've got him!' he exclaimed.

Bree stared at him. 'Who?'

'Ilyan Damesceau, the stray hair found on the girl, detained in Germany.' He pushed his phone back into his inside pocket, beaming at Bree.

'Problem is…' Bree reserved her euphoria. She continued tapping her fingers on the steering wheel. 'We can't extradite him.' She offered a dry smile to Nolan.

'Surely the nature of this crime…' Nolan's lips covered his teeth, the smile disappearing on the realisation.

'We'll have to build the case and present it to the European courts.' She shrugged. Nolan rested back in his seat, the cogs in his mind turning. 'Anyway, remember what we are here for?' Bree fixed her braids into a ponytail, getting herself ready. At that moment, Jorgi's sleek silver Mercedes rolled in slowly, parking only a few metres away from where their car was stationed.

'Hold up.' Nolan slid down in his seat, peering over the dashboard. 'That car is far too nice for a Kingfisher resident,' he commented, as Bree raised her phone and began to take pictures of the car and the driver. 'Check that number plate,' she instructed Nolan, who acted immediately, taking his phone out. 'I'm calling it in,' he answered, as Bree zoomed in, taking a series of snaps of Jorgi.

* * *

'Let me show you something.' Cindy halted Dwayne's departure, stepping back into the front room.

'Sis, I got to go,' Dwayne protested, closing the back door and watching Cindy scrambling to her laptop bag.

'Just give me a second.' She pushed aside the half-full Chinese takeaway cartons, making space on her table for the device. She quickly flipped it open and began to type frantically, much to Dwayne's annoyance.

'Sis, another time, yeah.' He moved towards the hallway.

'Look!' She spun the laptop around. The screen displayed the website of The Hive.

'What's that?' Dwayne looked at the screen, stepping forward and squinting.

'That's our future. Me, you and Cece.' Cindy's desperate voice exuded hope. 'It's beautiful. I've been there with Cece, look.' She navigated through the gallery of pictures, capturing Dwayne's attention.

'Yeah, it's nice, but we can't afford that.' Dwayne slammed down the lid, moving away.

'No, we can… well, nearly… I've been saving,' Cindy pleaded. 'I just need a bit more.' She looked at Dwayne. 'Look, I know whatever you're doing is paying you well. It's obvious.' Her almond brown eyes stared expectantly at her brother.

A silence ensued until his mobile phone rang again. Dwayne answered, 'I'm coming!' He sounded agitated. 'Can we do this tomorrow?' He shrugged.

'No! Give *me* your time for once, bro.' Cindy got up from the table and walked towards him. 'I don't want you to end up like Ricky. I need you. Cece needs you. Invest your money… in us.' She cupped his bearded face with her pretty hands.

Dwayne shook his head. 'You don't understand, sis. This is deep. It's fucked.' He removed Cindy's hands from his face and tried to back away, but Cindy hugged his broad torso. Instinct told her that he was holding back. She felt the vibration of his phone kicking into her body.

'Got to go, sis.' He tried to peel himself away. 'We'll chat later,' he confirmed, but Cindy clung even more passionately.

'We can do this, bro.' Her voice was muffled as her face was pressed into his chest.

'I really have to go.' Dwayne released himself. He looked directly into her eyes. She could see the pain in his eyes, condemned.

The sound of heavy knocking on the door sparked them back to reality.

'Expecting anyone?' he asked.

'No, not at this time,' Cindy replied, looking up at him confused. 'Stay here.' Cindy patted his chest, then walked to the hallway towards the front door. She arrived and peered through the peephole.

'Shit,' she uttered under her breath, quickly backtracking to the front room. 'It's them police again. Go to the balcony,' she whispered, waving him away before tiptoeing back to the door. She checked over her shoulder, making sure Dwayne was out of sight, before opening the door to reveal Bree and Nolan standing in front of her.

'Ms Cindy Harper, have you got a minute?' Bree's expression was stern as she flashed her ID badge. Darren Nolan straightened his coat as they put on a united front, staring directly into her face.

Chapter Twenty-Three

A Childrens Story

Reflecting on Berlin.

A cacophony of screaming, shouting, grunting and arose from the melee in the Schmidt hallway. A terrified teenaged Lena stood shivering uncontrollably as tears streamed down her cheeks below her uncool, nerdy glasses.

Dietmar rushed past her, his white school shirt undone and flapping. He screamed wildly, holding a half-full whisky bottle aloft in his hand, and aimed a devastating blow to the back of the head of a man who was grappling with their mother, who was spread-eagled on her back at the bottom of the staircase. 'Mama!' Lena screamed on watching the shards of glass explode around the bodies. A loud groan, followed by a long retching sound, reverberated through the night.

Dietmar continued to grapple with the man, using all his strength to roll his large body off his mother, who lay motionless except for shallow breaths and a twitch from her bare foot. The man did his best to fight back against the smaller frame of Dietmar, whose blond hair dangled over his face. He used all his might to free his arms, still holding the remains of the broken bottle in his hands.

Lena managed to steer herself away to a phone which was hung on the wall. Her hands trembled as she picked up the receiver, watching on. Her fingers clumsily attempted to dial. Dietmar let out a roar, plunging the jagged spikes of the bottle into the chest of the man, who let out a long, monotone wheeze, succeeded by Lena's ear-piercing scream.

A temporary silence followed, apart from Dietmar's panting. He turned to face Lena, his white shirt and face splattered with blood. He stared demonically at Lena, dropping the piece of broken bottle on the wooden floor and sinking to his knees with exhaustion.

* * *

A solitary beep from the heart monitor punctured the silence every few seconds. Tubes and wires from various medical machines were attached to Lena's mother's body. She lay motionless, her head wrapped in white bandages, her face flopped to one side, covered by an oxygen mask which barely covered the red bruising on her face.

Andersen, his face ashen, comforted a young, sobbing Lena he could only watch on seeing the sight of his oldest university friend lifeless in front of him, flashbacks of their time together studying on campus and her introducing him to her best friend Frieda at the student bar incited a restrained smile. Lena clung to her mother's body, still traumatised by the terror she had witnessed. Andersen's wife, Frieda, came rushing into the room, clinging onto her coat and bag, her blonde hair tied into a ponytail that accentuated her sharp cheekbones and ice-blue eyes.

'How is she?' She dropped her things onto the floor, gently pulling Lena away from the bed. 'Darling, come with me,' she said, trying to peel her away from her stricken mother. 'And Dietmar?' She turned to Andersen. 'Police,' he uttered despondently.

Frieda touched his arm. 'Take her. Go get some coffee.' Andersen grumbled, the shock still buried in his eyes, but he nodded, put his arm around Lena and led her from the room.

* * *

Dietmar sat alone in a small cube of a room—bland grey walls and a solitary metal table on which stood a can of Coke. He was still in his blood-stained school shirt, with splashes of blood across his face as if an artist had flicked a paintbrush at him. He stared blankly ahead, with no expression of hurt or remorse. Instead, he yawned, stretching out his arms as though he was being inconvenienced.

Andersen sat comforting an emotional Lena in the family waiting area. She continually trembled; the fear still raw in her being. Frieda entered the room, her face reflecting the news she was about to deliver. She could barely speak; she just covered her mouth, making a gurgling sound as she choked back her emotions. Andersen hung his head, clutching Lena tightly, stifling her cries on his chest.

***

Years had passed since that traumatic incident. Dietmar had got off lightly. Andersen had ensured his lawyer friends submitted a watertight case of self-defence for the murder of his stepdad who was drunk and attempting to murder their mother. There had been years of abuse, but this time it was fatal.

Andersen and Frieda became their legal guardians until they reached young adulthood. Lena had never forgiven Dietmar, even though he had been trying to save their mother. As much as he tried to convince her he had done the only thing possible, it was all in vain. She blamed him for her trauma. They had lost both parents but gained stability living with Andersen and Frieda. Moving to Holland to complete their education afforded both of them the private school experience.

Dietmar became an introverted loner, distancing himself from the family and eventually falling in with petty drug gangs within the Dutch community. He never again spoke about his actions on that day; he internalised his emotions, which fractured his already withered relationship with his sister. Lena recovered enough to go on and finish university, completing her degree in business, integrating herself into her new family and helping Andersen and Frieda with their young daughters when she could.

When Andersen landed his executive role at Schuster and Klein, Lena was excited to follow him and move to London. Dietmar instead went back to Germany and disappeared into the dark underworld of Berlin, only contacting Andersen when he needed money, which a guilt-tripped Andersen would provide, his own demons still haunting him. After some years, Dietmar turned up in London, but he was a different person—he was more refined and seemed to have somehow thrived on his underworld experience in Europe. The only link to his troubled past was Andersen.

Chapter Twenty-Four

Pray for me

Dwayne made his way back to Sasha's place. It was early morning, 6:00 am, cold, dark and wet. It had been another long night of making drops to Raz's strange client base across London. Jorgi was different to Ilyan—more militant and serious—so this felt more like hard work to Dwayne now. As much as he hated it, at least Ilyan had an inkling of a personality, which made his nights bearable.

He walked down the silent corridor, the wet rubber soles of his trainers squelching against the tiled floor which led to the front door. He was holding a leather bag which contained his payment for a night's work. He could barely drag his feet the final few yards, his mind weighed down with the visit of Bree and Nolan asking Cindy about the fight with L Boi.

Luckily, Cindy had managed to deflect them enough to avoid any suspicion but only at the cost of Dwayne's revealing to her what had actually occurred that night and promising to help her raise the deposit for the new house.

This was an added layer to his already stressed thoughts. He pushed the key in and unlocked the door with a gaping yawn. As he walked in, he stepped on a white envelope which had been slid under the door. He bent to pick it up, after looking behind him to check for anyone lurking. He closed the door and locked it with both the key and the security chain.

He dropped the bag to the floor and began peeling back the flap of the envelope freshly stained with his trainer sole imprint, curious as to who would even know he was staying there. He ripped the rest of it open and pulled out a black-and-white ultra sound picture with the fuzzy image of a growing foetus. 'What's this?' He stared at the picture, baffled, rubbing his tired eyes. He flipped the picture over and saw some writing on the other side. 'Soon x' it read, with a heart shape.

Dwayne stood rooted to the spot, studying the picture, searching for some sort of clue as to who had delivered it and when. He kept flipping it front to back, taking heavy breaths until the penny dropped. 'Fuck!' he exclaimed on the realisation it could only be Sasha. He kicked the bag in frustration. 'Fuck sake!' His torment showed no signs of abating.

* * *

Cece sat in front of the TV, her eyes glued to the large colourful screen as she ate some toast. The loud sounds of a children's show blasted through the surround speakers. Cindy, still in her dressing gown and silk scarf covering her head, paced in and out of the kitchen with the phone to her ear. 'Yes, I'm happy to confirm that,' she spoke confidently. 'I'll email over the details this afternoon. Thank you so much.' She seemed pleased as she cut the phone.

'Excuse me, Miss Cece, turn that down please; you're not deaf.' She came into the front room and sat at the dining table, flipping up her laptop and navigating to The Hive website. Once again, she clicked through each picture in the gallery, scanning every detail, mentally interior designing each room.

She knew how close she was now to fulfilling her dream and no longer cared where the money from Dwayne came from. She glanced at Cece and afforded herself a satisfied smile. 'Shall we go out for lunch?' she asked, her eyes still fixed on the screen.

'Yes, Mummy! Can I have McDonalds?' Cece jumped up with a spurt of energy and ran over to hug Cindy.

'Ok, then.' Cindy squeezed her. 'Go to the bathroom and get yourself ready.' She shooed her away.

'Yes!' Cece punched the air with delight before running out of the room and up the stairs. Cindy glanced back at the screen with a satisfied smile.

* * *

Lisa sat alone in her front room. She dabbed her nose with a tissue, sniffing back the tears as she held a printed eulogy with a picture of a young, smiling L Boi. His real name, Lyall, was written in italics beside two angel symbols. She sniffed again. Her hand shook as she put the leaflet down, picked up her phone and unlocked it with her fingerprint.

The phone screen lit up as she accessed her contacts and scrolled down to Bree's name. She hesitated for a few seconds, then pressed the video call symbol. After a few seconds, an image of Bree appeared. She was sitting in a deep, foamy bubble bath, hair covered by a large sunflower-print shower cap, surrounded by flickering tea lights.

'Hiya, babe.' She waved to Lisa, her face covered with an avocado green face pack. Lisa choked out a laugh on seeing her. 'Sorry, Bree, I can call you back.' She wiped a tear from her eye, trying to mask her sorrow.

'No, babe, it's fine. What's up?' she asked, seeing the hurt in Lisa's expression.

'Was Lyall's funeral today.' Her voice cracked; it was barely a whisper, etched with pain.

'Shit, girl, I forgot.' Bree perked up. 'Listen, give me an hour, I'll come over.' She sat up, the foam bubbles protecting her modesty.

Lisa pushed back her red hair, nodding. 'Thank you.' She sniffed again before cutting the call.

* * *

Dwayne was on his hands and knees counting out and stacking his money. He kept the savings from his ill-gotten gains in neat piles in various shoe and trainer boxes. Amongst the notes was the polaroid picture of the ultrasound scan, which, after every count, he picked up and studied again before placing it down to the side and counting some more.

Finally, he sat with his back against the wall, staring at the wads of cash in front of him. He scratched his head. 'Fifteen bags exactly.' He breathed out a heavy sigh. 'Gotta go harder.'

He sounded despondent, even though he was sitting in front of a small fortune.

'Ten for Cindy.' He started to pick up the money and stuff it into the leather bag, only to be interrupted by the funky house ringtone of his phone. He stopped and grabbed it from the bed. 'Speak of the devil,' he huffed, seeing Cindy's name on the screen. He answered, 'Yes, sis, was just thinking about you.' He put it on speaker mode, continuing to scoop up the cash.

'What you doing?' She sounded as though she was in a crowded place, the chatter of voices around her.

'Just sorting that thing we spoke about; gonna pop round later,' he continued, stopping to pick up the ultrasound photo and stare vacantly again.

'Ok, we're in McDonalds. Be back soon. Bye!' Her perky voice cut off and the call went dead.

Dwayne sat mulling, his eyes flicking between the stuffed leather bag and the image of the grey, almost cloud-like foetus. 'Where are you, Sasha?' he asked rhetorically, flicking the picture to the other side and staring at the heart-shaped symbol written with the word 'Soon x'.

* * *

It was now early evening. The skies had darkened to almost black, with a dense mist hanging between the high-rise rooftops. It was cold, winter in its infancy. Andersen sat alone in darkness in the Orbit office. His chair was swivelled towards the large glass windows that gave him a panoramic view of the bleak city beneath him. He sipped on a large tumbler of whisky, grimacing as the liquid hit the back of his throat.

For once he looked rough, embittered, his shirt hanging unbuttoned. He scratched his chin, the stubble coarse like sandpaper, making a grating sound as his nails connected. The glare from his large Apple Mac screen silhouetted his profile. He turned to glance at the screen. 'Man captured for murder of young refugee girl in the UK' was the translation of the headline of an online article in a German newspaper; there was a clear mugshot of Ilyan. He turned away, taking another mouthful of whisky. He grunted before putting the glass to his slightly trembling lips and downing the rest.

Andersen sat in silence, still staring out of the window, the cogs of his mind turning as he processed his options. He leant back in his chair, cracking the bones of his hands. A high-pitched bell disturbed him from his thoughts. He grabbed his phone from the desk and stared at the screen. A text message glowed into his craggy face. 'On my way to Dietmar's wish me luck. Lena'. He read it, then grunted again, reaching for the bottle of whisky.

He unscrewed the top then drained the remainder of the liquid into his glass, breathing heavily through his nostrils—a wheeze which steamed up the glass. He tilted his head and drank the full amount before throwing the glass across the room, his inner frustrations finally shattering his iceberg persona like the glass of the tumbler which smashed across the floor.

* * *

Dwayne walked slowly towards the dreary blocks of Kingfisher. It was a nasty night, cold and dreary, with fine drizzle annoyingly sweeping across his face. He wore a black padded Stone Island jacket with the hood covering his head. He was in deep thought, with the leather bag of money slung over his shoulder. He stepped off the kerb, about to cross the road, when the headlights of a car blinded him; the roar of a revved engine got louder, accompanied by the screech of tyres.

Dwayne froze as the vehicle hurtled towards him. His reactions kicked in and he started to run, darting away as fast as his feet would take him. Adrenaline rushed through his body, although his legs turned to jelly. He glanced back to see whether he could recognise the car or the driver, but the LED headlights dazzled him.

Hauling the bag, he stumbled towards the Kingfisher car park, knowing that if he could make it past the old broken barrier, he could make it to the arches, which would see him disappear into the maze of blocks. His breathing got heavier. He sprinted with every sinew in his body, sensing the car nearing.

Too scared to turn for a second glance, he skidded suddenly, taking a sharp left and hurling himself over the barrier, twisting his ankle in the process. 'Arrgh, shit!' he yelped like a wounded dog, scrambling on his hands and knees, clutching the handles of the bag and dragging it into his clasp before getting to his feet and hobbling away as fast as he could.

The car skidded to a halt, inches from the broken barrier. The driver's door opened and a shadowy figure emerged dressed in dark clothing. His outline and build resembled Trevor, but it was hard to tell due to the fine misty drizzle which swept across the asphalt.

Dwayne stooped along the balcony, crouching down until he got to Cindy's. He banged heavily on the bottom of the door with his fist until Cindy opened it, wearing a silk dressing gown and smelling freshly bathed. She stared down at her brother, who crawled in, shoving her out of the way, the hood of his jacket covering his head.

'What now?' she asked.

'Just shut the door,' he growled back, finally collapsing onto the carpet and catching his breath.

Cece heard the commotion and came down the stairs bleary-eyed, wearing her pyjamas. 'What's up, Uncle Dwayne?' She stared down at him. 'Why are you on the floor? What's in the bag?' She stepped down and went to look into the bag.

'No, Cee, back to bed please,' a stern Cindy interjected.

'But, Mum, I wanna see…' she moaned, beginning to sulk.

'We'll go for milkshakes tomorrow, Cece, ok?' Dwayne caught his breath enough to convince Cece. She nodded, then turned and trudged back up the stairs.

They both waited until Cece was back in her room. Dwayne was lying flat on his back, hood still over his head.

'So why the dramatic entrance?' Cindy sat on the stairs, fluffy slippers on her feet.

'I swear someone just tried to kill me, run me over.' He finally sat up, pulling his hood down, his face wet from a combination of sweat and drizzle. He puffed out his cheeks, dragging his knees up to his chest and rubbing his ankle.

Cindy sat silently in suspense. She rubbed her nose vigorously, trying to compute. 'How deep is the shit you're in?' She shrugged, clearly fed up with her brother's antics.

'Sis, I told you, the less you know…'

'The better. Yeah, I get it.' She finished his sentence.

'That's yours.' He dragged the bag towards Cindy. 'Open it,' he continued, wiping his face, staring at her. She unzipped the bag, prising it open to see the stack of notes. Her eyes lit up.

'Jeez, bro!' was her only response.

'Told you I'm a courier. I deliver.' A smart retort from Dwayne, who grinned at her. 'Sort that deposit out fast!' He finally regained the energy to stand up, tentatively hopping on his good leg. Cindy also stood and engulfed him in a long, tight hug. The two embraced for a few minutes in silence.

'Thank you,' she whispered, squeezing him tighter. 'I've one more favour to ask.' She pulled away, ruffling his hair. 'Can you stay? Look after Cece for a few hours please?' Her eyes were glassed over with tears. Dwayne broke into a cheeky grin.

'Going to see lover boy, huh?' He tugged her chin playfully.

Cindy shied away, embarrassed. 'Allow me, innit.' She tried to mimic him.

'You two are funny.' The sound of Cece's voice came from the top of the stairs. She had been sitting there, watching through the banister and listening. Dwayne and Cindy looked up at her and in unison shouted, 'Cece, go to bed!' before bursting into laughter.

* * *

'I ain't had one of these for ages.' Lisa glanced up at an unimpressed Bree as she put the finishing touches to a perfectly rolled joint. 'My cuz. He deals, so he gave me a bud.' She grabbed a lighter and sparked it, lighting the cone-shaped spliff and taking a long, hard drag.

Bree stared, her inner police instincts agitating to say something, but instead, she bit her lip, 'Where's Kai?' She looked around the small but cosy room. Lisa stared back, handing the joint to Bree, who hesitated before taking it.

'My mum took him.' Lisa's eyes closed as the weed hit. She leant back on the sofa, fixing her hair into a ponytail. Bree took a small toot of the joint and passed it back to Lisa, who giggled.

'You afraid of the kush?' she asked, placing it back to her lips and taking another long pull.

Bree shuffled back into the seat. 'So today was rough, yeah?' She quickly changed the subject. Lisa nodded, taking another drag.

'Thing is feds ain't got a clue. I mean this is murder!' She shook her head regretfully. 'They don't care, just another dead black boy, innit.' She passed the joint back to Bree, who refused.

'Nah, I'm cool, and you're wrong. We are...' She coughed, realising she had to choose her words. She waved away the misty smoke that floated in the air around them. 'I mean... I'm sure the feds are doing what they can.' She tried her best to sound convincing.

Lisa cracked up laughing. 'What planet are you on?' She sat up, staring, wide-eyed, her high gradually kicking in. 'You're different. Not from the ends, are ya?' She flicked the flint of the lighter repeatedly, sparking a flame and continuing to tug on the joint.

Bree rested back, fixing her braids. 'I am from the ends. Colindale, innit.' She threw up a pretend gang sign with her hand, making both burst into laughter. She cleverly diffused the tension. 'Let me hit that again.' She stretched her hand out, taking the joint from Lisa.

* * *

The chime of an old-school doorbell rang loudly through the wide spaces of the large house occupied by Dietmar. He sauntered down the stairs, cigar in mouth, dressed in his signature black outfit, this time, a T-shirt, jeans and socks on his feet. He swept his blonde mane back away from his eyes as he walked across the white marble-tiled floor to the door.

'You're early,' he said, swinging open the large, black wooden door, but to his total surprise, he saw Lena standing in front of him. Her tall frame was covered by a black coat, her blonde hair nestling neatly on the fur collar. She fixed her glasses.

'Expecting someone else?' she asked with a nervous smile.

Dietmar's jaw dropped. So much so, the cigar teetered from the corner of his mouth.

'It's cold out here.' Lena shuffled her way forward, slowly initiating her entrance.

'Sorry, come in.' Dietmar took the cigar from his mouth, stepping aside.

Lena stepped into the lobby-like entrance, surveying the grandeur of her brother's house; she nodded her head, impressed with the layout. 'Nice place.' She gave her seal of approval.

After closing the door, Dietmar stood with his hands on his hips. 'What are you doing here, Lena?' he asked her directly, his immaculate persona now slightly ruffled.

'That's no way to greet your sister... especially after how long?' She looked at him, hands still shoved deep into her coat pockets.

'What do you want?' he replied, walking past her into the large, modern, open plan living room, a plume of blue cigar smoke trailing behind him.

Lena followed him in, her eyes widening on seeing how nice his home was. Dietmar plonked himself onto a black velvet sofa and crossed his legs. 'So, this is what drug money buys then?' she commented, taking off her coat and throwing it next to him on the sofa, revealing her pale, model-like frame. She was wearing a body-hugging vest top, a mini jeans skirt and knee-length black leather boots.

'So that's what child trafficking money looks like?' Dietmar responded. She turned towards him.

'That's fucking below the belt,' she said, jabbing her finger at him and scowling as she walked over to him. Dietmar rested back on the sofa, arms spread out, a smug grin creeping across his face.

'But true, dear sister.' He sucked on the cigar like a goldfish out of water sucking for air. 'How dare you come to my home to pass judgement,' Dietmar continued. 'I certainly didn't invite you.' His cold tone cut through Lena's being. She folded her arms, pacing around away from him.

'You haven't changed. All this...' She waved her arms at the spacious room and expensive contemporary furniture. 'It's just BS.' For once, Lena's happy disposition was punctured.

'I would offer you a drink but I'm expecting company shortly.' An unflinching Dietmar rose to his feet. 'I need to get ready. Let yourself out.' He calmly walked past her into the hallway. Lena fumed, scrunching up her face and taking a deep breath.

'Stop seeing Cindy!' she blurted, straight from her gut.

Dietmar stopped in his tracks, his socked feet skidding to a halt on the polished floor. 'Andersen sent you, didn't he?' He slowly swivelled around to face her, sweeping back his hair.

Lena cast her eyes down and shrugged. 'She don't need to be mixed up in...'

Dietmar walked right up to her, inches away from her face. Lena flinched as he neared. 'Mixed up in what?' he hissed; the smell of cigar layered on his breath. Lena's eyes rose slowly back up to look directly at her brother. Neither of them blinked until the chime of the doorbell interrupted their standoff.

On her way home, Lena sat alone on the backseat of a car. The windows around her steamed up because of the cold, misty night. She pulled the furry collar of her coat tightly around her neck, her pale face stern and her lips pursed. Only a blush of pink coloured her cheeks, which were streaked with tears. She pulled her phone out of her pocket and began to type a message to Andersen. 'That was horrible...' it read. She sniffed, pushing her glasses up onto her face and wiping away the tears, before sending the message.

***

Cindy walked elegantly across the peppercorn marble floor in the entrance of Dietmar's home. Her face was a picture of delight, her eyes wide, marvelling at the exquisite detail of the decorations. Dietmar, still dressed in his black T-shirt, jeans and socks, took her hand, guiding her into the main living area. His cool mask had not slipped, although the presence of his long-lost sister merely minutes earlier still lingered in his mind.

Cindy felt his allure more than ever as he removed her coat from behind her, peeling it away from her shoulders to reveal her black roll-neck sweater. He leant in, putting his face to the nape of her neck and inhaling her sweet fragrance. 'Delicious,' he whispered. Cindy giggled, turning around to face him, her eyes sparkling like jewels. 'Delicious?' she questioned as Dietmar threw her coat onto his velvet sofa. 'Yes, you smell delicious,' he countered, his sky-blue eyes gazing into hers.

'Make yourself comfortable. I'll be back.' He smiled. A sheen of sweat covered his forehead, the only sign of his awkward reunion moments earlier. He left the room, leaving Cindy alone to nose around. She walked tall in her heels, clinking across the floor, feeling as if she was floating on air. It felt as though everything was coming together in her life, finally.

Chapter Twenty-Five

Run, run

The image of Ilyan gleamed from the screen of an iPad, but this time the headline from the German news source was different. 'Child murderer found dead in his cell.' The silver-ringed fingers swiped the screen, rolling it down to read the small print, only to be interrupted by the crackle of a baby monitor. A small gurgle came through, lighting up the small screen to reveal a newborn about to burst into tears.

Sasha put the iPad down and stood up from her chair. She had changed her hair—the peroxide had grown out, replaced by her natural dark tresses which flowed freely down her back. She walked barefooted across a wooden floor into a bedroom in which stood a white cot filled with a few colourful cuddly toys. 'Hello, beautiful. Hungry, huh?' She bent down to pick up her daughter, a cute, beige-skinned baby with curly black hair. 'Come on, let's go get some milk.' She snuggled her into her chest. Sasha looked tired, the strain of being a new mum showing on her clear-skinned face.

She stood staring out of a large glass patio door, viewing the lush green rolling hills, an idyllic country landscape draped in a gentle mist. The baby was cradled into her arms, sucking hungrily on the teat of the bottle. She glanced down, her brown eyes admiring her child.

'Can't wait for you to meet your daddy.' She smiled. 'And I can't wait to meet him again, too,' she said hopefully, retreating to her chair. She sat down, resting back as the baby continued to drink from the bottle. She turned to the iPad, touching the screen to activate it; the bright image of Ilyan stared back at her.

* * *

'Fuck! How convenient. Our only suspect and possible witness dies in jail!' Bree slammed down her laptop and put her head in her hands, her fingers scratching away at her braided scalp.

'Calm down,' Nolan's deep, authoritative tone growled from across the desk. He looked down at her through his glasses which were perched on the tip of his nose. 'We'll have to open a new line of enquiry,' he huffed.

Bree's head slowly rose, her eyes meeting Nolan's. 'We have no new line…' She stopped mid-sentence, trying to bite her tongue. 'That poor little girl's life means nothing now. She gets no justice!' Her voice was now raised a few decibels.

Nolan stood up, his semi-creased shirt untucked. 'I think you need to calm down, go for a walk or something,' he ordered, his hands shooing her away. Bree got up from her chair, grabbing her black leather coat from the back of it.

'*He* might be dead, but there are others involved, I know it.' She shot her remark at no one in particular, although Nolan stood in front of her, his arm still locked into position, pointing her towards the door.

Bree stomped out, her chunky Doc Marten boots squelching against the tiled floor. She was furious. She hated to be defeated; it didn't sit well. She threw on her coat, then tapped a number into her mobile phone as she strode through the corridors of the station building. 'Any lead on that Mercedes yet?' she asked in a determined tone. 'Great, send me the address.' She clicked off the phone, continuing to march away, fastening the buttons of her coat.

* * *

Fits of giggles emanated from the bedroom upstairs. Raz's wife sat at the kitchen table, staring at a laptop screen, reading the story of Ilyan's death. She shook her head numerous times, disbelieving what she was seeing. 'Raz!' she called out, turning her head towards the stairs. She got no reply, only hearing him continuing to play with the children.

She got up from the table, taking the laptop with her, and made her way up the stairs on her sturdy, chunky legs. 'Have you seen this?' she said, stepping into the doorway, viewing Raz tickling both of his children as they rolled around on the bed, laughing and fighting him off.

'Time for bed now,' she interrupted with a stern, motherly tone. 'Did you hear me? Raz collapsed onto the bed out of breath, his thick torso between his kids, who flopped next to him.

'What do you want, woman?' he wheezed. She frowned, flipping the laptop around to show him the screen with the headline.

Raz sat up, catching his breath. 'Come on, kids, time to sleep now.' He gathered them both into his strong arms, kissing them on the cheeks. 'Bed, come on.' He playfully pushed them away before getting up and walking towards her, swiping the laptop from her hands and brushing past her. She slammed the door to the kids' room, then confronted him.

'Ilyan is dead. They said he's a child murderer,' she whispered through gritted teeth, following him as he went down the stairs.

'What do you want me to do?' Raz snarled, making his way into the kitchen.

'Ilyan was your friend. How can this happen?'

Raz's eyes stared back at her coldly with an intense fury. He slammed down the laptop. 'Ilyan was a soldier; he knew the rules of war.' He clenched his fists, trying to suppress his anger.

His wife swept back her curly black hair. She sniffed up the last comment, trying to digest his harsh words. 'And Sasha? Is she the same?' she asked bravely.

Raz scratched the thick hair on his chest. 'Sasha… is a survivor,' he muttered, which didn't satisfy his wife.

'What does that even mean?' Her hands trembled, instinct tugging at her gut. She shook her head repeatedly. 'Where is she? Raz, just tell me.' She reached out, gripping his arm. He pulled away aggressively, pushing the chair away from the table. He stood up, rubbing his grizzly chin.

'Woman, don't ask me questions like this.' His squat physique loomed over her as she cowered under his tyrannical tones. He bent down, putting his face close to hers. 'Never speak to me like that again,' he hissed. 'I'll put you on the next flight to Romania to that shitty village where I found you.' His hot breath warmed the side of her face. She shuddered, nodding her head obediently, her hair covering her face. Raz grabbed his phone from the table and walked out, slamming the door hard behind him. She sniffed in a sharp intake of breath, covering her mouth to stifle her cries.

* * *

Cindy sat staring at a spreadsheet on her large Apple Mac screen. She hummed to herself, trying to work out the masses of figures in front of her. She typed a couple of numbers into it, but her mind wasn't really engaged with the tedious task. A loud, high-pitched alert from her phone gave her a welcome distraction. She huffed, picking up her phone from her clear desk and checking the message. A text from Dietmar. 'The other night was great hope you liked the gift.'

A smile broke across Cindy's face, the embers of her memory from that night still flickering in her thoughts. She placed the phone back onto the desk and tried to drag her mind back to work. A knock on the glass door distracted her. 'Hi. Busy?' Lena stepped in, smiling, all teeth, blonde hair straightened onto the shoulders of her pin-striped fitted shirt, fringe immaculate just above her black-rimmed glasses.

'Oh, just trying to work out these new sales reports—not happening.' She laughed.

Lena pulled a chair next to Cindy. 'Let me have a look.' She glared at the screen. 'Hmm, no, not happening.' She laughed too. 'Anyway, have you seen Mr D?' She spun her chair around to face Cindy, who took a sip of water from a clear plastic cup.

'Wow, straight in then.' She swallowed. 'Actually, I have,' she responded shyly, her dimples showing with the wide smile which crept across her face.

'So come on, what happened?' Lena eagerly shifted her chair closer. 'I want all the juice.' She crossed her legs, resting back.

Cindy picked up her phone. 'He bought me a gift.' She unlocked her screen and scrolled for a few seconds before showing Lena a picture of a sparkly black cocktail dress and a matching masquerade mask.

'Ooh, ok.' Lena's eyes widened. 'He's kinky, huh?' She touched Cindy's leg, trying not to laugh.

'I didn't think of it like that; playful maybe,' she countered, clicking off her phone.

At that point, a moping Andersen tapped on the glass door. He looked weary and unshaven as he poked his head into the room. 'Can I see you?' He nodded towards Lena, who jumped up on command. 'I'll be in the Orbit.' He barely glanced at Cindy as he left the door ajar and walked away.

Lena turned to Cindy. 'Sounds serious.' She shrugged before making a hasty exit.

Cindy sat for a few seconds; her inner antennae switched on. Something didn't feel right. She got up and left the room.

She walked quickly through the open plan office spaces, past the busy hub of employees, towards the lifts. She paused before approaching, peering around the corner to see Andersen and Lena having what seemed like a heated exchange before entering the shiny chrome lift.

Cindy followed them, curious as to why Lena also had access to the Orbit. She watched the green arrow flash on the mini display until it reached the floor. She then pressed the button repeatedly until the green arrow showed it was descending back to her floor.

The lift door slid open. Cindy stepped out into the atrium, her heels sinking into the thick carpet. She walked slowly across towards where his office was situated. She could hear their raised voices from behind the door. She paused, trying not to make a noise.

Lena sat on the cream sofa, watching Andersen pace up and down in front of her. 'So, what did he actually say?' Andersen pressed Lena for answers, scratching his chin.

'You know how he is—arrogant, defiant, he didn't care.' Lena sat back into the soft cushions.

'They can't be together, no. Maybe I will speak to him,' he replied, finally taking a seat at his desk. 'Something else.' Andersen peered up at Lena, pushing his blonde hair away from his eyes. 'You have to make another trip to the orphanage.' He tapped his fingers on the table.

Lena shook her head. 'No! I can't!' She stood up and walked over to his desk, her eyes wide through the lenses of her glasses. 'Don't send me back there!' Her voice shook with emotion.

Andersen put his head in his hands, his hair flopping over them. 'We have no choice!' he replied, his normally calm voice strained. He looked up at Lena, who instantly melted into tears, covering her mouth with her hand to stifle her sobs.

Cindy backed away from the door and quietly made her way back to the lift. Luckily the doors slid open instantly. She stepped in, her heart beating fast. 'Come on.' She pressed the button repeatedly to take her back down. She heard the sound of Andersen's door opening. 'Shit!' She pressed the button again. Luckily, the silver doors slid shut and the lift began its descent.

* * *

Bree's car crept slowly down a suburban cul-de-sac, the type that had mainly gated entrances and was lined with trees and well-trimmed hedges, the branches exposed as the autumnal weather took its toll. She looked either side of her at the numbers on the bronze plaques mounted on the brick walls next to the gates.

'One seventy-two, there it is.' She pulled over to the side of the road, cranking up the handbrake. The property was a large family home protected by a black and bronze gate. The hum of the engine was abruptly cut off as she pulled the keys out of the ignition.

Bree strode purposefully towards the house. She peered through the gate, sighting a gleaming blue Range Rover parked outside the large frosted glass-panelled door. She looked up at the windows before pressing hard on a modern intercom. The bell chimes rang out loudly.

'Can I help you?' A male voice crackled through the intercom. 'Yes. Detective Bree Archibald. Need to have a word with a Mr Cohen.' She stood back, expecting the gate to swing open, but it didn't.

Again, she pressed the intercom, then looked through the gate. She saw the door open slowly. A grey-haired man dressed in a green hunter's gilet, faded jeans and caramel boots stepped out of the house.

'What's this about?' he asked, his arms spread to the side. He walked down the concrete path to face Bree through the gates. 'Do you own a silver Mercedes E-Class, registration number…' Before she could finish her sentence, he interrupted, coughing loudly. His facial expression changed; the skin reddened as he choked.

'Not anymore… Ahem, I sold it ages ago. Got that now.' He turned, looking at the gleaming Range Rover.

Bree eyeballed him, digging her hands into the pockets of her leather coat. 'Who to? And when was ages ago?' She tilted her head with attitude, waiting for him to answer.

He shrugged. 'Can't help ya. My wife took care of it all.' He rubbed his nose, sniffing.

Bree laughed. 'Ok, then, is she about?' She looked past him, checking the house.

'She's abroad,' Mr Cohen responded, tucking his hands into his gilet pockets.

'Course she is,' Bree responded, rolling her eyes. 'Thanks for your time; been very helpful,' she said sarcastically, turning away and heading back to her car as Mr Cohen watched on.

Chapter Twenty-Six

Moment of clarity

Dwayne's reflection could be seen in the glass of the cube-shaped lift as it rose to the thirtieth floor. Dressed smartly, he adjusted his shirt collar and dusted down the shoulders of his grey tweed trench coat. Red neon lights shone around him as he looked out on the city below. The last time he had been in this space, Ricky's reflection had accompanied his. The silver doors of the lift slid open, allowing the thudding bass from the club speakers to reverberate, sucking him into the space.

Dwayne stepped out confidently, his black loafers camouflaging against the black onyx-tiled floor. It was pretty much the same as when he'd visited here before— the long, futuristic bar with colourful rows of liquor bottles above, a crowd of designer-dressed punters and sexy, stylish women.

He looked around the room, scanning everyone closely until he spotted the person he'd come to see—Paige. There she was thigh-high black boots with a silver jumpsuit which hugged her voluptuous curves. She was deep in conversation with a tall, lanky man dressed in red ruffled shirt and black leather trousers which were strangely tucked into black and silver cowboy boots.

Dwayne made a beeline to her. She had not spotted him approaching, too deep in conversation to notice. His broad frame strode confidently towards her. He looked at the man before grabbing Paige's arm. 'Need to speak with you.' His voice could just about be heard over the banging drumbeats. Paige looked shocked when she saw Dwayne staring down at her.

Quickly, she turned to the man. 'Excuse me please.' She smiled politely before pulling her arm away and giving Dwayne daggers, her brown eyes burning into him. 'What the fuck?' she said with a shrug, her peacock-coloured eyelids blinked furiously.

'Let's go' Dwayne insisted, allowing her to lead the way.

They sat in a rooftop courtyard. Cushioned wooden benches were surrounded by the greenery of plants in large marble pots scattered around the brown decking. 'What do you want?' Paige lit a cigarette held between her diamante blue nail polished fingers.

Dwayne sat calmly, holding a glass of Bacardi rum which he swirled slowly. He crossed his leg over his knee, brushing the suede of his shoes with his other hand.

'What did you tell Trevor?' His opening question was direct.

Paige rolled her eyes, blowing out a cloud of blue smoke, her irritation clear. 'He asked me about you and Ricky. I told him you were with him the night he died.' She shrugged. 'That's the truth, isn't it?' She turned to Dwayne, who uncrossed his leg and leant forward onto his knees, taking a slow sip from his drink before replying.

'I *saw* him that night…' He paused, rubbing his face.

'Thing is, he phoned me, spoke to me. I knew what he was up to,' Paige interrupted. She pointed at Dwayne, the half-smoked cigarette still clasped between her fingers, smouldering.

Dwayne looked up towards the clear sky. He stared at the full moon, which shone like a beacon in the distance. 'Trevor is trying to kill me; he's out for blood.' His voice cracked with emotion. 'Whatever *you* think, I had nothing to do with what happened,' he continued, turning towards Paige, who threw the remains of the cigarette to the floor and crushed it with the sole of her boot.

'Tell that to Trevor, innit.' She got up to leave, only to be pulled back by Dwayne.

'Where's Sasha?' His voice was laced with desperation. Paige tugged her arm away.

'Fucking hell! Do I look like the oracle?' she responded, accompanied by an ironic laugh. 'She stopped contacting me after she met *you*; bit like Ricky, really.' She shook her head and walked away, arms folded, shielding her from the late-night chill.

Dwayne watched as she re-entered the club. 'Fuck sake,' he murmured to himself, sitting back on the seat and tossing the remains of his drink down his throat.

* * *

Cindy scuttled back and forth between the kitchen and the hallway. She was dressed smartly for work, her cropped hair neatly in place, yet her face was knotted with frustration. 'Cece, hurry up, we'll be late,' she yelled up the stairs while stuffing a packed lunch box into Cece's rucksack.

Cece appeared at the top of the stairs in her smart green uniform, blazer, grey skirt and black stockings. 'I can't find my letter,' she said, stepping slowly down each step.

'What letter?' Cindy responded, pulling on a black fur-collared coat.

'From school for our field trip next week.' Cece reached the bottom, taking her coat from the banister. 'Miss Thomas said it needs to be in today. I gave it to Uncle Dwayne last time.'

'Ok, you put your coat on. I'll check in his jacket; it might be in there.' A harried Cindy began to check amongst the coats and jackets hung on the hooks.

'He always leaves his stuff here,' she muttered while digging into each pocket of Dwayne's jacket. She pulled out a letter. 'Think I've found it.' She turned to Cece with a smile then unfolded the paper. The ultrasound picture was wedged under a fold. Cindy gazed at it, stunned into silence for a few seconds. She flipped it over to see the word written on the back: 'Soon x'.

'Is that it, Mum?' Cece interrupted her mum's trance-like state.

'What? Oh, yeah, it is. Come on, I'll sign it quickly. Let's go,' she said, shoving the picture into her coat pocket.

* * *

Cindy encountered the usual small crowd of parents waving their children off to school as she rushed through to get Cece in on time. 'Ok, darling, have a good day.' She bent down to kiss her on the cheek then ushered her towards the waiting teacher, who stood patiently by the gate waving in her direction. Cindy waved back briefly before turning to walk away. 'Oh hey, Lisa!' she said, smiling, her voice high-pitched with surprise.

Kai looked up at Cindy and waved as he ran towards the school gate. 'Long time no see.' Cindy embraced Lisa gently, looking down at her stomach. 'How are you?'

Lisa nodded her head. 'I'm good,' Lisa replied with a bland expression, tucking her hands into her jacket.

'Well, just wanted to say congrats!' Cindy broke into a big smile. 'Can't wait to be an aunty. When are you…'

Lisa stared back at her with wide eyes. 'Wait what?' she replied aghast at Cindy's revelation. Cindy engulfed her with another hug. 'Look, I'm sure we'll all talk soon. Got to go, late for work,' she gushed, leaving Lisa standing frozen, unable to process the information fed into her ears. She could only watch Cindy walk away swiftly into the distance.

* * *

Only the hum of the smooth engine could be heard inside Andersen's Mercedes as it sat wedged in heavy traffic a few miles from Heathrow Airport. His ice-blue eyes stared straight ahead; his blonde hair swept back immaculately away from his dry face. Lena sat in the passenger seat, her pale face grim, with little to no make-up, just the thick black rims of her glasses contrasting with the definition of her face.

'It's just a week.' Andresen broke the silence, turning to her with a sympathetic glance. 'Just make sure the medication has arrived and shut down the orphanage. The kids…'

'It's that simple, right?' Lena interrupted, disappointment threaded through her voice. 'You don't know what it's like,' she continued, folding her arms.

'This will be the last time,' Andersen wheezed, pumping the car horn in frustration at the slow-moving traffic ahead of him. The blare caused Lena to shudder, tears rolling down her cheeks. Andersen punched the steering wheel and took a deep breath. 'Fuck!' He rested his head back against the cushioned headrest.

'You're being weird; what's going on?' Lena sniffed, placing her hand over his fist to calm him. Andersen continued to stare ahead. 'Just business.' Regretting his momentary loss of control, he was unwilling to look at Lena. He moved his hand away.

Lena tilted her head against the window, staring out to the road. She saw a little girl in the backseat of another car. The girl stared at Lena and began to wave and blow kisses playfully before the car drove away as traffic began to move. 'Promise me you'll wait until I get back before you see Dietmar.' Lena turned back to look at Andersen. He nodded reluctantly, sensing he at least owed her that one period of grace.

* * *

The swirling wind whistled around Dwayne's ears. He was seated on the edge of the roof of one of the tower blocks of Kingfisher

Estate. Still dressed in the clothes he wore to the club; he looked down between his suede loafers towards the miniature toy-like cars which drove slowly around the grids of the surrounding area. He sniffed loudly, shivering as the air cut through his body.

A half-drunk open bottle of Bacardi stood on the ledge beside him. He went to grab it but fumbled, knocking it clumsily with his hand, causing it to wobble and topple over the edge. Dwayne made a belated attempt to grab it, tilting his body forward. He clung tightly to the pebble dash concrete wall, gripping it with the tips of his fingers.

He remained seated, looking out at the bleak city horizon, which was shrouded by darkened grey clouds. He sniffed again, wiping away tears which flowed freely down his cheeks. 'Why you have to get me into this fuckery, man?' he said, glancing down at his phone clutched in his other hand. He stared at a picture of him and Ricky posing at the club, each holding a glass of champagne. He broke down, looking skywards. 'Bruv, talk to me!' his strained voice shouted out. He tried to control his breathing, but a combination of the cold and his emotions made that impossible. He continued to shiver.

'I fucked up… fucking fucked up…' he rambled. A slither of dribble hung from his mouth and landed on the phone screen, blurring a message which popped up from Jorgi. 'Car wash 7 pm' it read, causing Dwayne to suck for air. 'Hate… this… it's shit… fucking pricks,' he said, but the words made no sense.

Again, he sniffed up his runny nose, staring blankly at the jagged landscape in the distance. He dug into his inside pocket and pulled out a scrappy piece of scrunched-up paper. He placed his phone between his legs as he unfurled it. The ink had smudged but was still readable. 'Willy Notch 07922143280'.

'Yeah…' He laughed to himself, swiping his phone screen open and accessing the keypad. 'Fuck dem, fuck Raz.' He sniffed up his snot, pressing a digit at a time, his finger wavering unsteadily, his hand shaking. 'O… seven… nine…' He could barely count, slurring as he concentrated and wiping his glazed eyes. 'Fuck this shit…' he babbled.

Another text flashed up on the screen, this time from Cindy. 'Guess what? We got the house!!!' At that moment, a sharp gust of wind whistled around his head again. He began to laugh to himself between supressing the tears. 'Ricks, you are watching me, innit, bruv.' He pointed up towards the sky, wagging his finger. His phone began to vibrate on his thighs. He looked down at the screen and saw a private number. He picked it up, trying to compose himself before answering.

'Hello.' He put it onto speaker mode. At first nothing, just silence. 'Who's this?' he asked, slurring, lifting the phone to his ear. 'I said…' He was about to speak again but heard a baby cooing. He stiffened. Suddenly he perked up, listening intently. 'Say hello to Daddy.' He heard Sasha's hushed voice. She sounded happy and playful as the baby continued to make warbling noises.

Dwayne swung his legs back over the ledge onto firm ground. His eyes swivelled panoramically as he spun himself into some form of balance. A warped smile appeared across his face. 'Sasha… Is that you?' He raked his other hand through his curly afro. 'Say hi to your daughter… Mellieha,' she said softly, relief and joy in her voice. Dwayne sank to his knees. His body shook. He began to sob like a widow, hunched over as if he was praying in a mosque. 'I'll call you soon. Be careful.' Sasha cut the call, leaving Dwayne in a crumpled heap, blubbing from deep in his gut.

Chapter Twenty-Seven

Do you know?

A busy, crowded airport arrivals hall met a tired, hot and worried Lena as she stood in the queue for immigration. Her head was covered by a black scarf, which made the rims of her glasses protrude further from her face. She was nervous. It wasn't a trip she enjoyed; not now, not then.

The perspiration dribbled from her armpits down into her bra, and from her forehead to her top lip. She looked around, observing the militia-like security guards who patrolled and watched every single visitor intently. She inched towards the passport desk, dragging her suitcase. Each step made her heart bound out of her chest. The thought of the long journey she still had to make filled her with dread. The best she could do was to act cool in the sweltering heat.

Finally, she reached the desk. The black-uniformed customs clerk stared blankly at her passport. He flicked a few pages then looked up, his skin raisin-like, gruff from a long shift in the stuffy cubicle, eyes dulled. He stared at her for what seemed like an age.

Lena stood quietly. Her stomach churned until he stamped her passport with a thump. She bowed gratefully, taking her documents and shuffling out into the ramshackle arrivals' foyer.

A sign with 'Miss Lena' scrawled in black marker pen was held aloft by a tall, thick-set man with a greying, almost yellow, tobacco-stained beard. He wore a white tunic with a gold embroidered pattern and white trousers.

Lena nodded towards him, and he scuttled towards her. 'Miss Lena, welcome.' He bowed his head. 'It's hot.' He smiled, taking the handle of her case from her. 'Hi. Yes,' she replied quietly. She followed him through the hectic crowds of people and past overzealous taxi drivers pleading for their next fare.

'The vehicle is over here,' he said with his Arabic accent. As Lena followed, she was stopped by a young street urchin begging for money. He looked up at her tall figure, his wide, despairing eyes standing out from his dirty face and overgrown curly hair.

Momentarily Lena was immobilised; a vivid flashback of the little girl in the Mickey Mouse T-shirt was screened across her memory. 'Hey!' the driver shouted at the boy, waving his hand at him to move away. 'Sorry, Miss Lena.' Again, he bowed to her and ushered her towards a black Jeep.

Lena slowly wound down the window, took out her phone and sent a message to Andersen. 'I'm here en route now. Will let you know when I'm done.' She rested her head back, closing her eyes. The dichotomy of relief and fear gripped her, tinged with a sense of anger that Andersen would put her through this experience again. She tilted her head, looking out at nothing but desert and the shells of buildings, the sweat now dripping from her jaw line.

'Miss Lena.' The driver looked into the rearview mirror at a dozing Lena. 'I apologise to ask. It would be simpler to stay at hotel and travel tomorrow.' He paused, his eyes searching, waiting for an answer. He adjusted the mirror.

'No! I don't want to be here longer than I need.'

'But Miss Lena, we have long drive; it's better…'

'We continue through the night,' she ordered, her anger rising faster than the desert heat.

'Ok. Sorry, Miss Lena.' He switched his eyes from the mirror back onto the road ahead.

Darkness had fallen. The dusky sunset had now been replaced with a pale blue moon which shone clearly above the horizon. Lena had fallen asleep. Her heavy head bobbed each time the car hit a pothole in the dusty road.

The driver stared ahead in silence, barely able to keep his eyes open, until he saw the bright beams of multiple headlights speeding towards them in the distance. He shook himself awake and pumped the brakes firmly, causing the car to skid to an abrupt halt.

Lena jumped out of her sleep, the force of the stop throwing her forward. 'What's happening?' she asked, her mind still adjusting to her surroundings.

'I don't know, Miss Lena.' The driver sounded nervous as he watched their car being surrounded by four army-type Jeeps.

Several men jumped out of the vehicles shouting in Arabic, their faces covered by black scarves, their heads wrapped in black turbans. They wore military boots and carried AK47 rifles aimed at the car. The driver held his hands aloft.

'Not good, Miss Lena,' he muttered. Lena looked spooked. She fixed her glasses and adjusted the scarf on her head. The men, maybe eight or ten of them, all stepped towards the car, still shouting expletives. Their Jeep headlights shone like spotlights into the car.

The men opened the doors to the car, aggressively pointing their weapons at Lena. They shouted angrily, gesturing to her to get out. 'Ok… please don't…' She became tearful. Her body shook with fear. 'Don't hurt me… please,' she begged. One of the men pulled her by the arm and dragged her to the floor, her legs like jelly as she fell. Her glasses came off her face. She stretched out her hand to retrieve them, but the man stepped on them, the rugged sole of his boot crushing the lenses.

As Lena stared up, her headscarf unravelled, revealing her blonde hair. She held her hands out, pleading, 'Please don't kill me…' The man continued to shout at her until she was manhandled and dragged to one of their Jeeps. Her feet scraped along the gravel path. One of her flip flops was discarded. She was picked up and thrown into the back of the car. She screamed out loudly but was soon stifled by a black hood being shoved over her head.

Lena was crumpled in a heap in the footwell behind the driver's seat, feeling the weight of a hefty knee in the small of her back. The sound of voices and doors slamming was accompanied by a round of gunfire—quick, sporadic blasts that seemed to last for an age but was probably only a few seconds. She squealed, weeping uncontrollably, as her car sped away from the scene.

Chapter Twenty-Eight

Sober thoughts

Dwayne sat fidgeting in the comfort of a large brown leather sofa, his head full of a thousand thoughts. He was interrupted by a little girl bashing her plastic tricycle wheel into his Nike trainers. He looked down, smiling warmly at the toddler, who was bare-chested and wearing only a cute smile and a baggy nappy.

She giggled every time she reversed and repeated the same action. Her mother, a short, buff, light-skinned woman with electric blue braids, wearing an Adidas sports bra and cut-off jean shorts, came into the room.

'Sorry 'bout dat. Come, Chantel.' She dragged the little girl away from Dwayne. 'Him soon come,' she said, her Jamaican patois strong, while scooping up the girl. 'You want a juice?' she offered as she backed away into the kitchen where the aroma of Caribbean food lingered in the air.

'Ok, thanks.' Dwayne smiled politely, his eyes reverting to the large flatscreen television mounted on the wall in front of him, showing a Gervonta Davis fight. He rubbed his hands together, trying to wring out the overwhelming nervousness, distracted only by the buzz of his phone. He dug it out of his jeans pocket to see Lisa's name flashing on the screen. He sighed heavily before shoving it back into his pocket.

A few minutes later, a man entered the room, his chiselled body accentuated by a clean white vest. He wore tight, bleached, ripped jeans fastened with a classic Louis Vuitton belt. He waltzed in confidently, looking down at his phone then tapping in a message. He had short dreadlocks and a bushy beard, through which ran a thick scar.

'Mr Dwayne, wha gwan!' His loud voice commanded Dwayne to stand to attention.

'Yes, Willy Notch.' They touched fists as they greeted.

'Sit, man.' Willy gestured to Dwayne, who dutifully followed his instructions, sitting back down on the sofa.

Willy lit up a fat cone-shaped joint. He sucked on it hard as the orange tip glowed in the lighter flame. He made several sucking sounds before blowing out the thick smoke, the pungent weed smell wafting out into the room.

'Mi cuzzy tell mi you hold him down pon de wing.' He nodded in appreciation. His sleepy eyes looked at Dwayne and he pointed at him, his fingers laden with gold rings.

Dwayne reflected briefly. 'Yeah, Felix is cool. How's he doing?'

'Him alright.' Willy nodded, taking in the high as the smoke hit his bloodstream. 'So, you have business fi talk?' He looked at Dwayne, with an air of seriousness.

Dwayne sat up. 'Yeah.' He nodded with certainty.

Willy's smartphone constantly buzzed while Dwayne spoke to him. He watched as Willy answered call after call and several messages; he seemed like a man running an empire from the comfort of his home.

'So dem man have nuff keys?' he asked, his voice hoarse.

'I'm telling you, I'm their main courier, bro. They work out of that valet place next to the bridge.' Dwayne spilled all the beans on Raz's operation. 'They are on other shit too, kid trafficking and that.' His voice trailed off, realising that he maybe had said too much.

Willy sat mulling over the information while watching the fight on the screen. His girlfriend came back into the room holding a tray with some drinks. She laid it down on a large glass dining table, then handed one of the glasses to Dwayne.

'Thanks,' he acknowledged, spotting the little girl playfully hiding behind her mother. It made him think of his own newborn daughter, Mellieha.

'Ok, hear what. I want times, dates, addresses, everything. You can do that fi me?' Willy Notch got up from his seat and stood in front of the TV screen, the fight continuing behind his muscular silhouette. Dwayne took a large gulp from his drink, then nodded with a semblance of confidence.

'Yeah, I'll hit you with all that.' He craned his neck upwards towards Willy Notch.

'One other thing,' he added with slight hesitancy. 'I need someone else to disappear.' He took another sip of his juice. Willy looked at him, his eyes diverted from his phone. He stared down at Dwayne scarily. His girlfriend looked at them both before retreating to the kitchen, sensing this was not a conversation she needed to hear.

'Bwoy, Dwayne. Man is on some killer bloodclart ting, darg.' He broke into a chesty laugh. Dwayne shrugged. 'It is what it is.' He swallowed the last of his drink before standing up and embracing Willy, who held him closely. 'If this lick comes off, I'll do the other ting for free,' he whispered menacingly into Dwayne's ear. He stepped back with a sneer.

* * *

Lisa sat alone on a park bench, shivering in the cool wind. She watched as Kai played happily on the climbing frame. She checked her phone before stuffing it back into her pocket. 'Kai, be careful up there,' she shouted as he clambered across the various ropes and ladders. Again, she checked her phone impatiently, tutting under her breath.

The lone figure of Dwayne ambled along the path towards her. He didn't seem in any rush, much to Lisa's annoyance; she frowned on seeing him. Dwayne stopped at the bench and sat down, resting back, stretching out his legs and pulling his hood up over his head. 'It's chappin' out here.' He stared ahead, watching Kai.

'Took your time.' Lisa's frosty comment matched the climate. Dwayne nudged her playfully. 'Don't touch me,' Lisa replied curtly, shifting her body away from him.

'Jeez, did you get up on the wrong side of bed or suttin?' Dwayne turned to face her. Lisa remained quiet, staring ahead. He could tell she was in deep thought. 'So… spit it out.' Dwayne sat up, digging his hands into his pockets. 'What's up?' he prompted her, leaning in.

'Bruv, you a weirdo.' Finally, Lisa faced him, her voice full of hatred, her faced screwed up.

Dwayne burst into an uncontrolled laugh. 'What you going on about?'

'It's not funny—see what I mean?' She shoved him in his head. 'You're not serious, dickhead.' She turned her back in a show of disgust.

Kai ran over out of breath, slightly bedraggled from his exertions. 'Mum, I need a drink. Hi, Dwayne.' He caught his breath while Lisa dug into her bag and pulled out a Capri-Sun which he grabbed enthusiastically. 'Wait! Let me at least put the straw in,' Lisa snapped. 'Here.' She handed the drink to Kai, who gleefully took it from her.

After his quick break, Kai was back entertaining himself on the swings, watched by Dwayne and Lisa.

'What are we?' Lisa asked. An air of calm had now softened her voice. 'I mean, you act like my man but…' She paused, pulling her knees up to her chest.

'But what?'

'But you ain't never around when I need you, like, for example, my cuz's nine night.' The emotion crept into her voice although she tried to maintain her composure.

'I told you, was working that night.' Dwayne became defensive, knowing to tread carefully with any reference to L Boi.

'See, second best, innit.'

'Look, where is this all coming from?' He finally removed the hood from his head and looked curiously at Lisa. 'Talk to me,' he pled, sensing she had more to say.

Lisa tried to fight her emotions, but a lonely tear trickled down her cheek. She wiped it away quickly. 'I let you into my life, my son's life… I *actually* liked…' She sniffed, turning her face away so that Dwayne couldn't see her vulnerable.

'What?' He pulled her arm, trying to get her to face him.

'Saw Cindy the other day by the school.' She shrugged, pulling her arm away from Dwayne's clasp.

'Yeah, and what?'

Lisa finally turned around to face him. A mix of hurt and anger etched on her face, she managed to force a smile, a glint of her diamond tooth revealed.

'Kai, come on, we're going now!' she shouted out across the park.

'Wait a sec, what's going on?' Dwayne felt desperate.

'She congratulated me. Thinks she's going to be an aunty for some reason.' Again she sniffed back her tears, rubbing her nose.

Dwayne hung his head as the realisation hit him. He sat forward, hunched, the guilt pulling him down like an anchor. 'I can explain…' He spoke towards the ground, too ashamed to look at Lisa, who stood a few yards away.

'Come on, Kai!' she screamed, unable to hide her emotions.

Dwayne stood up and walked towards her. 'Wait! I beg you, just let me explain…' Kai ran past him and clung on to Lisa, sensing she was upset.

'Forget it. Stay away from us,' she insisted.

'Yeah, stay away from us.' Kai copied his mum, thrusting his finger at Dwayne.

'But… Hold up… Just give me…' Dwayne's plea fell on deaf ears; he watched Lisa walk away, arms folded, with Kai beside her chasing after a few pigeons.

Dwayne flapped his arms in frustration. His phone began to vibrate again. 'Shit!' He pulled it from his pocket, still gazing at Lisa in the distance. 'What?' he shouted through the device, only to hear, once again, the sound of a baby.

'You sound tense! What going on?' said Sasha softly, her Eastern European accent pronounced.

'It's nothing,' he answered, distracted. 'How is she?' he continued, trying to compose himself.

'She's beautiful,' Sasha replied. 'I need you here.'

Dwayne's head was in a spin. He went and sat on the bench again, head bowed. 'Give her a kiss from me,' he said gently.

'And me, do I get a kiss?' Sasha's husky voice turned seductive.

Dwayne broke into a confused laugh. 'Soon, babes.' He cut the call, resting back, looking up into the grey skies.

* * *

The sound of Bree slurping up the remains of her green juice smoothie irked Nolan as he sat opposite her, flicking through various papers. 'Do you have to?' he grumbled, adjusting his glasses. Bree gave it another couple of hefty slurps just to annoy him some more.

'Love when you get pissed off; brings out your macho side.' She chuckled to herself.

'Do some work!' he growled, banging down another thick file and searching through more pages.

'That car we saw on Kingfisher,' Bree continued, relaxing back and putting her shiny Doc Marten boots onto her desk.

'What about it?' Nolan lifted his head and looked at Bree.

'Well, I did some digging; was sold by a Mr Jess Cohen.' She sounded smug, wiping her hands with a clinical wet wipe.

'What have you done?' Nolan's tone was like a disappointed father waiting to be let down by his child.

Bree tossed the wipe onto her desk. 'I paid him a visit, sniffed him out.' She folded her arms, chuffed with herself.

'And…' Nolan leant in with intrigue. Bree's mobile ringtone burst into life; the high-pitched rhythmic tone jangled Nolan's nerves.

Bree looked down at her phone and saw Lisa's name in large letters across the screen. 'One sec.' She shushed Nolan, who groaned impatiently at being held in suspense. 'Hey, Lisa.' She played the bestie role, her voice high-pitched and girly. Nolan shook his head, knowing his partner was up to no good. 'Hey, slow down. Wait, what?' She smiled at Nolan, playfully relishing her deception.

'Ok, hun, I'll be there soon with a bottle of wine. Ok, bye.' She cut the call. Quickly she swung her legs down and stood up, grabbing her green parker coat. 'Got to go, speak later.' She hurriedly collected her things.

'But what about this Cohen character?' Nolan pleaded.

'Chat later,' Bree bellowed as she ran out of the office, leaving Nolan to get back to his pile of papers.

* * *

As always, the Schuster and Klein office floor was buzzing with chatter. Workers conversed while connected to wireless ear buds. Huddles of hipster-looking staff held meetings in the comfortable, arty, brightly coloured spaces around the open plan room.

Cindy walked through, holding her iPad and a cup of coffee. She smiled at some of the young workers as she headed towards her office. Her mood was upbeat, buoyed by the fact that her dream of leaving the bleak Kingfisher Estate was now a reality. She glanced over to where Lena usually sat, but her desk was empty.

Back at her desk and sitting comfortably, she sipped her coffee while checking a few emails, humming a tune to herself. The figure of Andersen pacing up and down past her window interrupted her. She watched for a few seconds, seeing him slightly agitated, head down, before he stopped and came into her office.

'Morning!' Cindy chirped brightly. 'You alright?' she asked, taking another sip from her cup. Andersen, dressed in his customary sky-blue trousers and white shirt, ran his fingers through his hair.

'Hmm… yes, I think so,' he replied, his tone low as he took a seat, eyes firmly locked onto his phone screen.

'Any idea when Lena's back?' Cindy asked, her question poking him to look up.

'Huh, no, not sure.' His words were hesitant, telling. Cindy could sense something was not right with him by the furrowed look on his face. She watched him for a few seconds, trying to figure out the reason for his distracted mood. His phone buzzed in his hand, and he saw Lena's name flash on the screen.

'Ahh, look.' He showed the screen to Cindy, who smiled back at him.

'Hi, Lena,'. 'Thought you was going to call me when you got to the airport…' Andersen's mouth dried up. 'She's not coming home.' The sinister reply caught Andersen off-guard. He stood up, the blood drained from his face. He turned away from Cindy, shielding his reaction. 'We know who you are,' the mysterious voice continued. 'One million pounds, she returns alive; we'll send the details,' he rasped before hanging up. Andersen's heart thumped in his chest. A cold shiver ran down his spine.

'On her way, then?' Cindy asked, excited to hear that Lena was returning. Andersen made an odd sound—a low, exasperated growl, his mouth unable to formulate any words. He grimaced before leaving the room without even a word.

* * *

The car valet site was awash with activity. Young men tended to the incoming fleet of cars, scrubbing and jet washing each vehicle as they lined up. On the other side, next to the portacabin, Jorgi oversaw operations as a couple of men loaded hefty sacks into the boot of a Land Rover Discovery.

Jorgi stood watching attentively, his tall, slim body cloaked in a big leather coat, his hair dangling around his bumpy face. He puffed on a cigarette, nodding in approval as the men loaded the last of the sacks.

Raz joined them, his stocky figure clothed in just a tight black T-shirt and jeans, braving the cold afternoon weather. They all gathered in a huddle, speaking in their native tongue. He was clearly in charge, pointing and gesticulating to the others.

After a few minutes of animated conversation, they all embraced then parted ways. The men climbed into the car and drove away. Raz patted Jorgi on the back before retreating into the portacabin.

On the street opposite, a black Porsche Cayenne was parked, the engine gently humming. Inside sat Willy Notch with another man, scoping out the movements of Raz and his cronies. He wore dark shades, even though the weather was cold and bleak. The other man was one of his generals, a tubby Jamaican known only as Dee. His frame cuddled comfortably in the driver's seat, a black hoody covering his head.

Willy stared through the smoked glass of his shades, puffing on a spliff, the dense smoke filling the interior of the car. 'So, Dwayne was right.' His voice was hoarse, his throat fighting with the inhalation of smoke.

'Seems so,' Dee concurred. They continued to watch on as the Land Rover drove past their car.

'Everyting set.' Willy smiled, sparking a big flame from his lighter and relighting his spliff. 'Let's go,' he ordered Dee, who acted on command, steering the car out and slowly past the car wash.

* * *

Low background music playing the sound of a weepy Drake song set the mood as Lisa sat at her dining table nursing a glass of wine. Bree sat opposite, staring at her empathetically. 'I think you dodged a bullet there.' Bree's short stint of empathy ended abruptly. She gulped a mouthful of wine.

'Yeah, maybe,' Lisa replied wistfully, her mind still half wishing things had worked with Dwayne.

'No! Definitely,' Bree interjected. 'Who knows what else he's been up to?' Bree played expertly on Lisa's vulnerable mental state.

Lisa put her head in her hands, her red tresses dangling over her face for a few seconds. She took a deep breath, then raised her head defiantly. 'I know *exactly* what he's been up to.' She nodded, affirming to herself that now was the time to reveal all to Bree, whose eyes widened in anticipation as Lisa spoke.

'You're right! I couldn't bring a man like him into Kai's life.' She took another gulp of her wine. The scorn she felt seared any fine traces of loyalty she had left, and the heady Merlot teased out her emotions.

'What do you mean? I thought you liked him, especially with Kai?' Bree did not let up; she took the bottle and eagerly topped up Lisa's glass.

'That's the thing.' Lisa shook her head, still trying to untangle her messy thoughts. She curled her lips, showing her diamond tooth. 'I feel so dumb, was willing to accept his shit.'

'What shit?' Bree jumped in, sensing an opportunity to squeeze more information about Dwayne from her.

'He's into dodgy shit big time,' a woozy Lisa blurted. 'And you know what?' She wagged her manicured finger towards a fascinated Bree. 'That guy who died in the car crash…' She took the wine glass and downed another mouthful. 'Now, I ain't no snitch, right, but he's mixed up in a lot. What was I thinking?' She stared sleepy-eyed at Bree regretfully.

Bree rested back in her chair, unable to contain a devious smile which snuck across her face. 'Aww, babe, you know you can tell me anything.' She reached out and held Lisa's hand, squeezing her silver-ringed fingers gently, her hollow sincerity lost on a fractured Lisa.

Chapter Twenty-Nine

Same problems?

Raz's wife sat alone in darkness at the dining table, only the glare from her laptop screen glowing on her face. She cried as she read the details of the little girl who had been murdered by Ilyan. She held a tissue to her nose as she scrolled through each news story. The vibration of Raz's car exhaust as he pulled up outside jolted her into action. She quickly closed the laptop, ran into the front room and switched on the television.

Raz trudged heavily into the house, switching on the lights. He walked into the front room. 'Hi.' His low growl was barely a greeting. She looked at him, offering a fake smile. 'Hi.' She was distracted but trying to act normally after digesting the chilling details of Ilyan's actions. 'The kids are asleep,' she added, watching Raz prowl around, grunting to himself, absorbed in his own mind, failing to even notice his wife's masked emotions.

'I'm going away for a few days on business,' he shouted from the next room before stomping up the stairs. His mood hung in the air like a dark cloud. She sat staring at the television, chewing her fingernails.

Raz returned, clutching a leather rucksack. He stood in the doorway, his stocky torso filling the width of the frame. 'See you,' he said with no emotion. She turned to him and smiled passively, removing her finger from her mouth.

Raz turned and left without another word, slamming the door on his exit. She got up quickly from the sofa and ran to the window, watching through the net curtains as the red rear lights disappeared from the drive.

She took her phone out of her pocket and scrolled hastily through her address book until she stopped at Sasha's name. She checked out of the window again before pressing the call button and putting it on speaker. The message came through: 'The number you have called is not recognised.' She gave a deep sigh. *Sasha, where are you?*

* * *

Cindy led Dwayne out of the show house. 'So… this is The Hive.' She spread her hands out to the nearly built brick houses growing out of the muddied ground of a building site. Dwayne put his arm around her.

'Yeah, sis, looks alright. I can see why you are so gassed.' He looked around at the large skeleton landscape.

Cindy beamed, leaning her head into her brother. 'Yeah, another few months and we'll be away from that place.' She squeezed Dwayne's arm.

'Thing is, sis,' Dwayne said quietly, sniffing up the cold air, 'I've got to tell you something…' Cindy swung around to him, her brown eyes twinkling.

'I know what you're going to say.' She smiled, tugging at his beard with her gloved hand. 'I'm going to be an aunty,' she sang playfully. Dwayne rolled his eyes, shaking his head. He swatted her hand from his beard.

'You already are, and it's not with Lisa.'

'What! Jeez, man, so who, when girl or boy?'

Dwayne hung his head. 'I can't say right now,' he mumbled, kicking some loose gravel away from his feet. Cindy pushed him in the chest.

'Better start talking now!' she demanded. Dwayne laughed to himself, wiping his nose as the cold bit.

'The less you know…' Cindy spun around, walking away from him back towards the show home.

'Not this shit again!' When you came out, I told you no more fuckery. Now it's the less you know.' She turned her back, folding her arms. Dwayne could only stand there in silence. He knew it was best not to aggravate an already sticky situation. 'You ain't changed.' Cindy spun back towards him. The joy had drained from her face, quickly replaced by disappointment. 'All this is for us to live like normal people.' She spread her arms out wide, again showcasing the potential of The Hive and the showroom behind them.

'Sis, you way too dramatic.' His petulant reply triggered Cindy into aiming a kick at him.

'Don't you get it?' she screamed, her frustration boiling over. 'I'm trying to protect us! Me, you and Cece,' she said through gritted teeth. For once her rational mind was close to breaking point.

'I get it, sis. Why'd you think I gave you that ten bags?' Dwayne stepped forward to console her. 'Trust me.' He put his arms around her. 'I'll explain everything; just need to tie up some loose ends,' he said softly. He felt deflated sensing his sister's disappointment.

Cindy pushed back from his embrace. 'So, I'm an aunty?' She looked up at him. Dwayne looked down, nodding, trying to resist a smile. 'Shit, I thought it was Lisa, and I told her…' Dwayne smiled.

'It's cool, sis. I know.' He gave her a reassuring squeeze. Cindy's phone began to ring, the harmonious ringtone interrupting the disharmony between the siblings.

Cindy dug into her handbag and pulled out her phone. 'Hello,' she answered, trying to sound professional. Dwayne stepped away, allowing her to take the call while he turned to view the show home once more.

'Pardon, when?' Cindy's voice sounded urgent, causing Dwayne to turn back to her. 'Ok, text me the address, thank you.'

'What's up?'

'It was a solicitor from the CPS. They need a statement from Cece. Leon's trial begins in a few weeks.' She gave a huge sigh, the weight of her world causing her shoulders to sag.

'It's calm. We'll deal with that later. Enough for today.' Dwayne put his arm around her, guiding her away from the site.

* * *

The city lights dotted below twinkled for as far as the eye could see. Andersen's reflection was silhouetted against the large rectangular window of his office in the Schuster and Klein building. He stared pensively ahead, both hands dug deeply into his trouser pockets. For once his shirt was untucked, unbuttoned, the slickness he usually displayed far removed from his rigid stance.

His phone began to buzz aggressively, vibrating loudly on his desk. It made him jump and shook him out of his trance. He spun around and picked up the device, checking the messages on the screen. They seemed to be video messages sent from a private number.

Andersen's hand shook as he opened the messages. He gasped on seeing the first video of a dirty, bedraggled Lena sitting uncomfortably on a dirty mattress in what looked like a derelict cave. Her face was red and she was without her glasses. The old bow-legged woman from the orphanage stood over her. His eyes glassed over like marbles as he glared at the videos. His finger shook, hovering on each play symbol he pressed, fearing the worst.

A man dressed all in black, his face covered by a black and white chequered scarf, stood behind a drowsy-looking Lena, holding a machete across her throat. 'You take our children; I'll take her life!' he screamed. 'You failed to send the money, Mr De Breuk.' His Arabic accent threaded through his hysterical pitch was distorted through the phone.

'Just need a few more days…' Andersen spoke loudly as if the person was in the same room. He squeezed the phone, his body tensing up as the video went black. Voices could be heard alongside Lena's whimpering. 'Don't hurt her, I'm begging you, please. I'll get you… the…' Andersen dropped the phone onto the desk. He covered his face with both hands, letting out a long, anguished cry.

Chapter Thirty

Tomorrow

Dietmar appeared from his kitchen carrying two cups of coffee. He looked as if he had been woken out of deep sleep, his usual slick blonde hair sticking out like straw. He walked across his floor barefooted, wearing only black shorts and a black silk dressing gown.

'You need to drink this, here.' He gave the cup to a ruffled, drunk Andersen, who could barely lift his head to acknowledge the gesture. He growled, waving away the aroma of the coffee steaming from the cup. 'Bring me a whisky,' he demanded, hunched over on the black velvet sofa where a smirking Dietmar joined him.

'Dear, oh dear, you're the last person I thought would turn up at my place.' Dietmar set the cups down on a glass table beside him. He turned and looked at Andersen, who was breathing heavily, pinching the top of his nose, his breath reeking of alcohol. He shook his head repeatedly as if he was trying to shake off the dark mood which hung over him.

'Listen to me.' Finally, Andersen raised his head, his eyes bloodshot, and gripped Dietmar's arm tightly. 'Lena…' He choked, swallowing dryly, unable to complete his sentence.

'She's…' Again, he stammered, searching his intoxicated mind for the right words.

Dietmar shrugged his arm away from Andersen's grip. 'She's what?' He gave Andersen a shove. 'Speak, man!' Andersen put his head in his hands, shaking. He mumbled, the alcohol affecting his speech.

'She's in danger.' The words tumbled out of his mouth. Dietmar stood up; his silk gown fell open, revealing his pasty chest and milk bottle legs. He hovered over Andersen, scraping back his hair.

'Ok, start talking. Where is she?' The vortex of his words sucked Andersen's head up towards his eyeline.

They eyeballed each other for a few seconds; an awkward silence ensued. Andersen cracked. 'I don't know,' he said. 'I need a drink.' He attempted to get up from his seated position but was pushed back down by Dietmar.

'Oh, the irony. My sister's protector has now put her in danger—pathetic.' Dietmar folded his arms. 'What. Happened. To Lena?'

Andersen let out a deep, gut-wrenching cry akin to that of a seal. He drawled as though he was suffering from a stroke. 'I don't know,' he grimaced through clenched teeth, looking up at Dietmar, his usual confident patter now reduced a pitiful plea. 'I need you to help me,' he begged, much to Dietmar's disgust.

'Look, just go, Andersen.' Dietmar took his coffee and retreated upstairs. Andersen attempted to get up to follow him but instead fell to his knees. 'Dietmar… don't… please, I need you.' He ended up crawling on his hands and knees across the marble floor.

* * *

Darren Nolan and Bree sat staring pensively at a large screen television mounted on a wall. They were playing mobile phone footage of the fight between Dwayne and L Boi taken from the window of one of the flats looking down towards the entrance of Kingfisher Estate.

They kept freezing the footage, frame by frame, peering intensely at the scene. It was difficult to make out all of the individuals in the melee. 'Hard to tell who's doing what,' Nolan mused, as the action continued towards the left of the screen. Two flashes of orange could be seen before L Boi's body jolted into the air from the impact.

'Wait! You see that?' Bree sat forward with excitement; her eyes lit up. 'Go back,' she ordered. 'Hold it; there, you see?' She got up and pointed to the screen where the flashes of orange originated. 'The shots came from someone else. We need footage of the car park. Who sent this in?' She stood in front of the screen, her body silhouetted against the backdrop of the footage.

Nolan flicked through some papers nestled in his lap. 'Oh, here it is. Barry Evans, one of the residents.'

'Get him in. I need to know what else he saw.' Bree turned back to the screen. She stepped closer, studying the images. 'Play it on,' she ordered, taking a few backward steps, captivated. The footage continued, showing the youths all running in different directions, leaving two bodies on the ground. L Boi's figure lay motionless, while the second person slowly rose to their feet.

'Hold it there!' Again, eagle-eyed Bree focused on every pixel. 'That's Dwayne Harper—it's him!' She turned back towards Nolan. 'Bingo, bango, bingo!'

'Let's not start sucking each other's dicks yet.' Nolan quelled her enthusiasm with a downbeat reply, holding up his hands. 'Let's watch on.' He pressed play again. Bree sucked in her excitement and sat back down.

'Such a passion killer,' she huffed.

As they watched on frame by frame, it was obvious that Dwayne was gesturing to someone else before eventually limping away from the scene. 'I say Mr Harper is our star witness.' Bree twirled her braid slowly around her finger. 'Bring him in.' Nolan froze the footage on an injured Dwayne and a dead L Boi.

* * *

The quiet sanctuary of a plush office was more than enough to pique the interest of Cece; she observed the swinging chrome pendulum balls, which made a ticking-type noise every time they touched. Cindy sat beside her, dressed smartly, as always, in a black fitted blazer and white silk blouse. 'Mummy, who we for?' Cece asked, still gawping at the framed art hanging on the grey walls.

A youthful-looking man in a dark grey pin-striped suit hurried into the office, clutching a folder. His round face was flushed as he closed the door. 'I'm so sorry, my last meeting overran.' He threw the folder down on the desk, turning to stare awkwardly at Cindy and Cece. He bent down, smiling at Cece; his slightly yellow-stained teeth stood out like dried corn on the cob.

'My name is Scott Doherty; you must be Cece?' He put his hand out towards her. She recoiled shyly, leaning into her mum.

'Say hello,' Cindy encouraged, nudging Cece.

'Hello,' Cece replied, holding her hand out politely.

'Lovely to meet you, and you are obviously Cindy.' He shook her hand before moving to his chair behind the desk.

He pulled the folder towards him, flipping the pages inside. He read through some notes silently, nodding his head, affirming with a short grunt every few seconds. 'So, let me explain.' He adjusted his glasses and looked at them. 'I have all your statements. The only thing I require now is your version of events.' He focused on Cece, grabbing a pen which was clipped to his blazer pocket.

'All I need is for you to tell me everything. What happened with your daddy?' Again he grinned, speaking playfully, doing his best to make Cece feel comfortable. Cece shifted in her seat, looking up at Cindy, who held her hand, rubbing it gently.

'It's ok, just tell him everything that happened,' Cindy reassured her. Cece took a deep breath then looked at Scott Doherty, her eyes widening before she began.

* * *

'Why should I trust you?' Dwayne held the phone to his ear while scuttling around Sasha's flat clearing away his debris. He swept all the takeaway foil containers and empty rum bottles into a large black bin liner.

He rushed around wearing only a white vest and blue gym shorts. 'You lied to me about your fucking brother, innit!' He stopped, spinning around, checking everything. 'It don't make sense for me to do that!' His voice rose as his anger built up. He stomped into the bedroom where a large open suitcase half-filled with his clothes sat on the bed.

'I know about the kids as well.' He put the phone onto speaker, throwing it on the bed as he continued to chuck the rest of his clothes into the case.

'I'm sorry… I promise I'll explain everything.' Sasha sounded exasperated, her breathing getting heavier. 'Ok, listen to me. Go to the kitchen and lift the countertop next to the fridge.' Her instructions were clear and precise. Dwayne picked up the phone and held it in front of him, staring at the screen. 'Private number' it read.

'What for?' Dwayne responded stubbornly, slowly walking out of the bedroom.

'Trust me for once, will you?' Sasha pleaded.

Dwayne made his way to the kitchen. He held the countertop, then slowly lifted it. 'Ok and what?' he responded.

'There's a metal box in there. Pull it out. It's heavy.' Dwayne tilted the countertop, which opened like a car bonnet. He leant it onto the grey tiled backsplash, then reached inside, feeling around. Sure enough, there was a black metal box. He dragged it out, his muscular arm straining slightly with its weight.

He put it on the floor. 'What the fuck is in this?' he asked. The sound of the baby beginning to cry could be heard in the background. 'Is she alright?' Dwayne's tone became more mellow on hearing his daughter.

'Now the key to the padlock is in the sugar. Pour it out… ssh, baby, I'm talking to Daddy.' She deviated for a second, tending to the crying child.

Dwayne grabbed the sugar container, removed the top and poured the contents onto the counter. A small chrome key was buried amongst the granules. Dwayne knelt and began to open the box. 'If I didn't love you…' Sasha paused, 'or trust you…' She sniffed, still shushing Mellieha.

Dwayne listened while jamming the key into the small padlock and twisting it until the lock opened. He lifted the lid of the box. It revealed rolls of cash all neatly stacked together like cigars, with black rubber bands holding each roll. He picked one up, his breath taken away at the sight of the pink notes vacuum-packed.

'Now do you trust me?' Sasha asked hesitantly.

'Yeah, I do,' Dwayne replied, kneeling over the box. He became emotional, as though a weight had been lifted from his broad shoulders.

'I'll send you the details later,' she said softly as Mellieha's cries simmered down to a few sucking noises. 'And, Dwayne, I trust you. Don't disappoint me.' She disconnected the phone, leaving him sunk on his knees, staring at the box of money.

A few seconds later, the sound of someone pounding on the door jolted him back into reality. 'Shit.' He jumped up quickly.

'Who the fuck?' he muttered. He tiptoed towards the door. The banging continued—heavy-handed thuds every couple of seconds.

'Sasha! Open the door,' came a gruff-sounding voice.

Dwayne stopped in his tracks. He recognised that voice. A hot rush of blood flooded through his body. He edged closer to the door, trying not to make a sound. Peering through the peep hole, he saw the warped goldfish-bowl image of Raz and Jorgi, both dressed in black, their figures magnified, consuming the view.

Dwayne ducked down onto his haunches, covering his mouth. He lay flat on his back before turning onto his stomach, stretching out on the floor and sliding his thick body along the laminated wood towards the kitchen. They continued to bang on the door for what seemed like forever until suddenly it went silent. Dwayne lay still, posed on his stomach next to the open black box full of pink notes like a candy floss treasure chest.

* * *

Seated alone in the clinical interview room, Barry Evans looked nervously around, wringing his hands. He was still in his post office uniform fleece top. He fidgeted, anticipating the worst, unsure as to why he had been called in. The door swung open with force as Bree stepped in wearing leather trousers, her Doc Marten boots and a green camouflage T-shirt. The only thing that identified her as a detective was the black police lanyard hung around her neck with an ID badge.

Barry swallowed hard, intimidated by her bolshy aura. 'Mr Evans. Detective Bree Archibald.' She shoved out her hand for a shake, gripping Barry's sweaty palm. He nodded, almost in awe of her presence. Bree put her iPad down, swivelled it around and touched the screen into life, playing the footage of the fight between L Boi and Dwayne.

Barry looked down at the screen. He nodded on seeing the footage. 'You recognise that footage, Mr Evans?'

'Yep, I remember that night. Always something going on round there, but this...' He pointed to the screen then looked up at Bree candidly. 'This was out of control.' He shook his head as he reminisced.

'How so?'

Barry wiped his face with his hand. 'I mean Kingfisher... well, you know.' He shrugged with a crooked smile. 'But this one was a bit crazy.' He looked back at Bree.

'Do you recognise anyone?'

Barry squinted at the screen, shaking his head. 'It was dark; just heard noises and got me phone out.' Bree touched the iPad, forwarding the footage to the part where the bright flashes of light appeared. 'Did you see that?' She froze the footage on the image. Barry wiped his face again.

'Nah, what am I looking for?' He looked up at Bree, his mind void of any details.

'Gunshots... Two of them,' she retorted, her frustration surfacing. 'Do you remember seeing anyone else over here?' She pointed to the area where the gunshots had come from. Barry sat back, scratching his head, his memory recall buffering.

'Oh yes! I saw the front of a car just in the car park.'

Bree sat up. 'Make? Model? Colour?' She clung to any morsel that Barry could muster.

'Black or dark blue; Mercedes, I think. My mate Stumpy would know; he's a grease monkey…' His mind drifted.

'Registration number?' Bree interjected to keep him on track. Barry shook his head, his mind now vacant.

'Nah, didn't see that, sorry.' He shrugged.

'Ok, Mr Evans, I think I have it all.' She dragged the iPad towards her.

'Actually, I see you live in Gordon House—is that right?' Bree's intuition forced her to probe him again.

'Yeah, been there for years.' Barry rested back in his chair.

'Do you know Cindy and Dwayne Harper?'

Barry was about to answer then held back, sensing the question was trying to lure him into a space where he didn't feel comfortable. 'Erm, don't really know them. Keep myself to myself… work a lot.' He sniffed, wiping his nose with his sleeve.

'Thanks, I'll see you out.' Bree smiled, pushing back her chair, getting up and gesturing towards the door.

* * *

A gust of wind blew the crisp winter leaves across the patchy grass knolls of the graveyard. Trevor knelt in front of one of the headstones, which were lined up like grey teeth fillings consigned to the earth. He scrubbed away vigorously with a brush, his hands covered by yellow washing-up gloves, which showed up starkly against his thick black bomber jacket. He sniffed heavily, inhaling the cold air, watching the soapy suds slide down the black marbled headstone.

'Hope you can see me doing this, bro?' He chuckled to himself, taking the utmost pride in his domestic duties. 'The gym's going well… Yeah, trying to stay fit you know,' he said aloud, his intimate musings the only way he could feel connected to Ricky's spirit.

He plunged the brush into a bucket of water then took a cloth to wipe away the excess water from the headstone. 'And you know what? I'm about to be a dad.' He wiped his brow then proudly patted the head stone. 'Yeah, Alicia's four months now,' he said with a smile.

The figure of a cyclist on the path through the memorial gardens leading to the graveyard seemed innocuous as Trevor continued to clean and fuss around the grave. Another gust of wind caused the stripped branches of the trees to bend and sway.

The cyclist entered the graveyard a few yards away from where Trevor was crouched, clearing away the leaves. Still in deep conversation with Ricky, he did not notice the rapid approach of the rider.

'So, yeah, hoping it's a girl, really. Always wanted a…' He paused on hearing the tyres on the tarmac path and the squeaking of the chain. He turned slowly, his thick torso twisting to view the cyclist.

The rider wore a black parker jacket with the hood pulled over his head. A black scarf covered most of his face, showing just two piercing eyes that locked onto Trevor. As he neared, he slowed down, pulling a black gun with a short silencer nozzle from the inside of his jacket and aiming it directly at him. The blasts of two quick pressurised bullets were lost in the swirling wind.

Trevor's body slumped onto the grave; his heavy head angled against the side of the bucket. His gloved hands were twisted underneath him. Blood was splattered across Ricky's newly cleaned headstone, with the drops of excess water still rolling slowly towards the heavy body motionless in front of it.

* * *

'Hi, sis, I'm on my way. Should be there in a bit.' Dwayne cut the call and rested his head back onto the headrest of a clean, pine-smelling Uber car. He gave a huge sigh. A message pinged onto his phone screen. He looked down to see a postcode and underneath the message 'Soon x'.

Dwayne pulled the hood of his jacket over his head; his thick beard protruded. He seemed occupied. A million different thoughts swam through his mind as he peered out to the darkening clouds gathering in the sky.

'Can you put some music on?' he asked the driver, a small Asian man with glasses who looked back at him in the rearview mirror before reaching over to twiddle the knob on the car stereo. A high-energy pop tune came through the speakers. Dwayne checked the time on his phone; 18:10 the large white numbers showed. He rested back just as the tower blocks of Kingfisher could be seen in the distance.

* * *

Bree sat, her legs stretched out along her black leather sofa, sucking hard on a straw which was planted in a thick strawberry milkshake. She looked at her phone screen, viewing a row of multiple missed calls from Lisa. She tossed the phone to the side, finally taking a breath from sucking at her beverage. She picked up her laptop, flipped it open, and began to click on various files until she found the picture she had taken of Jorgi sitting in the Silver Mercedes parked in the Kingfisher car park.

'These cars don't belong here,' she muttered, trying to zoom in on the picture as best she could, analysing Jorgi's profile. She picked up her phone, the cogs whirring in her mind. She quickly tapped in some numbers then waited while continuing to zoom in and out of the image.

'Hi, yeah, anything on that CCTV?' Really? Send to me now!' She clicked off the phone, sitting up eagerly and belching loudly before an email popped onto her screen. She clicked on it. Her eyes widened with glee. She slammed the screen shut, took another long suck of the strawberry milkshake and got up from her comfortable position. She picked up her phone again and pressed a few buttons. She waited for a couple of seconds. 'Glad you're awake. Get your coat; you've pulled.' A sly smile crept along her mouth.

* * *

Background mood music played in Cindy's flat, 'On and On' by Erykah Badu. The sweet combination of coca butter and perfume lingered in the air. Cindy sat in front of her dressing table applying the finishing touches to her make-up. Her hair was freshly cut in her signature cropped bob. She hummed along happily to the tune while staring at her reflection in the mirror.

She looked regal in the sparkly black cocktail dress Dietmar had given her. She picked up the masquerade mask and placed it on her face, turning her head from side to side. She giggled, shaking her head in disbelief.

A knock on her door interrupted her moment of indulgence. 'Dwayne, where's your keys?' she muttered and went to answer the door. Cindy opened the door, expecting to see her brother, but instead saw Bree and Nolan standing in front of her.

'Miss Harper, well don't you scrub up well!' Bree looked her up and down as Nolan stood on, impassive and bleary-eyed.

'What do you want?' Cindy sighed, heavily disappointed to see them again.

'Where's Dwayne?' Bree retorted, her tone uncompromising and official.

* * *

The Uber taxi pulled into the car park of Kingfisher Estate and slowed to a halt. 'Wait here, I'll be two minutes,' Dwayne instructed the driver, unlocking the door and getting out, pulling his large bag with him. He quickly made his way towards the lift, lugging the bag on his shoulder.

Standing alone in the cubic corrugated box, he checked the time on his phone. The lift doors opened and he stepped out, but as he was about to make his way to the flat, he noticed the figures of Bree and Nolan outside Cindy's front door. 'What the…' He backed away, peering around the corner. 'Fucking feds,' he said under his breath and turned back towards the lift.

* * *

'So, when was the last time you saw him?' Bree continued her inquisition, eyeballing Cindy.

'Look, he's an adult, not my child, and I'm on my way out, so are we done?' Cindy responded in frustration.

'He may be connected with a murder which happened on this estate a few months back.' Nolan decided to cut in to add more authority and weight to their cause.

'Murder?' Cindy laughed on hearing the word, folding her arms defiantly. 'Well, I don't know anything about that.' She looked at them both, her threaded eyebrows knotted across her forehead. 'Do you have a warrant for his arrest?' Cindy asked, knowing their random visit was more speculative than certain. 'No? Well, as I said, I have places to be.' She stepped back and slammed the door in their faces.

Bree frowned, annoyed. She looked at Nolan, who shook his head, his patience now reaching its limits with Bree. 'Let's go,' he grunted, his eyes shooting daggers in her direction.

* * *

Dwayne scuttled back to the waiting taxi, crouching down as he approached the car door. He quickly pulled it open and slid into the backseat, holding the bag to his chest. The driver was confused by his actions, turning his head to see Dwayne's sizable body scrunched in the car.

'You ok, sir?' he asked.

'Yeah, just drive. Let's go, go!' Dwayne shouted in a panic.

'Ok, sir, no problem.' The driver slammed the car into reverse, did a U-turn and accelerated out of the car park.

As the car left, Bree and Nolan emerged from the stairwell and headed back to their car. Bree dug her hands into the pockets of her green parker, her head hung low. 'We need to tread carefully. She could do us for harassment,' came Nolan's voice from behind her, his grated words pushing into her back.

Bree turned around to face him. 'She's lying, man! I know it,' she said, her eyes boring into Nolan.

'Ok, calm down.' He pushed his silver-rimmed spectacles up on his nose. 'We'll put all units on alert, distribute his details.' He tried to reassure her, but Bree's anger was boiling.

'I'll get him, and I know how.' She turned away but Nolan grabbed her arm, hauling her back.

'Bree, wait… Look, I'm not pulling rank on you, but you need to—'

'I need to *what?*' she fired back at Nolan. 'We've got two murders, two!' She stuck two fingers up at him.

'That little girl who will *never* get justice and that young man… They were somebody's children.' Her voice trailed off in pain. She relaxed her hand, putting it down on the realisation that her emotions were, for once, overriding her bolshy exterior.

Nolan stood, arms folded, confronting her verbal barrage. 'We're on the same team, but let's be diligent.' He cleared his throat, then walked past her towards the car, leaving Bree standing alone in her feelings.

* * *

Cindy approached the glossy black door of Dietmar's house. She could hear music playing and chatter coming from inside. She wore her black faux fur coat and carried a black clutch bag. The glittery black and silver masquerade mask covered half her face.

Her nerves were getting the better of her as she pressed the bell. She felt excited but slightly anxious about what was to come. The door was opened by a tall blonde girl with red lipstick, who was dressed in the same outfit as Cindy—the sparkly black cocktail dress and a glittery black and silver masquerade mask.

'Hey, I'm Ingmar. So glad you're here. I need a hand serving these drinks.' She ushered a bemused Cindy in. 'No, I'm not here to… I'm Dietmar's… I mean I'm here to see Dietmar,' she semi-protested in her moment of confusion. On entering, Cindy saw a crowd of well-heeled people in evening wear—men in tuxedos and women in draped silky dresses, all wearing Venetian and masquerade masks.

Her eyes panned around the room, and she could see a few women dressed similarly to her. 'I didn't think you were coming,' a familiar voice whispered in her ear. She turned to see Dietmar, his piercing blue eyes sparkling at her. 'Look at you.' He took her hand and spun her around.

Cindy removed her mask, her eyes signalling disappointment. 'What is this?' she asked directly.

Dietmar was collected. He smiled. 'It's a party!' He began removing her coat. Cindy pulled away.

'Why are all them girls dressed like me?' She clutched her coat to her chest, doing her utmost not to reveal her dress.

The tall blonde Ingmar walked over to them holding a large tray of flutes filled with champagne. She looked at Cindy. 'Come on, get started; there's another tray in the kitchen.' She waltzed away towards the guests and continued serving them.

'We need to talk,' Cindy said through gritted teeth.

Dietmar looked back at her with a silly smirk on his face. 'Ok, go to my bedroom. I'll be up in five minutes.' He leaned in for a kiss, but Cindy recoiled.

'Five minutes,' she ordered, then turned and went up the stairs.

* * *

Two black Range Rovers snaked their way from the dark country lane onto the smooth tarmac outside Dietmar's house. They stopped next to the water feature and cut the headlights. A group of men dressed in black outfits, leather gloves and balaclavas stepped out of each vehicle. They resembled an American SWAT team, holding guns and rifles.

Some of the men ran around the back of the house, while the rest stood around the front door. They signalled to each other, taking up position. One of the men pressed the doorbell then held his hand up, signalling to the other men to wait. Once again, the door was opened by Ingmar, who was not expecting the nozzle of an AK47 to be stuck in her face. She yelped as the men rushed into the house, brushing her aside.

They stormed into the hallway then into the main room where the party was taking place. 'Everybody get pon de rarse floor now!' one of them shouted, his Jamaican patois booming over the background music. The guests at first hardly noticed what was happening, but the screams of the waitresses soon raised the alarm. One of the men smashed the butt of his rifle into a man's face, knocking his masquerade mask to the side.

Dietmar was seated at a large table with some other businessmen. They all froze on seeing what was happening. Two of the men rushed over to their table. 'Where's de bricks?' one of them shouted, sticking his gun into Dietmar's face. 'Mi seh, where de food, deh?' his gruff Jamaican accent threatened.

Dietmar calmly held his hands up. 'I don't know…' Before he could finish his sentence, the butt of a gun smashed into his face, the impact knocking him back off his chair. 'Tek arf all ya watches and jewellery and put them pon the table,' the man ordered the businessmen.

Dietmar cowered on the floor nursing his injuries, his face splattered with blood. The snivelling and whimpering cries of the other guests replaced the music as some of the masked men ripped watches and necklaces from them as they huddled on the floor.

Cindy snooped around Dietmar's bedroom, checking out his collection of expensive watches and cigars placed neatly on a dark wooden table. She had taken her coat off and laid it on the bed. She slid open his wardrobe, which was filled with his all-black attire, shirts, polo necks and T-shirts. She swept her hands over them before being disturbed by a loud scream, followed by the sounds of heavy footsteps coming up the stairs.

She moved to the door and opened it slightly, expecting to see Dietmar, but through the narrow slit, she saw one of the masked men dragging Ingmar by her hair, holding his rifle against her chin. Cindy's heart pumped ferociously in her chest. She quickly and quietly closed the door then tiptoed back into the room. She looked around, seeking somewhere to hide. The only place she thought of was in the wardrobe.

Cindy quickly took her phone from her bag and sneaked into the wardrobe, crouching down amongst Dietmar's clothes, which still carried his dusky fragrance. She switched on the torch on her phone and saw a large leather bag lying a few inches from her. She leaned over and reached for the zip, her hand shaking as her palpitations increased.

She pulled the zip slowly, taking care to make minimal noise. The torch shone onto the contents of the bag, revealing a stash of fifty-pound notes. She gasped loudly, then covered her mouth. Her eyes widened in the glow of the light until she switched it off.

* * *

The car valet building was still active, even at such a late hour. The floodlights shone above the blue canopy which covered the jet wash area. The minions were still scrubbing and wiping down a sleek vehicle. Willy Notch sat in a black Porsche Cayenne a few yards away with his chief cohort, Dee. He sat slumped down in his seat, puffing on the obligatory spliff, watching the workers clean the cars.

'Call the man dem, mek sure dem in position and ready,' he said sideways from the corner of his mouth. A message pinged loudly on his phone. He read the message then showed it to Dee. 'De man dem ah clean up at the rich bwoy's yard. Dem ah search the rest of the place!' He cackled, touching fists with Dee.

'Yes, Willy, and we about to clean up this place,' said Dee, pulling on a pair of black leather gloves with a hearty chuckle. He pressed the car touch screen, initiating the phone system. It rang loudly as Willy slid down the tinted window, tossing the remains of his spliff out onto the road.

The call connected, with background noise of street traffic and footsteps. 'Yo, man dem ready or what?' Dee shouted, pulling his hood up over his head. 'Yeah, man, we dehya,' a voice responded.

Willy pulled a black balaclava over his dreadlocked head, leaving only his eyes visible. He stared ahead, spotting the other men in his crew advancing towards the valet. 'See dem deh.' Willy nodded towards the men, who were in position across the street, just beyond the bridge, close to the portacabin.

'Showtime.' He nodded, opening the glovebox and taking out two handguns. He handed one to Dee. They opened the doors of the car and got out simultaneously, slamming the doors behind them.

They walked menacingly in the chilly night air towards the valet entrance just as the last car pulled out. The workers were talking, cleaning up and washing down the premises, not noticing the two shadow-like figures approaching swiftly.

Willy held his hand up to signal to the other men waiting. They began to make their move towards the workers, entering underneath the canopy. They rushed in, yelling, 'Get on the fucking floor!' and the men dropped to their knees.

Willy's men moved in closer, guns pointed. 'Lay on the ground, hands behind ya back!' Again, the workers complied, lying on the wet floor where the suds from the last wash were draining away. Willy and Dee arrived, guns drawn. 'Hold dem there,' Willy shouted while he and Dee ran around the back to the portacabin.

Dee kicked the door open with a heavy size twelve, nearly breaking it off its hinges. Willy rushed in first, shining the torch from his phone. The bright light revealed a desk and chairs, a metal filing cabinet and a large safe. 'Dee, search the cabinet. I'll check the safe.' Willy bounded in, kicking over the chairs and pushing the desk aside.

He dropped to his knees, then noticed the safe door was already open. 'Yo, you find anything?' he shouted at Dee.

'Nah, the ting's empty,' Dee replied, slamming the last draw.

'De safe bloodclart empty too.' Willy stood up, turning to Dee and removing his balaclava, his locks springing back into shape, sweat dripping down his angered face. Dee and Willy looked at each other in the ransacked room.

'Dat lickle bloodclart, Dwayne, he set me up!' His face contorted with fury, his eyes laser-focused, searing into Dee. 'We gaan find him and kill dat pussyhole.' Willy pulled his balaclava back on, then marched out. Dee pushed over the empty filing cabinet, slamming it onto the floor, before following Willy.

* * *

Loud, raucous laughter bellowed through the kitchen in Raz's house. He laughed hard until he choked, wheezing, his thick hand pinching the corners of his eyes, trying to stop the tears flowing down his face. Jorgi and three other men sat around the table. A pile of playing cards, half-full glasses of whisky and loose fifty-pound notes were scattered on the glass surface in the blue haze of cigarette smoke.

They continued being boisterous, much to Raz's wife's annoyance. She was sitting alone in the front room, trying to tolerate the noise but itching to interrupt and chewing nervously on her nails. Finally, she got up and walked to the other room. 'Keep the noise down; the kids are in bed.' She tried to be assertive, her voice momentarily silencing the men, which surprised Raz.

He turned, giving her a death stare. Jorgi and the other men watched on nervously for a few seconds, unsure of Raz's reaction. He picked up his glass and downed the rest of his drink before bursting into a fit of laughter again, belatedly followed by the rest of the men.

Raz's wife huffed and went back to the front room. She picked up her phone, staring at the screen. As she tried to hold back the tears, the embers of humiliation burnt in her gut. Her hand shook as it hovered above her phone keyboard. She looked up quickly, checking that Raz had remained where he was.

She dialled 999, turning down the volume enough to hear the call connect and start to ring. She wiped away a tear as the call was answered. 'Hello, emergency services… Which one do you require?' Raz's wife tried to speak but hesitated on hearing Raz's voice raised in the other room.

'Hello, which service do you require?' the female voice repeated. Raz's wife tried to speak again, but no words came. She held the phone to her ear, breathing heavily, glancing up, her eyes catching a photograph of her two children. She quickly cut off the call, burying her head in her hands, sucking back her emotions and weeping silently.

* * *

The loud beeps signifying the closing of the train doors mixed with the din of the train announcer. Dwayne barely made it on board, squeezing his frame, suitcase and heavy leather bag onto the train. He looked around, found a seat, chucked the bag on the seat next to him and lifted the case onto the opposite seat. He gave a sigh of relief, resting back into the chair.

His phone buzzed in his pocket. He pulled it out and saw 'Willy Notch' flashing on the screen. He stared at it for a few seconds just as the train started pulling out of the station. He switched the phone off, put it back into his pocket and closed his eyes.

'Good evening. You are on the Great Western service from London Paddington to Torquay. Our journey will take approximately…' Dwayne pulled his hood over his head and placed his hand on the leather bag beside him. He opened his eyes and could see the darkened skyline of London through the window as the train picked up speed. He watched for a moment as that world moved away into the distance. Again, he breathed a heavy sigh before closing his eyes and resting back.

***

Bree stood outside the red door of Lisa's flat. She was flanked by two uniformed officers. She took a deep breath before banging on the door. They waited a few seconds before movement was heard inside. Lisa opened the door dressed in black velour shorts and a white crop top with the words 'Chic Chick' emblazoned in pink across her chest.

'Bree! Been trying to call you…' Her sentence tapered off as she registered the two officers either side of her. 'What's going on?'

Bree flashed her police badge in Lisa's face. 'Lisa Walker, I need you to come with me to the station. I believe you have information concerning a murder.'

'Murder? Wait… what? Is this a joke? Bree, what's this?' She shrugged, waving her hands at Bree.

Bree remained unmoved. 'Sorry, babe, but business is business.' She offered Lisa a fake smile before nodding to the officers to advance.

'You're a fed, Bree? Am I under arrest or suttin?' Lisa raised her voice as the officers moved in. 'Don't touch me, man!' she yelled at the uniformed men. 'Kai's sleeping. What about my son?' she protested, pushing the officers away.

'We'll contact a relative at the station. You got five minutes.' Bree stared at her stone-faced, her betrayal not even troubling her.

* * *

Cindy took her time creeping out from the wardrobe. She wanted to check on Dietmar but dared not risk it. She stepped out into the bedroom, dragging the bag with her. She tiptoed across the room to the door and again pulled it slightly ajar.

The loud rants and horrified screams could still be heard coming from the hallway and main room. Cindy gently closed the door, trying not to panic. Her eyes scanned the bedroom. Following her instinct, she picked up the bag and heaved it over to the large arched window. She peered through but could not make out anything in the dark.

She knew she had little time to contemplate her next move before the intruders searched the rest of the house. She gripped the metal handles of the frame and used all of her strength to pull up the weighty panel. She managed to wedge it up a few inches but at the expense of creating a loud screech.

Beads of perspiration formed across Cindy's forehead as she struggled to pull up the jammed window. 'Come on, come on!' she said through gritted teeth. She heard heavy footsteps and voices coming from the stairs. Her hands shook as she pulled the window up just enough to be able to squeeze through the gap.

Looking down, Cindy saw that she was a couple of storeys up from the ground. 'Right, Cindy, come on.' She psyched herself up before grabbing the bag and lobbing it out, then she straddled the sill.

She heard raised voices on the landing just outside the door. Fearlessly she climbed out until she was hanging from the windowsill. Looking down and to the side, she noticed a black pipe a few inches to the left of her. As she stretched out her leg to grip it with her foot, one of her high heels scraped against the exposed bricks and fell to the ground.

'Shit!' Her fingers were losing grip, so she let one hand go and tried to use her momentum to swing to the pipe. She let go just as the bedroom door burst open.

Cindy fell, her hands scraping over the bricks. Her leg snagged on an exposed rusted nail which was poking out of the wall. 'Owww!' she involuntarily screamed as she crashed to the ground, her body half-cushioned by the bag, which took the wind out of her.

She lay still, sprawled on the cold concrete, dazed. Her eyes rolled back into her head, which pounded from the impact of her fall. Her eyes began to flicker, staring upwards, adjusting to the image of one of the men leaning out the window looking down at her.

'Yo, one of de gyal dem downstairs!' he shouted, pointing his gun in her direction. Cindy began to cough and splutter. As she gasped for breath, she felt as though the image of the masked man staring down at her would be the last image she would ever see. She rolled onto her side, still coughing and wheezing. She felt a searing pain in her leg. It felt as if it was on fire, but with the adrenaline surging through her body, she managed to lift herself into a seated position.

Cindy staggered to her feet, grimacing as her leg throbbed. She hobbled, trying to establish her balance, having lost one shoe. She looked down. The blood streaking down her leg made her dizzy, but she knew she could not dawdle. She grabbed the bag, straining to lift it off the floor.

She stumbled through the garden trees into a thickly wooded area. The cold air cut through her but she struggled on, trying to keep out of sight. Looking back, she could see tiny phone torch lights shining into the garden and heard voices shouting.

Tears were running down her face, but she knew she had to keep going, even with the weight of the leather bag impeding her progress. Cece's face flashed into her mind, a reminder that she couldn't get caught. No matter what, she had to get home.

The End

The next instalment:

La Maison de Allure

Written by Lyndon Haynes

All rights reserved 2023 ©

Chapter One

Addicted

Five years later.

Cindy sat alone in the garden of her home in The Hive. She rested back on a recliner, soaking up the rays of the sun which shone brightly onto the lush green lawn. Her hair had grown now; it was golden brown and tied into a ponytail. She was reading a book through her designer sunglasses. She wore a white vest and white shorts that revealed a thick scar on her right leg. A tall glass of orange juice with ice was perched next to her on a rattan table.

The sound of her mobile ringing disturbed the silence of the summer's day. She placed the book on her lap and picked up the phone. It was a Facetime call from Dwayne. She answered, sliding the accept call button. The image of Dwayne, Sasha and Mellieha appeared on the screen. They were on a beach, all squeezed together on a sun lounger, looking like the perfect family. Sasha's skin was brown and tanned, her hair back to the short peroxide blonde that was very much her signature.

'Hey, oh my God, look at you lot!' Cindy's happy remark was greeted by Mellieha, her cute face and black ringleted hair showing her growth.

'Aunty, we on beach!'

'Yes, my darling, I can see that. Hey, Sasha, hope he's treating you well.' Cindy sat up, picked up her drink and took a sip.

'I'm good, Cindy, and yes, he's been a darling,' she replied, giving Dwayne a kiss on the cheek. Dwayne's body was in shape. His dark skin had a healthy glow, his hair was shaved low and his beard was neatly trimmed. He seemed happy and content.

'We good, sis. This little one is keeping us busy.' He scooped his cute daughter up in his arms as she playfully giggled, then wriggled away. 'Where's Cee?' he asked, tilting down the large sunglasses from his face.

'At school.' Cindy stood up and began to walk around the lawn.

'Cool. Is she good?'

'She's a moody teenager,' Cindy responded, laughing. 'But yeah, she's alright.' She nodded.

'Ok, we'll shout you soon. Take it easy.'

'Bye, Aunty Cindy,' they all shouted before the call cut off.

Cindy turned towards the house, staring at the modern property, which stood alone in front of a large wooden deck flanked by a long, neat, colourful flower bed. She let out a satisfied sigh. 'It's good to be home.' She went back to the recliner, plonking herself down and getting back to her afternoon read.

The corridors of the St Anne of Nazareth girls' private school began to fill with hot and bothered students, signalling the end of another round of lessons. The volume of excited chatter and laughter rose a few decibels as the end-of-week excitement crept in. Most of the girls were aged between twelve and sixteen; they were all dressed in white shirts, blue and red ties and matching checked skirts. The majority were white English girls, except for the tall figure of Cece, her brown skin and braided hair sticking out like a sore thumb.

At fourteen years old, she was now a smart, confident teenager. As she had matured, her features had come to resemble Cindy's. She was popular with most of the pupils, especially with her classmates, Phoebe and Tallulah. Since she had settled into St Anne's, they were the ones who had gravitated towards her naturally.

Phoebe was smart, the bookworm type. Her parents were bohemian but successful in the publishing industry. She was pretty. Her uncut dark tresses flowed down her back, she always wore a psychedelic headband, and she knew most of the answers to many different subjects.

Tallulah was the epitome of the spoiled little rich kid. Naturally pretty, she looked slightly older than her fourteen years. Her Mediterranean looks stemmed from her rich Sicilian father, the owner of a large shipping company, and her English mother whom he met while she was a student in Italy studying Art and Design.

Tallulah had all the latest gadgets—the newest iPhone, a slick laptop, the latest earbuds and clothes. She knew her dark, mysterious features drew envious glances from some of the other girls but, when out, also drew admiring looks from the boys down at St Joseph's, which she played on hard. Tallulah was a rebel, headstrong and a leader. She knew what she wanted out of life, even if in reality she didn't have to work too hard to get it.

'So, what's the deal for the weekend?' Tallulah asked as the three of them walked out into the sunshine towards the school gates.

'You guys could come and hang out at mine,' Cece suggested casually, eager to impress.

'Yeah, we can sunbathe in your garden and listen to Billie Eilish,' Phoebe chimed in excitedly.

'Yeah, bitch, you need some colour on that pasty skin.' Tallulah's dry remark punctured Phoebe's enthusiasm.

'Oi, don't be rude.' Cece slapped Tallulah's arm.

'It's ok. I know she's just joking,' a red-faced Phoebe acknowledged, checking the colour of her arms.

'Well, I've got a busy weekend, doing that online thing I told you about,' said Tallulah, nudging Cece. 'Remember?'

'What's this, then?' Phoebe looked at them both.

Cece stared at Tallulah. 'Tell her, innit.'

Tallulah took her phone out and scrolled through it for a few seconds before showing Phoebe a screen grab of a site. 'Youngerfans. Talk to a schoolgirl hottie' it read. 'Ew, please tell me you're not…' Phoebe looked up at Tallulah, who shrugged.

'Yeah, it's a laugh. Stupid pervy men paying for me to chat shit and show a bit of boob. So what?' she responded defiantly. 'Plus, I make good money.'

'And what, you too?' Phoebe turned to Cece.

'Nah, not me.' She shook her head emphatically.

'Make good money,' Phoebe repeated. 'Like you really need it.' She turned away disgusted.

'It's *my* money, not my parents',' Tallulah continued, taking a rolled joint from her school bag. 'So, while you're tanning, I'll be having fun.' She walked on ahead.

Phoebe looked at Cece. 'How long have you known about this?'

'Not long. I was gonna tell you, but she…' Cece shrugged her shoulders, her golden braids glistening in the sunshine.

'I'm going to the fields. Are you lot coming or what?' Tallulah waved the joint in front of her face with a cheeky smile.

To be continued.

Printed in Great Britain
by Amazon